KU-054-085

THE
SMALL DARK MAN

ST/Sa/Me

LEABHARLANNA ATHA CLIATH
CASTLETYMON LIBRARY
ACC. NO.   0550 204121
COPY NO.   TE 2018
INV. NO.   BACKSTCK
PRICE IR£   3.50
CLASS   F

by Maurice Walsh

The Key above the Door
The Small Dark Man
Trouble in the Glen
Blackcock's Feather
While Rivers Run
A Strange Woman's Daughter
The Road to Nowhere
And No Quarter
Danger Under the Moon
The Hill is Mine
The Man in Brown
The Spanish Lady
Castle Gillian
Green Rushes
Thomasheen James, Man-of-no-Work
Son of a Tinker and Other Tales
The Honest Fisherman and Other Tales
Son of Apple
Sons of the Swordmaker
The Smart Fellow

THE
SMALL DARK MAN
Maurice Walsh

CHAMBERS

This edition

© Maurice Walsh, Ian Walsh and Neil Walsh 1979

All rights reserved. No part of this publication may be
reproduced, stored in a retrieval system, or transmitted, in any
form or by any means, electronic, mechanical, photocopying,
recording or otherwise, without prior permission of
W & R Chambers Ltd

Printed in Great Britain
by T & A Constable Ltd, Edinburgh

ISBN 0 550 20412 1

CHAPTER I

Where Fate has touched
Thou art blind.
In toils of Fate
Rest thou resigned.
" Free am I to come and go."
But Fate moves thee so—and so.

I

THE small dark man came round the corner into the village street and halted. A group of three people stood before the doorway of the post-office, and he could not get inside to send his wire without shouldering past the tall young fellow who glanced at him with a casual and intolerant blue eye, and made no least offer to give space. The postmaster, a lank man with a bloodless face above a fringe of blue-black beard, was giving particular route directions in a soft Highland *blas*, and the small dark man, leaning a shoulder against the red letter-box let into the window, waited patiently.

". . . Down the road—the only road it is, anyway— till you come to the high-cocked bridge over the Croghan-moyle, and at th' ither side of it there'll be a nice path up through a bonnie bit birch woodie. Don't be misled by that path. It will land ye in a corrie of screes and boulders, and fair wander ye. Keep the road another mile, till the big rock of Craigvhor—ye canna mistake it —a big humploch o' granite standing two hundred feet up off the left of the road. At the hinner end o' it there'll be a path winding up and up—stiff, stiff; but at the top there's the easy face of the mountain, and ye canna go wrong till the second cairn."

5

"Thank you," said the tall young man.

"Mind you," said the postmaster, a forefinger raised in a restrained gesture, "this is no' the time o' year for climbing Cairn Ban. No' the time at all."

The tall young man lifted a blonde, hawk face to the serene July sky, and his well-opened eyes opened a little wider in confident disbelief, and then narrowed to slits as they failed to focus into that tremendous blue abyss.

The postmaster, Highland and wise, did not fail to notice that unbelief. "I'm tellin' ye," he said firmly. "From July on it is a rare day that doesn't wrap a birl of mist round Cairn Ban of an afternoon."

The young woman smiled at the postmaster. "I know," she said in a pleasant voice. "But we have been climbing all the week—Cairn Dearg, Stob Mor, Ben a Mhuic—and there was never a shred of mist." She pronounced the Gaelic names without the southern click.

"Cairn Ban is the hill for mists, young lady," said the postmaster, a trace of protest still in his voice. "Cairn an Cludaigh Bhain, the Hill of the White Mantle—and the mantle is not snow. If ye will be risking it——"

"We will," said the tall young man.—"Come on, Fred." He turned abruptly, and, after a moment of hesitation, the young woman turned too. The two strode off down the village street, and the fine white dust of the road made a little mist round their brown shoon.

The postmaster shuffled a single stride into the roadway and stood looking after them, reproof in his eye. The young man, striding hugely, was tall and strongly built; his wide shoulders were high-set and rigid under heather homespun, and yet his hips and legs gave the impression of being too bulky for his shoulders, perhaps because of the baggy knickerbockers he wore and of the heavily-muscled calves above light ankles. The young woman

6

was tall too, but slim and supple, and carried herself with a litheness to move a pulse.

"You are right," spoke a resonant baritone voice behind the postmaster. "She has good legs on her, that one."

The postmaster turned with remarkable quickness for his years, and there was startled surprise in his deeply blue eyes, and a trace of discomfort too. "I wasna observing her legs," he disclaimed, but without heat.

"Maybe not, then, but I'll wager my new hat you and I could tell the colour of her hose without another look." The rich timbre of the deep voice was a delight, and the dark eyes, half-closed, smiled between black lashes.

The postmaster looked at him for a space of two seconds and smiled back, the clean pallor of his face crinkling about his mouth. "They are light brown stockings she's wearing—almost cream," he said, "and there's a seam down the back of them—silk they would be, maybe——"

"Not to climb hills on—merino wool, more like."

"What I was observing," the postmaster hastened to elaborate, "was that her brogues were no' a comfort to her, and she by way of hiding the beginning of a limp. See how she bears on her crook. That lad with her is not the sort would be noticing a small thing like thon, and she'll have a sair bad blister when he does."

"The blonde beast!" remarked the small man speculatively.

"No' that exactly. A pair of honeymooners they might be."

"Honeymooners! No. I was observing her eyes." He was no longer speaking to the postmaster, but meditating aloud, his voice rumbling. "She has the tell-tale grey eye. She is surely in love with him and hungry. His wife, and she might still love him; but—anyway,

7

hunger is man's duty, and that lad has not that on him
—he's too damn sure."

"You know them, I'm thinking?"

"Never saw them before, and never want to see them
again. He and I would not get on well together, and
it would be a great pity for him."

The postmaster glanced from the small figure leaning
against the letter-box to the powerful figure dwindling
down the road.

"True for you," agreed the other frankly. "He is
a big lad, and I'll never love him—or her either. I don't
like her colouring. Too fair in the hair below that wisp
of silk, and her skin turns ashen under the sun. For all
that, she has her looks; but I must have red hair, and a
skin that freckles new farthing pieces."

"A queer lad this," considered the postmaster,
"wherever he came out of." And aloud he commented,
"That kind can be got too."

"But not held." The small man jerked his leaning
shoulder from the letter-box and cocked a dark eye
interrogatively. "Would you have a brother, by any
chance, and he a policeman in Dublin?"

"No," answered the surprised postmaster. "Yon's
no' a place for anyone's brother."

"As they have taught you. No, I suppose not. Queer
thing race. It was the way you gave those two trampers
directions: first telling them what to avoid. I mind
once in O'Connell Street—you won't object if I call it
O'Connell Street?"

"Is that the name of it?" wondered his puzzled
listener.

"Honest men used call it Sackville Street. A game
we play. Anyhow, I asked a policeman the way to
Mountjoy Prison—nice name for a jail, Mountjoy—where
a friend of mine was at the time, and deserved to be.

8

'Do you see the Parnell Monument up there?' This was the policeman. 'I do.' 'Don't take any notice of that; but do you see the clock up above beyond it?' 'I do.' 'That's the clock of Findlater's Church—don't take any notice of that either, but go straight on till you come to Dorset Street Corner.' 'Will I turn there?' 'No, No. Keep straight on till you come to the canal, and at Dunphy's Corner there'll be another policeman. Ask him and he'll tell you—unless it's Shawn Doherty that's in it, and he won't know. Go on, now.' A tall black fellow he was, with a northern accent."

"He was no brother of mine, yon," the postmaster assured him smilingly. The rich, flexible baritone brogue had been worth listening to.

"No. I liked the way you caressed that nice path up through the birch woodie. I'm tempted to set foot in it."

"And repent it. Are you for Cairn Ban too?"

"I am so, but I'd like to send a wire first. Can it be done?"

"Surely. Come away in and I'll telephone down to the Kirkton for you."

II

The shop was one step down from the street. It was wide and low, and, after the glare of the white road, dusky and cool and with a pleasantly mixed odour of raisins, tobacco, nutmeg, bacon, leather, and toilet soap. A wonderful shop containing everything that a man could need, down to spare washers for soda-water syphons. The post-office business was confined to a high-railed corner near the door, and in there the postmaster slipped and, after fumbling through a unique disarray of official papers, tendered a telegraph form.

The small man did not hesitate over his wire, running

9

it off in one scrawl and not pausing to count the words. "There," he said, sliding the form across the counter. "That will apprise Tearlath that I am here and coming."

The postmaster fitted on his spectacles and read it aloud slowly: "*Charles Grant, Innismore Lodge, Balwhinnie. Coming over the hill on two feet, Tearlath son. Six leather suit-cases, steamer trunk, and hat-box at the station. Get them.—Aodh MacFirbis.*"

The Highlandman, head bent, looked over his spectacles at the small man and hid well his surprise and unbelief. He had already noted the uncreased flannel trousers with the careless triangular rent at the side of a knee, the Donegal tweed jacket so unmistakably hand-me-down, the cheap mat shirt—clean undoubtedly, but collarless and unbuttoned at the neck, and a good neck too, long and broad-throated, finely brown above and with a film of black hair in the white V of the breast—and the brand-new, furry-black velour hat aslant on the back of the head and over one ear. Across one arm was an old burberry, and under the same a seasoned ash-plant.

The postmaster looked again at the wire and wondered. Six leather suit-cases, a steamer trunk, and a hat-box!

"Well you may doubt it," said the small man agreeably. "The one case that's in it looks like leather anyway. You see that's the sort of wire Tearlath would be expecting, and far be it from me to disappoint him or any man. Money it costs me often."

"Wicked waste in a telegram," said the Scot, pencil running along the words. "Suit-cases! Hat-box! Wonder do them words count two or four?"

"Hit an average."

"Long enough as it is. I'll warrant the Postmaster-General will let me know about it if I'm wrong." He lifted his blue eyes and hot grievance flashed in them. "Them Post-Office people are a dam' nuisance," he said warmly.

"Not every one of you."

"Accounting and reckoning and explaining even on—and me a busy man. A shilling or sixpence, ay, or a bawbee more or less, and down comes a yellow sheet long as that, and another after it, and a 'phone message like as not, and will I explain this and will I explain that, and t' ither—and about nothing at all. A penny too much, and couldn't I be using a stamp when I need it? A sixpence out, and couldn't they be taking it off the few pounds they pay me?—" He stopped, and a slow smile crinkled his face. "Man," he said in a changed tone, "I'm sometimes tempted to write them the letter the Sutherland man wrote them."

"It would be a useful letter. There's a Board in Dublin often troubles me——"

"I'd warn you against using it. The old fellow had a post-office like myself and the same bother with it, and in the heel of a temper he sat down and wrote a word to the Postmaster-General. '*Dear Mister Postmaster-General, you and your post-office can go to hell.*' That was it."

"It was enough," said the small man solemnly. "Brief and with the devil's own kick."

"Ay, and they took the post-office from him." The Highlandman threw the subject behind him with a lift of one shoulder. "Ye ken the laird of Innismore?" he inquired.

"Young Tearlath? Fine that. Himself and myself and a fellow by the name of Allenby captured Jerusalem together, and two of us got no credit for it. I am for over this hill of yours to spend a week or two with him."

"The long, hard road you're on."

"Wait, now. I was coming up the Highland Line reading a guide-book and Sir Walter Scott and looking over a route map. There I was, in a coop of a railway carriage, going down to a place called Muiryside and

11

changing there for a place called Dalbeallachie—that how you call it?—Yes, Dalbeallachie! and changing there for Balwhinnie, and a long dozen miles short of Innismore at the end. Whilst outside was the sun shining, and the moors lifting, pinewoods on the slopes. and a white road winding, and Innismore over there, twenty miles as the crow flies. So here I am. Well?"

"That crow would need the wing of an eagle," said the postmaster. "Did you reckon the miles set up on end?"

"I could see them, and I come from a land of hills."

"Out of Ireland you'll be?"

"Whether you hold it against me or not, but I used to be taken for a Jew in Palestine."

The postmaster looked at the wire that was in no hurry to go. "Aodh MacFirbis," he murmured.

"Hugh Forbes you would say in the English."

"I ken, I ken. The Forbes is a good Scots clan— Tomintoul way."

"And a good Irish clan, too—though not so good, maybe. There are many of the name where I bide, and that's Glounagrianaan—the sunny glen—where the brown hills rise up on either hand like the blue hills of Donegal."

"Not hills like Cairn Ban?"

"Not so big, but big enough. And what is one hill— or two hills—to a hillman in a long summer's day?"

"Ay so," agreed the postmaster.

III

Hugh Forbes went to the door, and his dark eyes stared boldly at the grand mountain that towered above him. The postmaster leant his broad hands on the counter and curiously examined the profile of this strange friendly man. Hugh Forbes, an Irishman! A queer breed thon, and black-avised by all accounts. But this was a friendly lad—and queer too. A lad with a skilly tongue and a voice to praise the Lord. Talk he would and could, and he had the art of winning quick confidence—like meeting a fellow-mortal in a lonely place and not being beholden to any secret small quirks o' the mind. A foreign look he had as well, with that bloodless clear skin and that black crisp hair in a point on the forehead. The face of a fighting man it was, but the mouth was wide and kindly and a muscle twitched at one corner, and the long-lashed eyes had the soft dark fire of a woman's. . . . Stare away, bonny lad! A hill or two hills might be nothing to you, but yon's Cairn an Cludaigh Bhain.

"I must be wrong, I know," said Hugh Forbes from the doorway; "but it looks an easy climb from here—straight across the stream and up over that wooded shoulder."

The postmaster came to his side and looked at Cairn Ban with him. The great bulk of the mountain towered close above them, and the summer sun poured all its light on the swelling basalt ribs of it. Three thousand feet above, the pinhead of a cairn stood out against the abyss of the sky that no shred of mist clouded. The foot of the first rise was a bare hundred yards away and was a temptation to foot and eye. Across the road from the post-office there was no house, but only a slope of grass, grey-green with dust, running down to the singing waters of the Croghanmoyle, and beyond the stream the steep breast of a perfect birch wood swelled upwards to a shelf that seemed to tail off into the face of the mountain. The drooping branches and heart-shaped leaves slumbered in the heat, but ever and again some small swirl of hot air turned, here and there, a leaf on edge and made a blink of silver.

"Wrong you are," said the postmaster. "That first ridge is a snare. It drops into a valley of bare stones—flat slabs cheek by jowl with wee pools scooped out—and you'll find yourself brought up by a two-hundred-foot wall. A waste of time and shoe leather."

"Is that the top of the mountain up there?"

"The first cairn. Three of them there are in a mile triangle, and the farthest one away is the highest—the one you'll be aiming for if your mind is set on going that road to Innismore."

"It is."

They were silent then, and the old postmaster leant a shoulder against the jamb and admired the mountain that he had been admiring for half a century. "A grand hill," he whispered.

A musing baritone murmur reached his ears. "I wonder why Cairn an Cludaigh Bhain wraps itself in a white mantle of a summer afternoon?"

"I've heard it explained. The forehill of the range—the warm breeze off the Firth strikes the cold front of it——"

"Any damn fool can give the scientific reason." Hugh Forbes stopped him. "Would you be knowing the real reason?"

"The real reason?"

"Yes, then. What the gods or devils or little people of the hills play at behind their white mantle?"

"We don't be heeding them old tales any longer," said the postmaster a little uncomfortably.

"I thought there would be old tales."

"If you are going that road," said the Highlandman quickly, "I will just give you the advice yon other two didna bide to hear."

"Well, oh well!" shrugged Hugh Forbes. "What the Highlandman has visioned the Irishman might see. Give me your wine of advice, wise man."

"It is worth notice. If you get up to the cairn—and you will—don't delay there. You'll be sore tempted, with half the broad of Scotland under your eye; but just take ae look, and four long breaths that you'll need, and hurry your road. If the mist comes down on you at the cairn, sit on a stone and wait; and if a mist smothers you across the flat, stick your ash-plant in the peat—mostly peat under a powder of granite—and if you have time, put up a stone ten feet away on the line you are going and keep your feet between the stone and the stick. Something calls you to move and, if you wander, the mist—" He paused and went on—"the mist will hang about you. Bide your place and the mist will move off before the wind in half an hour or less and you'll have a clear bit—but no' for lang. Go then as if claymores drove you. And ae thing above all—don't you attempt the descent unless you see your road. The first of it looks easy and it is that, but Glen Dhu drops a thousand feet as sudden as the edge of the counter there. Ae step over that——"

"It would be the devil of a long step," said Hugh Forbes. "Is there a road down there?"

"Every here and there the snow water has bit a channel down the cliff, and any of them makes a fine ladder—no trouble there and you with a steady head. Down below by Loch Dhu—black it is, I tell you—you'll have to watch your step. It's level there and thick with old heather, but the heather hides hummocks of stone that are aye ready to twist an ankle. Haste ye, but cannily, for it's a chancy place and night comin' on, as it will be by then. At the foot of the loch where the Abhain Ban leaves it you'll come on a path—a track Laird Grant made for the ponies—and, your feet on that, you'll have only walking before you. Ay, walking! the river down below and the brae at your shouder and the track white in front of you mile after mile—sixteen o' them, and no' a house the whole way except an empty bothy half-roads that they use for the stalking. You have it now, Mr Forbes!"

The small dark man had listened with attention, his eye flickering in visualisation. "I have indeed. No blame to you if I fail to strike Innismore."

"By the light of the moon you'll strike it. Have you a piece with you?"

"A piece! Ah! you mean provender. No, then— but suppose you give me four ounces of Bendigo plug."

The two grinned together, and the postmaster turned back into his shop. "Tam o' Shanter I keep," he explained, reaching for a flat yellow tin. "I smoke it myself, and I'll warrant it to stave off the hunger."

"No harm to give the hunger something else to bite on. What have you?"

"A bit tin o' meat?"

"Not ever. I read Upton Sinclair's *Jungle*, and after that lived for three years on bully-beef. Oh cripes!"

"A skelb o' cheese?"

"The kind that stays put."

"And Abernethy biscuits—the best made."

"So my wife would say."

The postmaster was surprised, but the glance under his eyebrows scarcely showed it. "Man," he said easily, "I would never take you to be married."

"Neither I am. But my wife is going to be Highland as well as red-haired—when I find her—and 'tis the thing she'd say."

"Ay indeed! The red-haired ones are hard to come by—but you might be lucky as you are."

"You may well say it," agreed Hugh Forbes.

He packed one of the side pockets of the old burberry with biscuits and cheese and reached a brown square hand to the postmaster.

"Good-bye now," he said. "You have been the best man on the road this side of Glounagrianaan, and there are no better men there. The next time I come your way we'll talk together."

"Ay, will we."

The postmaster stood at the door and watched Hugh Forbes depart, and, when he was gone ten yards, gave him the supreme Scots valediction: the final salute, that is never given except where liking is.

"Haste ye back."

"To be sure," called Hugh Forbes, and swung into his stride.

A small dark man was he, but well put together, his shoulders moving in a forward thrust, and his legs, that were slightly bowed, swinging from the hips.

CHAPTER II

O'er mountain walls
Your road lies steep.
Down dim dark glens
That road you keep.
No fear or foe your road may bar—
But Fate has lit a yellow star.

I

DOWN the white road marched Hugh Forbes, the swift Croghanmoyle singing on one hand with the birch trees leaning down to listen, and, on the other, a brown moor rolling up to the horizon. Sturdily he went and fast— and yet he gave the curious impression of being unbeholden to time, space, or goal. At the high-cocked bridge, a mile down the road, he leant over the ancient stone parapet and looked down into the river, here feet deep in a still pool and showing every pebble in its green-grey bed. A ten-inch speckled trout seemed to soar fin-still half-way down, but, the moment after the dark head appeared, it darted, too quick for eye, under the blackness of a ledge.

"Clear water of the Croghanmoyle," he murmured sonorously, "I give you best. The hills that ring Glounagrianaan are hills of my heart, but the waters that slide down the wide aprons are the sad brown of peat. Well, one can't have everything, even in Glounagrianaan.

Sad I was and sore I was,
And lonely to the bone.
Grey o' grass and green o' grass
And water over stone,
Set a dream upon a dream
And washed away the lone."

The bass drone of his singing seemed to vibrate in the grey stone of the bridge. And for long after the song was done he leant on the parapet in some quiet apathy of thought—or no-thought.

The road beyond the Croghanmoyle swerved in towards the foot of Cairn Ban, and the armies of drooping birches flanked it closely. In time he came to that nice but traitorous path winding enticingly upwards among the trees and bracken, and halted at the mouth of it. "The wayward devil you are, Hugh Forbes!" he addressed himself frowningly. "I know you. You hate trailing after that blonde lad and his blonde woman. In spite of anything I can do you'll set foot on this path and break your damn neck. You will? Go and have a look, then."

In addressing himself he gave the odd impression of addressing a man he knew well and had no great liking for. It was something more than ordinary thinking aloud, for he seemed to project a personality outside himself and make it the butt of criticism and comment. A man like that might be remote, but never would he be lonely.

Grumblingly he stepped off the road, but, once in the path, resigned himself to himself and buckled down to the work in hand. He climbed well, lifting springingly from heel to toe and placing his whole foot on the upward slope. The path steepened as it ascended; the birches that first brushed him with trailing fronds receded and thinned; and at last he came out on a dome plumed only with grey grass. It says well for his wind that his first deep-breathing halt was on the crown of this dome. He smiled pityingly. He was looking down and across a wide tilt of stone at the impossibly steep face of Cairn Ban. The outline of it was an almost perfect triangle, shaved as with a mighty plane except for a narrow boulder-filled corrie that gashed upward a little to the left of the middle line. That corrie had to be his road—or else he must circle round to an easier face of the mountain.

"Try it, you devil!" he urged warmly, and obeyed that urge.

Out on that hot tilt of stone he found the going not so easy and yet not too difficult. The surface had been split and twisted by primeval fires, and it was pitted with scooped-out basins varying in diameter from inches to yards, and all mysteriously full to the brim of limpid water—water as clear as a blue diamond, so nearly invisible that the eye could not gauge it but for the exquisite refraction of light playing through it when some faint tremor of air shivered across its surface. Once the small man lay full length and drank out of a tiny basin. "Wow!" he cried, "but it's cold. A gallon of good whisky in the punchbowl of it and I'd climb that mountain up there and two more on the top of it."

At a distance of half a mile the gash in the face of Cairn Ban seemed to be forbiddingly perpendicular, but on a nearer approach it promised better, and actually leant back so that, standing upright, a man could touch the rock with outstretched hand.

"A cataract of stone," he murmured, his head back into his shoulders and his eyes tracing the terrifying slant above him. "A pebble loose-footed up there, and give me back the cliff at Suvla Beach."

He tied the sleeves of the old burberry round his neck, drew in a full breath, and started to climb—a persistent grey ant crawling doggedly up the huge, calm face of the mountain. Head steady, hand and foot cunningly seeking sure grip, he went upwards, boulder over boulder, while the valleys and moors below him sank and widened and dwindled.

Two hours later Hugh Forbes was on the shoulder of the mountain a bare hundred feet below the cairn. He had safely surmounted the corrie, and his troubles seemed over. The ridge he was on ran straight up to the cairn, and he had but to make sure of his hand-grips and keep going.

And then it was as if a cold grey finger moved across the eyes that were intent on the rock before them. He steadied his grip and looked sideways into a pearly, opaque swirl that, next instant, poured over him, swallowed him, shut him in a narrow world where some devil whispered that everything was safe and without fear.

"Blast it! I can make the cairn," said the small man in his throat, and he went on climbing, his face to the rock and his eyes on his hands. He did make the cairn, but he almost butted into it before he saw it. And there he sat on the bottom stones, propped his elbows on his knees and his head on his hands, and drew in hard breaths. The air was thin and chill, and the blood beat painfully in his ears. It was long before that hissing thud died down.

In time he lifted his head and looked around. He could not see ten feet. A steady breeze blew from the north, and the mist went by him with the smoothness of flowing water. It could not flow for ever at that rate, he considered; and what was it the postmaster had said? "If a mist comes down on you at the cairn, stay there." He would do that, and meantime fill a pipe—and save his Abernethys for later on.

As he slowly ground a flake of brown plug between his palms, and stared unseeing into the opaque flow of mist, there came to his ears from somewhere far below a small sibilant whisper, and then something near said "hu-u-sh" warningly, and after that a booming note, weirdly hollow, lifted and went by—close by—and died away, and again came that warning hush. Only the swirl of the breeze in the gouged-out face of the mountain, but the Gael sensed something inimical, and his back hairs lifted.

"They are gathering about," he whispered, "but they have no power unless I yield it." He lit his pipe steady-handed and ᶜʰᵉred his hardihood close about him.

In less than half an houɪ ᴛ.e mist cleared off as quickly as it had come. One moment he was staring into nothing-ness, the next into immensity.

"Thunder o' God!" he swore aloud. "'Tis some devil lustful of beauty that drops a curtain and lifts it to get a sudden blink."

For the mist actually rolled up like a curtain without leaving even a fringe trailing among the rocks, and the sun-bathed width of Scotland burst on the vision. The startling change from opaque littleness to sunny im-mensity was dizzying. The eye swooped down and over the dark of woods, the sheen of water, the purpling brown of moors, the green of Moray Lowlands, the steel mirror of the northern firth, and, far beyond, the strung purple of the northern hills.

After a long look Hugh turned east and south and realised desolation in its ultimate. The mist that, a minute before, seemed to enshroud the world was now no more than a thin band of pearly cloud low down against the blue of the sky, and below it was a far-thrown welter of mountains: peaks and ridges and gashes flung to the horizon, dull brown, solemn grey, sombre black, swallowing and denying the sunlight, mocking the blue deeps they crouched under, weighing on the mind with some inscrutable content in their own abiding sterility. The stark white of an occasional patch of snow made that sterility all the more appalling.

"I will go now, in the name of God," said Hugh Forbes, "for beauty and terror should not be looked upon for long."

III

He did not delay long at the real summit. Twice the mist had rolled over him as he crossed the hollowed-out plateau to the summit-cairn, and twice he had waited grimly while the mist-whisperings approached and went by and died out. And always he had felt a great desire to crouch and move away from something that was creeping up behind him.

He had seen all he wanted to see that day; the sun was far down in the west; and somewhere below was Glen Dhu and sixteen miles of winding track. And so from the summit-cairn he went long-strided down the easy eastern slope, his old coat flapping like a mantle behind him, and his eyes watchful for the canyon of Loch Dhu. Presently the gentle slope he was on levelled out and even lifted into a slight ridge, and, thrusting upwards to the brow of it, he stopped dead. The whole side of the mountain was cut sheer away at his feet, and he looked far down into Loch Dhu, a long splash in the deep gut of the mountains. No sunlight shone on it— no sunlight ever did shine on it. In places it was black with depth, and in places purple, and in places dimly grey where basalt ledges came near the surface. At its upper end a fifteen-hundred-foot precipice lifted out of huge boulders into the breast of mighty Ben a Mhuic— a forbidding black precipice slashed with the red of iron and the white of snow. Where Hugh stood was the still

23

clear light of the gloaming, but all Glen Dhu, as far as he could see, was in shadow, though, across the mile-wide chasm, the tops of the peaks stringing northward were lit with orange, a wild glare of colour over the gloom of the glen.

He had no trouble in finding a way down the pitch to the loch side: a stone ladder with the tilt of a steep roof, where a trickle of water slid and fell and tinkled and frail ferns drooped and nodded in the crannies.

When at last he reached the made path at the foot of the loch there was no glow on any hill, and the even hush of twilight was over all that heaped land. And yet the awesomeness had gone out of the landscape. There was no disturbing whisper off the heather, no wailing note from the cliffs of Ben a Mhuic, no sense of an inimical presence tugging at reason. Fifty yards below him the swift Abhain Ban, the clear-running river, ran checking and gurgling over its white-pebbled bed, and a green ribbon of grass looped in the windings of it; the great breasts of the hills, solemnly brown, lifted in a smooth swell to the immense blue arch of the sky where already a star was shining; and the white path of disintegrated granite, winding out of sight round a curve of the valley, called him forwards to a secure haven.

All that was demanded now was steady walking and, at the end, a meal and a drink with his great Tearlath. And meantime, by way of company, he would nibble an Abernethy biscuit and a scrap of cheese, and thereafter light a strong pipe of Tam o' Shanter. It had been a hard afternoon: a four-thousand-foot mountain, climbed the long way, was behind him; sixteen miles of track curved in front of him; the dim shining night of the north was down on him; but he had still a kick left. A small dark man he was, who had gathered hardihood of mind in a hardy body, and made it natural and unassuming and almost secret. And though he was in a strange upheaved land, on a road he had never before set foot on, with no known landmarks to guide him, he was complete master of himself and not awed by his surroundings. He was a hillman.

Around the horn of that first curve was another curve exactly similar, and beyond that another and another—world without end. In the declining light, with the dim white line of the path ever tailing away in front of him, this similarity grew irksome in time. "A day or half a day might be pleasant on this road," he said to himself, "but a man condemned to walk it for ever would choose some other hell. 'Tis, surely, a terrible hell that begins by being pleasant."

The zenith was scattered with faint stars, and the sky above the eastern ramparts aglow above a rising moon, when, at last, he won out of that first series of curves into the mouth of a side valley. And there he halted. A quarter of a mile away a small square window glowed at him with a dull-red light.

"The deer-stalkers' bothy," he spoke aloud, "and someone in it—two probably, and I'll be damn'd if I'll love them."

CHAPTER III

In blood or bone
They are not kin.
The pull of Race
Is strong within.
Love limps slow behind hot Hate,
Yet is the weapon tried of Fate.

I

CHARLES WILLIAM VIVIAN STARK, standing upright, dropped three peat sods on the fire, and raised a mist of ashes and a drove of sparks. The sparks went up the wide chimney above the open hearth in pleasant darts and spirals after the manner of peat sparks, but the ashes found Stark's nostrils for his foolishness. He stepped back, sneezed, said a word under his breath, and then stood, head adroop, and watched in glum silence the small tongues of flame already licking round the black sods.

Frances Mary Grant opened her mouth to tell him that that was not the way to treat a peat fire, but thought better of it. Instead, she said in a tone of well-assumed disgust, "I am ashamed of myself, Vivian—and we so near home." But there was no trace of shame or chagrin in the face she turned to him.

She sat back in an old and decrepit wicker-chair, and one knee was lifted over the other. Her eyes left his face and followed her shapely, cream-hosed leg from knee to foot, and there rested. That foot was without its brown shoe, and, instead, a flimsy silk handkerchief was tied under the heel and over the instep. She moved her toes, turned ankle back and forth, and took breath

26

with a little grimace. "Rotten of me to fail you," she said, and looked up at him.

If silence means consent, Stark agreed that it was rotten of her to fail him so near home. Perhaps she hoped that he would say something agreeably excusing, for the firelight revealed a beseeching look in her glistening grey eyes and a smile faintly wistful on her lips. But his chiselled profile was turned obstinately to her and his eyes remained sullenly on the fire. Indeed this girl had tell-tale eyes. Anyone looking at her then would admit that she liked this young man—at the very least. Liked him for his physical beauty, surely not for his manners!

His eyes still on the fire, he spoke at last out of some context of thought not difficult to follow. "You should have told me earlier, Fred. At Croghanmoyle—we had time then to catch the train at Kirkton."

"But you were so keen on doing the four big peaks inside the week." Her voice grew cheerful. "And we have done them, you know. I didn't want you to miss Cairn Ban."

Even now he would not commend her. "I could have seen you to the station, climbed the peak, and been home before you." It was the unkind truth.

"I never thought." Her voice was quiet, but the sudden creak of the chair showed her discomfort.

"Of course you did splendidly, Fred," he said, relenting a little. "But this is—I am sorry this happened."

"So am I, Vivian; but, really, there is no harm done. This old bothy is quite cosy, and after a rest——"

"No, no. A blistered heel is not to be trifled with. The moon will be up in a few minutes, and I can easily make Innismore in two hours, and be back with a pony in other two."

"After such a hard day——"

"No trouble," he said shortly. "We must get to Innismore to-night."

"I suppose so." She was a little piqued now. "Really, I don't mind. I am used to these hills, and have stayed a night in a bothy before now."

"Hardly do, would it?"

She chuckled pleasantly. "Not with a conventional young man like you. I don't mind."

He made no reply to that. He moved across the floor to a black doorway in the rear wall and scraped a match on the jamb. "I'll get you a store of peats," he said over his shoulder, and then she heard him fumbling in the lean-to back place. He returned with an armful of black sods and built them up on the brick hearth. "That will keep the fire going till I return." She did not care to tell him that several armfuls would be required to keep a peat fire going for four hours. "You won't mind being alone, Fred?" he inquired.

"No-o. I can stand it. I am not afraid—in my own hills—of loneliness." A careful listener might have gathered that she would prefer company—this man's company.

Perhaps Stark gathered that too, for he turned to the door and spoke briskly. "And there's the moon—" And there he halted, his mouth half open and a sudden, small, psychic fear in his Nordic heart.

"What is it?" whispered Frances Mary Grant.

II

From outside, across the heather, came the sound of a voice singing. Out of that valley of loneliness and silence came a man's voice in a slow tune that was old as the hills, lonely as the hills, sad as the sadness that lurks in heather valleys. The great long roll of that baritone

28

voice filled rather than pierced the air, and the gutturals of the Gaelic held the rumble of heavy water. Before Sulcoid, before Clontarf, before Largs, Nordic fighting men had heard songs like that song drifting down from the night camp of the Gael, and, having survived the long day's fight, could never hear again a Gaelic air without remembering the carnage and the defeat.

> No home have I, no dear one,
> No friend, no kin to cheer one,
> No foe to fight or fear one,
>   Nowhere to go or stay;
>
> My life is reft of laughter,
> My clan gone down in slaughter,
> Yet in some dim hereafter
>   Is dawning of the day.

Close outside, the song stilled on a long middle note, and then a small dark man leant in the doorway. The blonde young giant at the fireside felt a prickling at the back of the neck, and something stirred at his roots. For the waving yellow flame from the peat showed the black V of hair on the wide forehead below the tilted head-gear, the black pools of eyes that drowned the light, the wide-winged nose flatly aquiline, the broad flat chin, the bare neck like a white pillar; and what looked like a saffron-yellow cloak was thrown carelessly over the wide shoulders. Leaning in the doorway, hands hidden, the peat flame in front and the wan moonlight behind, that figure might have stepped out of the remote past. A small dark man! One of the small dark men that possessed the land before history, and that persist!

"God save all here," saluted the vibrant deep voice, and waited for a response. It did not come. "'God save you kindly' is the reply to that. Pity that ye should forget." The voice mocked them.

Hugh Forbes had taken in the situation at a glance.

29

The blonde young fellow—beast or otherwise—and the blonde girl, who had now drawn a shoeless foot under her chair. "A sair bad blister," the wise Highland postmaster had said, and she had brought it over bad territory. Game she must have been! And now they were sheltering in the old bothy, and had built a fire. He could sniff the faintly sour odour of old soot, the mustiness of a house long disused. But it was comfortable too. The ruddy glow of the fire set shadows wavering on the lime-washed walls and vanishing in the smoked blackness between the rafters. There was no furniture except that old chair and a deal table against the wall. On the wall, above the table, was a heavily-lined crayon drawing not quite distinguishable. A bare room, yet the firelight made it cosy. Queer how a peat fire had that effect! And it was a poor fire at that.

"The man who built that fire did not know one damn thing about peat fires." He spoke the last words aloud, but as if still musing.

Charles William Vivian Stark came out of his uncomfortable trance. He felt a sudden twitch of anger and resentment at being, for a few seconds, under psychical durance, and his voice showed it. "Do you usually swear in the presence of a lady?"

The man in the doorway considered that. Swear? When had he sworn? An odd expletive was not swearing. He knew and could use a swear or two: splendid fine swears—do any girl's heart good to hear them—learned in the Tenth Division in that retreat down to Salonika when, instead of meals, they had bayonet fights three times a day with that very adequate fighting man, the Bulgar. And, anyhow, if he wanted to swear he would not let any dry small convention stop him. Startled you were, my lad, and bluffing to hide it—"No blame to you either," he said aloud.

He stepped into the room and walked evenly to the fireside between the man and the woman. "I am used to a turf fire," he said. "This is the trick of it." He went on one knee, laid down his ash-plant, and picked up two black divots. "Stand the sods against the hob, keep the red coals in the middle, hedge 'em in like that— with a gap in front for draught. You'll see the blaze in a minute." He turned his head and looked over the bulge of his shoulder at the shoeless foot under the chair. "'A sair bad blister,'" he quoted—"and we knew you'd have it. Spirit you had to bring it this far."

"You were at the post-office at Croghanmoyle," said Frances Mary Grant. She was slightly amused at the bold coolness of the small man.

"Probably followed us over the hill." Stark addressed himself to the girl only.

"My own road I came," murmured Hugh Forbes, "and heard the bad gods whisper in the mist," and forthwith went into one of his reveries, his eyes on the fire, where a valley glowed up a long mile and then a long mile, with broken castle walls at the end. So this hay-head had seen him at Croghanmoyle. The lad had looked at him with a look that did not register, but her eyes had never once seemed to observe him. Women were the very devil. . . . Pleasant voice the girl had too; soft and round, with the words slightly drawn, but not with the drawl that spoiled the Dublin voices. A Highland voice? And the man had a Rathmines accent. Oxford that would be. . . .

The tall man looked down and smiled, and in his hawk face was a trace of contempt for the small man and for his own recent feelings. Strange the tricks the fire-light played on one. The saffron cloak of the Pict was only a rusty old trench-coat thrown loosely on the shoulders, and the clothes beneath it were modern and shabby—frayed at the wrist, a rent at the side of the lifted knee. That hat was new—one of those furry black things affected by the vulgar—and the brown shoes were strong and well made. Probably lifted at a back door! A tramp, very likely—and Irish—who had seen better days! Charles Grant had mentioned that wandering men sometimes used the glen and the great pass of Sealig to cross over into Deeside and Aberdeen. Trying him for a touch in another minute! Damn him! He did complicate things. Couldn't very well leave Fred now unless . . . "Are you alone?" Stark queried suddenly.

As from a mile off in his musings Hugh answered casually. "But not for always—if there's a red-haired woman in all Scotland." He was watching the castle walls crumble at the end of the glowing valley and was stringing queer little rhymes in his mind:

> The red strong valley of life shall flatten in dust.
> The red long rally of steel shall crumble in rust.
> The red strong pulse of the heart shall falter in lust.
> The red . . .

"The red what? bust, trust, confust, must—elephants go must—that last line is going to be the devil."

Frances Mary, too, was observing the small man resting on one knee, and she was thinking along a line of her own. She, also, put him a sudden question. "Are you going on down the glen?"

"I was thinking of doing that." He had not raised his eyes.

"Could you do me a favour?"

"To be sure—if I can."

"Will you call at Innismore—the first house you come to, the big house on the right over the footbridge—and tell my brother Charles—Mr Charles Grant . . ."

Hugh Forbes for the time did not hear another word. He had a trick of concentrating on his own thoughts or problems and breaking contact with the outside. He did that now. Her brother Charles! So this was Tearlath's sister. Frances Mary! That darling name! He had heard this big lad call her Fred; silly ass to shorten a name like that. But of course she must be Frances Mary—Tearlath's only sister. How often had he heard Tearlath speak of her, his fine kid-sister! There was that heart-opening bad day when they were trapped on the wrong side of the Jordan and the Turkish snipers hitting close. Over the Jordan but not into camp-ground—not by a long shot—not by a long shot. Four hours among the hot stones till night came—and half the company gone. And Tearlath and himself talking so as not to think too much—picking their words slowly. "It would be no harm to say, Tearlath boy, that if that fellow lowers his front sight, the valley of Glounagrianaan will be needing another schoolmaster." And Tearlath, his great body flattened out and his cheek to the stones, smiling at him! "Never mind, Aodh, you've the soul of a teacher; and little wee imps in hell will learn things from you." Ay, the hot stones beyond the Jordan and the angry sun, and he minding the green valley of Glounagrianaan below the heather, and the kindly sun on the amber river where the trout lay! And then Tearlath spoke of his very wonderful mother who was nearly blind. "Ah well! she has Frances Mary, and as long as she has Frances Mary no harm can come to her." A darn queer thing race! Scot and Irishman with the same turn of speech and the same twist of mind. And this was Frances Mary! Somehow he had pictured her as little and red-haired, with live blue eyes and a skin liable to freckles. And instead she was a long-limbed, tow-headed—no, not that word—female. Good-looking in a way, with nicely curved lips, and the cheek-bones of the Scot, and those grey wide-set eyes that could never hide any feeling—love or dislike or——

"Answer the lady, fellow!" rasped a cold voice above him.

Hugh Forbes, whose eyes had never left the fire, woke up. "Excuse me," he said, turning to her. "A bad habit I have. What did you want me to tell—your brother?"

Frances Mary Grant had been observing the small man curiously, and now she smiled to him. "That I am here in the bothy at Aunbeg, with a blistered heel, and that he is to send up a pony. You can see we are all right, but that a pony will be necessary, sometime to-night—no hurry."

And still Hugh Forbes looked at her, and still he did not reply.

"Are you deaf, fool?" barked Vivian Stark exasperatedly.

The small man turned his head up with remarkable suddenness, and the shock of his dark eyes met the shock of the blue ones, solid as a bar. And there was a hard note in his deep-toned voice. "Blast you! Wouldn't you give me time to think?" He turned and again looked amongst the coals, and Stark, strangely startled by that shock of eye and tongue, took time to think too.

Hugh Forbes told himself that he did not like this tall fellow. Somehow he did not like him one damn bit. He never did care for big blonde men who had no vision but one, who would ignore the gifts of the gods—till they were ready to accept, and be not nice in their manner of

34

acceptance. Autocratic bounders, stupidly unable to get the other fellow's viewpoint! And, moreover, he did not care for long blonde women who could not hide strong feeling below the deeps of their eyes. But then, this one was Frances Mary who could keep all harm away from a nearly blind and wonderful mother. Tearlath Grant's sister! Tearlath Grant!—the finest man on top of the world. The most comradely of men! In the press of war, in stress of peace, drunk or sober, a hell of a good man to rely on! A reliable man and yet not a stupid man! A man you could put your finger on and say, "Tearlath may say this, and think thus, and curse hither and yon, but this is what he will do." The great big quiet boy—and not always that blame quiet either! Yes, and Tearlath had somehow put trust in a small devil of an Irishman from Glounagrianaan, who looked like an Israelite and had the reserve of an irate jackdaw. Therefore he had to do the right thing by Tearlath's sister—now, this minute. And what in thundering blazes was the right thing to do? Go on down to Innismore and send up a pony? That was the obvious thing, but was it the right thing? Was it, now? Why could not this big lad go? Probably he had been going. If so, Hugh Forbes coming in on them out of the night had made them change their plans. Was he to be the *deus ex machina* in some small game set by fate? He would see! He would see!

And all this consideration on Hugh Forbes's part was probably no more than an excuse to hide the fact that, instinctively disliking Vivian Stark, he hated like poison to act deputy for him. His next question seemed to prove that. He looked sideways at Frances Mary, and the half-humorous half-cynical quirk came and went at a mouth-corner. "Tell me, now; what were ye going to do?"

Where another might have bridled, she answered frankly and at once. "Vivian—Mr Stark was going."

And that was that. The obvious thing for Hugh Forbes to do now was to go canny, to be no interloper—to let things go the gait they were going, and all good luck to them. He looked up at Vivian Stark and grinned. "Time you were off, Vivian—Mr Stark."

"What?" The word snapped. Stark's temper had been growing warm, and now it grew no cooler.

"The sooner you start the sooner you'll be back, and a sair bad blister is a sair blister to-night or in the morning."

There was a silence that seemed to wait, and then came the tall man's voice, quiet like frost and as cold. "And what do you propose to do?"

"What the devil is that to you?" That voice sounded like tuck of drum.

"I'll show you," said Vivian Stark grimly, and his hand came down and gripped. No one can blame him. He had been provoked needlessly, and, worse, his sense of superiority had been outraged. The old burberry bunched under his fingers, but the force of his grip went deep to jacket, shirt, and skin, and Hugh Forbes was jerked to his feet as if he had been a mischievous urchin; jerked and held with a ruthless force not to be resisted. The black velour hat fell off and came to the floor with a soft whuff.

Frances Mary stirred restlessly, and the old chair creaked, but she remained silent. She could not help admiring the force of Vivian Stark, and the face of him. The beauty of that forward-thrown head thrilled her. It was not the face of a hawk now, but the face of a great eagle, the brows in a straight bar, the half-hooded eyes gleaming in the firelight, the strong arch of the nose curving over the line of the mouth. And yet, at the same time, she felt sorry for the little trampish man who had been at once impudent and intriguing. There was some texture in him, thought and speech, that appealed to her, something that she could dimly follow, something sib. And now he looked so helpless in the grip of this young giant. His back was turned to her, the gripped shoulder was lifted to his ear, the other drooped helplessly, his unclenched hands hung limply at his sides, and his feet were ridiculously intoed below slightly bowed knees— altogether like an urchin in the grip of an irate senior, deserving and expecting a lesson. But not to be grievously hurt—surely not to be treated with abasing indignity. That was why she stirred restlessly.

But Vivian Stark, having achieved mastery, had his sense of contemptuous superiority thick upon him. He would do no more than was necessary. He looked at her over the small man's head and smiled reassuringly, and his voice, when he spoke, had its usual reserved drawl. "It will be all right, Fred. I shall go on to Innismore and take the little tramp along." He referred to the little tramp as if he were at the end of a mile-long arm.

Frances Mary Grant nodded her fair head. She could not think of anything to say, and Vivian Stark would take his own strong line, anyway. He always did, and his appeal suffered nothing thereby.

Stark, having decided, did not hesitate. "Come on," he ordered shortly, and gave the small man an admonitory shake, an unmistakable intimation that in all things he must obey.

Hugh Forbes felt that forceful grip painful on his shoulder, but he did not wince. "Shake hard," he said in a startlingly unperturbed voice. "It will make it all the easier."

As they reached the door he turned his face over the

37

ungripped shoulder and grinned at Frances Mary. And that grinning face surprised her, because it was not the face of an about-to-be-whipped urchin. It certainly was not the face of an urchin: black brows, wide-winged nose, broad chin, and that queer sardonic quirk at mouth corner—a whole man's face; and though it grinned at her, there was below the grin some magnetic force of hardihood held in leash.

And then they were gone, and in the oblong of the doorway was nothing but the pale, bluish, wan glimmer of night lit with moon.

CHAPTER IV

No leaf shall fall,
No shadow flow,
But was thus doomed
To fall or flow
Before Time winged its little flight
Or God created Life from Light.

I

THE path down the glen, a white line fading along the
breast of the brae, started again at the corner of the
bothy, and the two men set foot on it and went on marching. Hugh Forbes went first, or was propelled first, for
Vivian Stark still grasped his shoulder. The small man
seemed to suffer no embarrassment, and his head moved
freely as he looked down and across the great valley.

"Thunder o' God!" he whispered; "what a night,
and what a glen!"

The moon had risen above the mountain ramparts
of the east, and that side of the glen was black lightening
to soft purple. High up against the glow of the sky,
right and left, ran the serrated midnight-black silhouette
of the great peaks, hushed and stark. Down below in
the bottom of the valley the Abhain Ban chuckled
subduedly over its shallows, and gleams of silver showed
and shimmered and vanished over the white stones.
The western slope of the glen, where the moonlight
shone, was ghost-like in that pale glow—grey, sub-
stanceless, without perspective, scarcely less dark than
the star-dusted sky and scarcely less remote. Except
for that subdued chuckle of the river there was no
sound, no hu-u-sh of air over heather, no cry of bird, no

snort of stag—no sound at all. But silence was there, a presence.

"Move on," ordered Stark, thrusting the shoulder he held.

"Time enough for to admire and for to see," said the small man calmly. "Let us hurry, then." He strained at the long arm like a dog on a leash.

They went on thus for perhaps two minutes till the curving path took them out of sight of the bothy, and then went on another minute till no sound might reach the bothy. And there the small man, with a twist that seemed easy and even nonchalant, brought his shoulder away from Stark's grip, leaving the old trench-coat in the clutching fingers.

"Let us talk," said Hugh Forbes, his voice deep and grave.

But Vivian Stark had no intention of talking. He threw the old coat aside in the heather and clutched at the shoulder that was still within reach.

The small man, nimble as a cat, was out of distance. "Don't be a blasted fool," he said very rudely. "Listen to me for a minute."

But Vivian Stark had become obsessed by the sense of power that that shoulder-grip had given him. Free, this little thug had an outrageous manner of speech: in leash he was subdued and obedient. Therefore, Stark did not heed the small man's exhortation. This time he sprang forward and his hand pounced.

"Hell!" snapped the other, and his hand was the quicker. It got first wrist purchase.

The two men came together, breast to breast. . . .

II

Hugh Forbes crouched on the edge of the path and looked down the steep heather-slope towards the river.

"He never went the whole way," he rumbled. "I never heard him souse—and maybe his neck isn't broken either. Ah! here he comes, and in a hurry."

Vivian Stark clawed up the slope, and there was fell purpose in his coming.

"Make it a game, son," called Hugh Forbes happily, "and don't be so dashed serious about it. I'm the king of the castle, and you're the dirty rascal."

Somehow, as he crouched there, he was no longer a small man. Rather was he a squat and powerful figure —force carried conveniently. His black head was sunk between great shoulders; his arms, bent at the elbow, reached his bowed knees gorilla-like; his legs were sturdy as towers. No urchin this.

Ten feet below the edge of the slope Vivian Stark paused for a moment, gathered all his poundage of bone and muscle, swerved a little to one side, and charged for the level ground of the path. Hugh Forbes side-stepped on nimble feet to meet him—met him solid as iron. . . .

Again the squat figure crouched on the edge of the slope. A glutton, that fellow down there. Barring the mercy of God, he'd be climbing up the bank and rolling down again the rest of the night. That last one was a clean "flying-mare," and if he had any wind left in him he'd need it.

Stark did need his wind this time. He came up slowly, and, in the stillness of the night, the hissing draw of his breath came before him. A little nearer, and the man crouching above could see the white teeth gleam between open lips. He made no swerve and charge this time, but came on doggedly, almost dazedly, until his head was over the edge of the slope, and there he was gripped and held, one unforgettable clutch at his neck and one at wrist, so that his breast was pressed into the ground and a heather stem tickled his chin. The figure

41

crouching over him was more gorilla-like than ever—a squat gorilla holding a frail human under a forelimb.

"And now we'll talk," said Hugh Forbes in his throat, and forthwith he had Stark on his feet on the path.

Charles William Vivian Stark could not talk yet awhile if he wanted to.

"And one of us will go down to Innismore. You or I?"

Stark did not deign to answer. Who could think of leaving a young girl alone with a savage and dangerous tramp—a plug-ugly—a tough trained in beer-house rough-and-tumbles? Loosed from Hugh's grip, he swayed and steadied himself. The moonlight shining on his face gleamed on clenched teeth. He would have his wind back in a minute and——

"Did you ever hear Tearlath—Charles Grant—speak of Hugh Forbes?"

Vivian Stark did not need his wind any longer. "You!"

"Yes; I am Hugh Forbes."

Stark did not doubt it. He had heard Charles speak of Hugh Forbes. Everyone had heard Charles Grant speak of Hugh Forbes, the black Irishman: frank as the day, secret as the night, of outrageous speech out of profound silences, gentle as a lamb, terrible as wrath—not to be forced, yet yielding his soul's worth at a friend's asking or an enemy's pain. . . . So said Charles.

"This need not have happened," said Stark.

"And it wouldn't, if you took a man as you found him."

And, oddly enough, that was the very thing that poor Vivian had done.

"Damn'd folly!" cried Stark angrily.

"It was all that," agreed Hugh. He paused, and in

42

that pause his whole manner and outlook changed. His voice showed the change. "It was damn'd folly, come to think of it. And maybe I was as much to blame as yourself. That wicked tongue of mine!" And now he grew cheerful. "Ah well! Sure, no harm is done. Only a bit of a wrestling match and never a blow struck. Man, if you had only used your reach and clouted me one!"

And there was Hugh Forbes forgetting to be ruthless, lightening his opponent's discomfiture, putting himself in the other fellow's place—after putting the other fellow in that place. A good right to be angry, the long lad had. Bad enough to be cross-buttocked and flying-mared by an insignificant tramp—and what else did he look like?—when a man upheld virtue, and defeat had an honourable sting; but to be stood needlessly on one's ear by the friend of one's friend—Murder! The boy's mind must be taken off such contemplation.

"What do you propose to do now?" Stark asked that question shortly. He was in a predicament that he was not used to; he did not know what to do. He knew exactly what he would like to do, but for once in his life he doubted his ability to do it. He desired most urgently to hit this small scoundrel a thundering and demolishing blow that would flatten nose and drive teeth into throat—but—but—but would it be safe to try it, to risk a counter that might rend flesh from bone like the drawing stroke of one of the great apes? He had felt the wrenching quality of the small man's grapple.

"Look you," said the penitent Hugh, "this thing that happened—it was nothing; only you and I know, and let us forget it. Now that we are acquainted, let us make a fresh start. You go back to Frances Mary, and I'll go down to Innismore and send up a pony."

"Go to blazes!" said Stark with hot force, and, without

43

another word, turned and strode down the glen, on the road for Innismore.

"Well, now!" said Hugh Forbes, and scratched the back of his head.

He stood leg-wide on the path, fingers smoothing his short hairs, and watched the tall figure fade into the grey of the hills. He was gone now, as if propelled from behind, and Hugh Forbes had to decide on his own course. That was not so easy. First of all, he would pick his old burberry out of the heather and see what damage had befallen his Abernethy biscuits and cheese. They were not *bruisther* at any rate. Ah! but where were his hat and his ash-plant? His fine new hat! Twenty-five shillings at Liam Flannery's sale—forty-five in Grafton Street, Dublin, Liam had said, but he was a thundering liar. Fell on the floor, it had, back there with that long-legged—female. And why did it fall off?—it had a bad habit of falling off at the wrong time. Perhaps some god or imp flicked it with a finger . . . not a leaf shall fall . . . not a leaf shall fall. Still, it was his own and only hat, and—in spite of the devil's mother—he would go back for it, and his ash-plant too. And, anyway, he could come away his own road when he liked, and he could be very circumspect and say nothing, or next to nothing. Ay, nothing! Damn you, Hughie, when it comes to saying nothing you talk like hell. Queer, all the same, how that long fellow went off down the glen and a good-looking jade—good-looking enough at any rate—back there in the bothy and not averse to his company. Maybe that was the reason. . . . A great pity that grey eyes held no secret! Fred he called her. Something wrong with a man who would shorten a

44

grand name like that. Frances Mary! A darling name. . . .

He plodded slowly, one foot over the other, back up the glen, his eyes downcast and his mind pursuing thought into the byways where philosophy is only folly, and reason a shadow, and cause and effect reach fore and aft into infinity—and do not matter.

CHAPTER V

Grew there no rose,
No flower fine,
No thistle spike,
No dandelion.
Yet was a seedling planted there
By moon of feet and sun of hair.

I

FRANCES MARY GRANT, that girl with the darling name,
sitting alone with her thoughts in the basket-chair, one
long shank see-sawing, heard the crunch of feet in the
gravel outside the window and turned her head to the
door expectantly. Alas! the figure that appeared was
not a tall figure to fill the eye—if not the heart—but,
well, Hugh Forbes, his own, normal, small self. He stood
very still in the doorway, and the glow of the peat flames
seemed to wash over him as water washes over stone.
His stillness and some emanation of force from him disturbed her for a moment. Had he escaped—run away?
He did not look like a man who would run from anything.
Where— Her thoughts found words. "Where is—
Mr Stark?"

"Gone down the glen," said Hugh Forbes, who was
to be very silent as well as circumspect. " '*Ah! down the
glen—rode Sarsfield's men—and they wore their jackets green.*'
We talked things over a piece down the path, and—he
saw things from several aspects not usual to him. Sensible
we were, the two of us. 'Excuse me,' he said, 'and
forgive me for my strenuous invitation. As you have
pointed out, to insist on your leashed company on this
narrow and precipitous path would be inconsiderate

46

—and uncomfortable. With your favour, and things being as you say, I will forthwith hie me for Innismore; and you—you can go to—' And there's the truth for you."

Frances Mary considered that. She did not quite understand how things had happened or what had happened. She realised that the two men had come to terms—not as this man related certainly, but in some workable way. And yet she was not pleased. It was distinctly unpleasant not to have her wishes considered. She had requested this man to leave word at Innismore, and yet Vivian had gone. That pricked her, and she did not hesitate to show her displeasure. Already somewhere deep down she realised that she could be devastatingly frank with this stranger. "What are you doing here?" Every tone in that query implied that his presence was needless, unpleasant, and impertinent.

"Me!" cried Hugh Forbes; "I only came back for my new hat." He looked along the floor. "Bloody wars! someone has stood on it." In two long strides he was at the fireside and sitting on his heels over the velour hat that had been distressingly flattened under some male heel. "My fine new hat!" he grieved comically, "and maybe 'twas myself tramped on it." He punched out the dents, patted it smooth, and twirled it on a finger. "Forty-five shillings—and I'm telling no lie—and a heel on the crown of it! Wo! Wo!"

Frances Mary looked down at him, her mind active on a new line. This was no ordinary tramp. This was no tramp at all. From the very beginning she knew that he was never a tramp. An Irishman! Ah! An Irishman! And, added to her intuition, some thought lifted at the back of her mind and grew. Her mood changed. She found herself smiling, and decided there and then to play a game until she had made sure. "You know," she told him coldly, "velour is quite out of date. It is never worn now."

He held up his hat and looked at it. "I wouldn't doubt you, Liam." He spoke as if to a man present in the room. "I might have known. 'Twenty-five shillings to a friend, and there's not a better hat in Grafton Street.' Yes, so!" His tone changed. "Still and all, 'tis a nice enough hat." He threw it on his head, and it fell naturally over one ear. "And there's my ash-plant." He went forward on one knee, propped the ash-plant in his oxter, and arranged the last of the peats round the fire. "Where's the peat rick?" he inquired.

"There's a stock in the back place—in there." She had been watching with curious intentness, noting every turn of his great voice, wondering what he would do and say next. She was not one morsel afraid; but then she was seldom or never afraid. Only here she knew that there would be no calls on her courage.

"I'll get you some," he said, turning to her. He saw that she had again drawn her shoeless foot under the arch of the chair. "Tell me, now," he inquired, his voice rolling gently, "was it a sair bad blister?"

"It was."

"And did it break?"

"I fear so."

"And you bathed it in warm water?"

"No."

He was on his feet on the instant. "Well, now!" he exploded. "Aren't you the damn'd little fool?"

"Thank you," said Frances Mary Grant politely.

"For nothing. . . . Any household utensils kept in this place?" he questioned brusquely.

"I believe there are a few—in there with the peats, on a shelf."

There would be. There would be. A flick of finger,

and back he had to come. Not a leaf shall fall . . . not a leaf shall fall. And why? What had he to do with another man's woman? Not quite that, perhaps! And still, flaxen hair and all, she was Tearlath Grant's sister, and the right thing had to be done by her; and done would the right thing be.

He went round behind her to the back place and scraped a match on the jamb. Vivian Stark had done that too, and Frances Mary remembered it. Then she heard him kick amongst the clump of peats, and the rich roll of his voice came through to her. "A kettle and a pan—no! A griddle and a pan it used to be, in that old story. From a woman from a man, from a griddle from a pan, from two barn thrashers, from four well-washers — and-from-you-if-I-can. W-u-u-ff! And the fox had it. And here's a gridiron. Would you lend me the loan of your gridiron? . . ."

He came out with an old tin kettle in one hand and an enamelled basin in the other. "You'll bathe that heel, young lady," he said briefly, and went out into the night.

II

The old wicker-chair creaked and a stocking-suspender snapped. Frances Mary knew that she should lave that foot, and she felt that she must. Already she was forming opinions about this man. He disliked her, and there was no harm in him. Gentle he was, and tenacious too, for he would persist in the face of odds—and suffer. A pity Vivian had gripped him so relentlessly—a wrathful young god in his invincible strength. There was really no need for such violence, though the little man's wicked tongue well hid his harmlessness. Wonder what he said out there to Vivian? She knew that too—exactly.

But why had Vivian not stayed? There was no need to go—or stay either. . . .

Poor Frances Mary! A gentle, wicked-tongued, harmless, small man! And she simply could not imagine gorilla shoulders yielding cunningly to the unwitting strength of her invincible young god and catapulting with enough explosive force to break both arms, and a neck with luck.

Hugh returned with the kettle full and the basin quarter-full of cold burn water. He laid the basin at her feet and fitted the kettle amongst the peats with the spout away from the smoke. "A grand night outside," he said conversationally.

"A grand night for walking down the glen," she said gently. "When are you going?"

"When God lets me," he told her, his voice coming from a mile down.

The unexpected reply always brings silence. Frances Mary leant an elbow on the frayed arm of the chair, rested her temple on her finger-tips, and looked sideways and up at him so intent on watching the flames lick round the belly of the kettle. A few minutes before and she had no desire to be in the least friendly with this man; now it was he who evinced no desire for friendliness. That was putting a "dare" up to her. Well, she could bide her time and say nothing. She could be very quiet, this girl; and, being quiet, she had a charm that was not obtrusive, yet had power. She looked at him and wondered in what valleys his thoughts ran as he gazed at the fire. Queer valleys where his thoughts ran and stilled!

A drift of steam came from the spout of the kettle. "It is hot enough," said Hugh Forbes in his throat. Without pause or thought he pulled off his fine velour hat and, using it as a holder, whipped the kettle off the fire. "Mind your feet, Frances Mary." And boys! it was a lovely name as he said it.

She looked down, and he did not see her smile. Frances Mary! But of course he would know her name, though that was the first time it had been spoken that night in that room.

He poured into the basin some of the hot water, and felt the temperature with the twiddle of a little finger. "Warm enough for a beginning," he murmured, laid the kettle within reach of her hand, and straightened up. "You will bathe that heel now," he told her, "and after a piece add a small drop more of the hot water, and then a drop more—until it is as hot as you can bear. And then wrap that wisp of silk round the sore place and slip the stocking over it. If you're not able to do all that, I'll help you."

"Thanks. I'll manage."

Praised be the saints for that! He, Hugh Forbes, did not want to have anything at all to do with a woman's feet. They were strangely disturbing things. No doubt the toes of that foot there would be pressed close together, but the instep would be arched and devastatingly white, and a thin delicate blue vein would reach over to the terrible curve of an ankle. And the smoothness of it: smoother than velvet, cooler than linen, and—"Hotter than the hob o' hell," said Hugh Forbes gloomily, and turned to the door. He went out from the hearty, ruddy, unsafe glow of the peat fire into the colder but not safer light of the moon.

The moon was well up now, and the mountains over there were no longer a ragged black silhouette. The black was purple and the purple pearl, and away in the south, high up on the shoulder of Ben a Mhuic, a bank of snow glistened white and aloof. He stood on the brink of the burn that ran gurgling down the brae to the

Abhain Ban and let his eyes wander over mountain and sky and finally come to rest on the river below him where silver streaks ran and vanished with the current.

As he stood thus, watching the roily glisten of the moonlight on the water, there came to his ears the sound of a long-drawn breath out of the hills—from near or far he could not say, but it made his neck hairs tingle. He faced round, head forward, shoulders hunched, feet planted. There it was again, back there in the lift behind the house—a long-drawn breath that filled the hills, a little laboured, and with something sibilant in it. Resolutely he walked up the burn towards it, and at once it stopped. He waited a full minute, but the hush of empty night was again supreme, drawn out thin and tense like a fine wire. "Stay in your own place," ordered the bass of his voice.

Frances Mary had heard that breathing sound too. It could be heard in a tomb. "What was it?" she asked him quietly, as he appeared in the doorway.

"A deer, a hawk, an owl, and the hills turning over in their sleep."

"A white owl, probably."

"Whatever it was, it won't hurt you." Perhaps the *you* was slightly accented.

"Oh! I'm not afraid."

"I am, like hell." But he did not tell of what he was afraid. He did not know—something elemental that underlay life.

He came to her side and saw the bottom of the pan shining through the water. "Woman!" he boomed, "did you bathe your foot at all?"

"I did; and made the water hot as . . . Look!" she thrust out the foot quickly and withdrew it again, but he saw where the silk bandage bulked under the stocking at the ankle.

"Are you feeling better now?"

"Splendid, thank you."

He took the basin outside the door and poured the water from shoulder-level on the grey grass, and the vanishing curve gleamed in the moonlight. "Let a rose grow there," his voice rumbled, "or a dandelion—or a thistle." He dropped the basin and went round to the back of the bothy.

III

When he again entered the room he carried in both arms a bundle of long grass and heather tops. "Could you be standing on one foot for a minute?" he requested, and without demur she obeyed, leaning on one foot, the other tip-toe, and a steadying hand on the arm of the chair. In that posture—in her cunningly shapeless frock —it would be no easy matter for any man to contemplate her reasonably. Hugh Forbes did not contemplate her at all.

He laid his bundle on the ridged seat of the old chair and shook it up loosely. "Wait now." He picked his coat off the floor and emptied both pockets on the table. There were two packages. "My luggage," he explained. Then he threw the coat over the chair so that it covered the seat and the open-back, and with a gesture of the hand that somehow displayed the tensed strength of his arm invited her to be seated.

Without a word of thanks she dropped into the chair, but she smiled softly into the fire, and, anyway, her thoughts were too busy for words. A woman must always discover a man's soul for herself—or his heart. Even her great brother, Charles, must not be allowed to impress his own impressions on her mind. And Charles was sometimes mistaken—as in the case of Vivian. He did not care for Vivian, and was inclined to be rude. A remote young god! Remote my eye! Only too damn cocksure to be inquisitive. That was her brother's opinion. Vivian could be mistaken too. He had despised this man here and had treated him as he would treat an impudent tramp. But she was discovering him for herself, outrageous tongue and heart of gold. How sure he had been that her heel needed laving, how closely and kindly he must have considered her to know that the old chair was uncomfortable! Vivian would never have thought things out in that way, and it was a pity that Vivian had made the kindly little man suffer under a strong hand. . . . He would be so very sensitive under his seeming bluntness.

Hugh Forbes did not think that he was being kindly. If he knew her thoughts he might say, "Kindly, hell! I am only trying to do the right thing by Tearlath Grant's sister." He kept on doing that. First he remade the fire, and then brought two armfuls of peat sods from the back place and built them up on the hearth. Thereafter he paused to think.

"I am quite comfortable now, thank you," said Frances Mary. "Don't let me detain you any longer."

He did not answer. The great hurry she was in to be rid of him! But he would go when he was ready to go, and not before. He felt a feather of chill air from the outside on the back of his neck, and looked over his shoulder at the open door. "The night air is bad for one," he remarked and went and shut the door, and then sat aside on the table. He placed his black hat over one of his paper packages. "Are you hungry?" he asked her.

"Don't mention it, please," she besought him, an eager eye on the hat.

"Would you like an Abernethy biscuit?"

"Only one thing I would like better."

"Two—and a skelb of cheese. There, then." His
hands juggled with the hat.

"Oh, you dear man!" Her white teeth bit cleanly, and
not a flake fell. "We finished our sandwiches early, and I
was ready to cry with hunger," she told him, her mouth full.

The healthy hungry young body of her! It would
transform dry biscuit and dull cheese into warm flesh,
and the light in grey eyes—and into soul, for all he knew.
Himself was not hungry any more. Never again, on top
of God's world, would he really hunger for anything—
food or wine, or even whisky, or—except, maybe, a girl,
and she with red hair. And that might only be a pose
after all. For a long time now the fear had been growing
on him that he was no more than a small collection of
poses hiding an emptiness that wanted nothing. "Lose
hunger and you lose God," he said gloomily.

"Eat, then. You have some there."

"Plenty. I ate my share coming down from the loch.
Here are two more for you, and we'll hold the others
as an emergency ration."

He picked up the kettle and again went out into the
moonlight. At the burnside he rinsed the old vessel
thoroughly and filled and refilled it under a miniature
cascade. When he got back Frances Mary was picking
the last few tiny crumbs off her lap, and not wasting any.
He laid the kettle by her chair and went into the back
place. "Neither a cup nor a saucer, a mug nor a glass,"
his voice rolled back; "but the gridiron is still here—
you could never drink out of a gridiron. Yes! and a
packet of damp salt! Devil the thing else." He came
out empty-handed. "I thought you would be needing
a drink of water," he said.

"I would like one," she admitted, and smiled confidently. Already she felt that she could dip into this
man's resources and find no lack.

He looked down at the kettle and smiled too. "I mind," he rumbled musingly, "Hugh Quigley of Glencroidhe—the heart's own glen—having a motherless half-bred foal, and he used feed her out of the spout of a tea-pot." He looked at her interrogatively.

"I am ready to taste any drink once," offered Frances Mary.

"Same as old Jurgen?"

"Oh! You know the American classics?"

"And you should not—the old helion he was." He picked up the kettle. "Mind you, you'll have to be careful," he warned her. "One splutter, and you'll have a pint of it down your neck."

Frances Mary flushed a little as her lips touched the spout. For a time she was concentrated on controlling inflow and outflow, and then happened to lift an eye. His face was as grim-set as a hanging judge's, and his whole being was welded to the job of holding the vessel at the right angle. That serious face was too much for her. She spluttered. And a tiny spurt of water leaped for her bosom before Hugh could tilt away the kettle.

"The devil mend you!" he said hotly, clamping the kettle on the floor. "See what you're after doing!"

"Wow!" she exclaimed. "That was cold." She lifted the top of her dress and shook herself like a puppy, and Hugh could not help glimpsing the exquisite white contrast of her breast below the cream of her throat.

"Many a man would be jealous of that drop of water," he said, calmly brazen, and left Frances Mary unutterably silent.

IV

Hugh Forbes sat on the table, leaning forward on his hands and his legs swinging. There was no more to be done and he would like to be doing something. He might be going on down the glen if he wanted to, and he told himself he wanted to, but he could no longer leave Tearlath Grant's sister—she was only that—alone in the aware wilderness. The wilderness was never dead—only sleeping, and once to-night it had turned over in its sleep. This young woman might not be afraid, but there was worse than fear. There was possession, and possession was hell.

"You tempt me grievously," said Frances Mary out of the silence.

Hugh looked at her puzzledly.

"What I have needed you have supplied," she explained, "and we are never happy till we get to the end of a man's resources."

"And ye wouldn't be happy then either."

"Probably not; but how much unhappier the man would be. What do you propose to do now?"

"I am going to have a smoke to myself." He took an old bent Peterson pipe from one pocket and an old leather pouch from another.

"You might have asked——"

"I might, then. With your permission——"

"Tut! I didn't mean that. You might have asked me to have a cigarette."

"Oh! is that it? Wait, now. I'm not beyond having a whiff sometimes." He thrust his hand into his breast-pocket and brought forth a battered but massive silver case. "Catch!—and there are the matches."

As Frances Mary lit her cigarette her downcast eyes caught a glimpse of a monogram engraved on the convex of the case lying in her lap. Without appearing to look, she examined it closely before the match burned down, and, though it was scrolled intricately, to her it was plain as print: "F. M. to C." Frances Mary to Charles! A girl of twelve, she had presented that case to her

57

brother Charles when he went to war in 1914. She gave no sign. For a time she sat very still, gazing into the fire and a finger smoothing over the dinted surface of the case. And then she smiled to herself. Let this small dark man be as secretive as he liked—and really he was simple—she would discover him for herself, and all that was in him. Why, she had probed him already and knew his capacity and his limitations. Charles might regard him as invincible but she had seen him under Vivian's hand. She knew that he could suffer. Vivian was so terribly strong! . . . Could they ever become friendly after what had happened? Vivian must be always a little contemptuous and this man a little shamefaced. . . . She must try and change that.

"I will not ask any more," said Frances Mary. "I should be afraid."

"There was never a woman yet," he rumbled, "who was ever afraid of asking, one way or another—tongue or eye."

"Yes," said Frances Mary agreeably.

"Yes so," he affirmed. He pivoted his legs on to the oblong of the table and lay on his back, his new hat crushed comfortably under his poll. The length of him fitted the board, and his chest stood up above his flat stomach.

"First you stood on it——"

"Or that long lad of yours——"

"Then you used it as a kettle-holder, and now you make a pillow of it—your fine velour hat."

"The man I bought it from said I could do what I liked with it and it would still remain a hat."

Her low chuckle was very pleasant. "You are due to prove him wrong—given time."

"Time! 'Tis all I have. It stands still all round me." He twisted the bowl of his pipe on the stem so that it hung at one side of his chin, and smoke drifted steadily to the black rafters. "Twisting it that way," he explained, "you don't get the ashes in your eye."

Frances Mary knew that. Charles had the same trick, learnt or taught.

For a time silence settled down between them. The fire burned without a sound, as peat fires do, and grotesque shadows danced solemnly on the lime-washed walls. In that soft dusky glow the room was cosy and satisfyingly mysterious, a small safe ark in the emptiness of the mountains, a haven where one could relax and snuggle down and dream as Frances Mary was dreaming now, her shoulders resting on Hugh Forbes's old coat, and her cigarette reddening and dulling lazily. She felt very safe and even a little happy: a sort of surprised happiness that had in it the faintest thrill of expectancy. She had always felt safe, of course, in her own hills, but of late happiness had stood off from her, and was only to be contemplated with a sudden, blinding sensation that was exquisite but painful.

Hugh Forbes, one knee drawn up, was thinking, too, in his own whimsical way. He was thinking of Tearlath Grant and the holiday they had contemplated—the two of them together on mountain, loch, and river. Ay! the two of them together! And here was himself, true to form, already complicating things. He never could help complicating things—no more than could a red-setter pup in a chicken-run. Tearlath Grant would be always Tearlath Grant, the friend of his heart; but now there was this girl here, Frances Mary of the darling name! Lying there on the table, his mind running back over the evening, he had to admit that this girl was not so very poisonous. Quiet she was, and what she had said had been quiet too, and had quality in it. As she sat there in the old chair, her long slim figure leaning back, and her head poised forward so that the line from crown to shoulder was graceful and alluring, there was a quiet dignity about her. No hoyden this. Was it she that gave a sense of comfort to the room? . . . This girl could not be easily ignored in the household of Innismore. . . . And then there was this fellow Stark, Vivian Stark. He would have to be considered, too, as a man who would have a very natural prejudice against being stood on his ear and rolled down a brae. "Damn!" said Hugh Forbes.

"Whom?" inquired Frances Mary.

"Myself, and Mr Vivian Stark, and you too, a small little bit. Would you mind telling me who this Mr Stark is?"

"My cousin. Charles William Vivian Stark. We call him Vivian so as not to confuse him with my brother Charles."

The devil himself could not do that wrong. "Your cousin? Is he ever called Bill?"

Frances Mary chuckled. She could not imagine the aloof Vivian called the devil-may-care Bill. "No."

"No. No one would ever call him Bill."

"It might be unwise. Vivian can be very autocratic." She did not add the "as you know" that was on the tip of her tongue.

Autocratic? *Autos*, self, and *kratos*, power. A man who holds all power in his own hands. Power over men? Well, now! Women? It could be. He had the build and the face and the intolerant blue eye. And her cousin, too! Cousins are naturally intolerant and unchivalrous, and that is perhaps why he trotted away down the glen. Surely he could hardly be so stupid as not to notice the warmth in a limpid grey eye? Whether or no, it was no business of Hugh Forbes; whose only business at present was to do the adequate minimum and keep a check on his disparaging tongue, if he could. Queer, all the same, that a fellow should run away from a good-looking young woman—not bad looking, anyway, in spite of her colouring. . . .

v

Hugh dropped one knee and lifted the other, and turned his head sideways to look at Frances Mary. Her eyes were on the fire and her face very still. That face had a good line to it; a self-reliant face but for the tell-tale eyes that were now hidden. Pity about those eyes. They made him feel uncomfortable. Youth displaying its high dreams to intolerance! He turned his head and looked at the wall at his other side. On its white surface was a drawing in carbon that dulled and sharpened in the pulse of the peat flames—a great sweep of hills in firm black lines, the royal tips of a stag's antlers against the sky, and a stalker and his gillie crouching flat and waiting.

"Landseer did that," came Frances Mary's quiet voice. "He did many of his sketches here."

"I thought you were looking at the fire," said Hugh, without turning his head.

"It made me feel sleepy."

He rolled off the table as handily as a cat. "Wait, now, and I'll make up the fire, and then I won't risk wakening you later on. You've had a long day and there are still hours in front of you. Foolish you were, and obstinate besides, and your pride sinful; but you had the pluck of the devil to bring your blister this far."

"It was sair," admitted Frances Mary softly.

He twisted on his knees at the fireside, and his black eyes flamed. "That man that was with you," his voice boomed, "was a blonde beast."

61

"No," she denied. "But he doesn't notice little things."

"So. 'Twasn't himself had the blister."

Yes, considered Frances Mary, this man could not be expected to know Vivian, and he would naturally be resentful. Men were slow to appreciate Vivian's qualities. Even Charles, who had known him for years, couldn't, or wouldn't. But she could and would; the aloof, high spirit, the mind and body that ignored in others what he ignored in himself, the austerely beautiful face with the clear but cold eyes. Ah! would she ever see warmth glow deep down behind the ice of those eyes? . . .

Hugh was again flat on the table, his eyes on the carbon drawing. "The dignified Landseer!" he mused aloud. "Even he would enjoy a holiday here. A good place for a holiday, this bothan."

"Yes, if you could produce biscuits, cheese, and tobacco out of your hat. I believe you could."

"Fish in the water, deer in the hills, coney, maybe, in the valleys and red stoat after them; a snared hare or a grouse, ptarmigan—heaps of things. One could do without bread and cheese—and even kisses."

She chuckled pleasantly. "Not for long. A straight meat diet palls, and bread and cheese are nearly as essential as kisses." She would have said that to no tramp, and no tramp would have snorted as Hugh snorted. "But you seek kisses, do you not?" she calmly answered that snort.

"I?"

"From one with red hair?"

"Cripes! Who said that?" This girl frightened him. He blinked rapidly, and his mind fell into caverns.

"You did, yourself. You said you would not be alone forever if there was a red-haired woman in Scotland."

"The tongue I have will be the ruin of me."

"It will," agreed Frances Mary. It had brought him disaster once already that night.

Hugh was relieved. He did not remember saying anything about red hair, but, in his time, he had said many things that he did not remember and did not worry any more when his words were brought home to him. He smiled across at her. "Maybe you know one with red hair?" he queried quizzically.

"There is one at home—at Innismore, now."

"Let her stay there, meantime," said Hugh coolly.

"I know a man who would like her to stay there all the time."

His mind twisted through and over and under that reply. A red-haired girl at Innismore and a man who would like to keep her there! Would that be Tearlath? Tearlath was never one for the girls; he could not be bothered, he often said. And yet! it might be Tearlath. A woman with red hair could knock a twist out of tougher material than went to his friend's making. Or it might be this Vivian—Bill Stark; and that might explain his coldness to warm grey eyes. This affair was getting complicated. And that was always the way with him. Before his eyes could behold the old house of Innismore, Innismore was entangling him—or he was entangling himself, the damn fool. And his holiday was to be an intrigue of tow-heads and redheads and. . . .

When next he looked at Frances Mary she was asleep, her head against his coat and her mouth with a gentle droop. Every now and then a wavering peat flame set her profile clearly against the far wall—clean fine lines from flaxen hair to long throat. Her face in sleep had grown very young and heart-stabbingly innocent; only once or twice the sweetness of her lips twitched into a small smile that was sad with regret or wistful with

63

anticipation. Queer how he felt that sense of possession and protectorship! And why not? He had fed her, and warmed water for her feet, and bedded her down cosily, and held fear away from her. Sleep on, then, little one—and not so blame little either—and if he could not help her dreams he might help her waking. If she wanted that long fellow let her have him, or let her find out before too late that he was not worth having. Tearlath Grant's sister! That was all she was, and it was a good deal. Youth wanted much and took it without thanks or lost it with clamourings. Himself was no longer young, thank God, and he could do without red hair or kisses —or any damn'd thing at all—he that was no longer hungry. . . .

CHAPTER VI

In grey stark dawn
　　Your glamour lives.
In slack of mood
　　Your beauty thrives.
His freedom feels like mountain air—
And yet you hold him with a hair.

I

WHEN Frances Mary waked, the fire was low in dull ash and high dawn had come in over the mountains. The tonelessness of it filled the room that was no longer cosy, but only drear and a little strange. Half-stifling a yawn, she turned to the table, and her teeth clicked sharply. The small dark man was not there. Had he ever been there? Was he only a unique creation out of dreams? But how could she dream so uniquely?—and here was his coat, and there on the table-end was his crumpled velour hat, out of which he could conjure biscuits and cheese, but not kisses. Where was he, then—and where was Vivian? It was full dawn and Vivian should have been here hours ago. She sat aside in the old chair and wondered, and in her mind Vivian Stark and the small dark man got curiously entangled. One was not here, and the other should be here. Where were they, then? Leaving her alone behind a shut door! And at once she knew anxiety. Those two men together! . . She leant over the other side of the chair and picked up her brown brogues.

The door yielded to her touch, and, supported by her long hazel crook, she limped out into the vastness of the morning. The great Glen Dhu curved away right and left and the mountains lifted themselves hugely into a thin sky. Over all that vast panorama was the even, still light of dawn, and life had receded to its last ebb. The brown of heather and the grey of rock were washed over with a toneless purple, and where the peaks gathered in about the gut of Loch Dhu a great rope of pearly mist bridged the glen and trailed round the shoulders of Cairn Ban. Above that band of mist the ridge of snow on Ben a Mhuic was a dead and appalling white. The babble of the little burn cascading down to the river was subdued to a whisper, and the voice of the river was only a murmur in a great emptiness. And the dawn wind was dead.

Frances Mary went to the edge of the brae and looked down towards the Abhain Ban. It ran swift and coldly over cold stones, and a great stag stood on the farther bank and stared at her. For half a minute he faced her as immovable as a statue, his grand head thrown high and his sweeping antlers patched with brown velvet, and then and suddenly he swung round and went loping up the far brae with indescribable ease and grace, silent as a shadow.

There was neither sound nor sight of the small dark man on the river front of the bothy, but, possibly, he was at the rear up the burnside. Frances Mary limped round the gable-corner and stopped dead. "Oh!" she gasped. And then in alarm, "What is it?"

Hugh Forbes, leg-wide, was lying on his breast on the very brink of the burn, an ear to the ground and his face turned towards her. His jacket was off and the sleeves of his mat shirt folded above the elbows. One shoulder and upper-arm were out of sight below the overhang of the bank and the other arm was propped from the elbow, the brown fist gripping a heather tuft and the muscles of the forearm standing out below a

66

film of black hair. It was his face that frightened her. It was wiped clean of all expression, the mouth was half-open, and the fully opened eyes looked at her and did not see her. A dead face might look like that—or the face of one concentrated so deeply on listening to some faint and unspeakable whisperings from the very bowels of the earth that the surface of life had stilled and steeled. It was those black eyes staring through her as if she were glass that forced that cry from her. "Oh! What is it?"

And then Hugh Forbes came alive. His eyes blinked, his teeth clicked, a muscular spasm twisted his face, and the arm that was over the bank scooped out of the water. Something shining black-and-gold curved through the air and fell at her feet. Frances Mary, arching her body inwards, screamed heartily.

Hugh twisted himself over with supple ease, propped himself on his hands, threw his head back into his shoulders, and his great laughter lightened the dawn. In that posture his long broad neck looked as massive as a tower. "There, now! I lay half her breakfast at her feet and she only screeches."

An eight-inch trout was flapping out its life on the grass between the heather-tussocks. Frances Mary looked down at it and drew in a deep breath. "You startled me," she said in a small voice, and the startle had not yet quite vanished from the wide-set grey eyes she turned on him.

"Did I, now," said his softest rumble. "I wouldn't like to frighten you, Frances Mary." His eyes travelled from her face down to the loosely-laced shoes. "And is the blister sair this morning?"

"Not a bit. I believe I could walk all the way to Innismore. But, how is it that Vivian—no one is back with the pony?"

67

"He'll be." Hugh spoke carelessly, though he was wondering too. "You said yourself there was no hurry, and 'tis barely morning. First we'll have a good breakfast to ourselves, and then hold council; 'tis bad to think on an empty stomach. I guddled three more besides that one."

She looked down at him and smiled, and in her smile was marvel and admiration and something that was a shade too warm for respect. Oh, you adequate small man that can produce things out of your hat, or out of nothing! "What is it you cannot do?" she wondered softly.

His eyes travelled back to her face. It was a little grey and weary this fine morning, the eyes gone pale and her hair without its lustre; but it was not a weak or petulant face, and the body below the shapeless frock had the long lithe lines of resilient youth. "I cannot wash your face for one thing," he told her; "and, God knows, it needs washing."

"I am sure it does," she agreed, her finger-tips rubbing her cheek. "I do feel gritty. I see you have already washed—but you might have shaved too."

"That can wait." His palm grated across his broad blue-black chin. Above the blue-black film his face, though bloodless, was healthy cream, his eyes clear, and his black hair crisp in damp bunches.

She thrust a hand towards him. "Let me have a nice diaper towel, please?" she ordered with mock imperiousness.

"Wait, now." He was on his feet in one complicated effort of muscle and away round the corner of the bothy and back again in five seconds, carrying one of his paper packages. "My luggage," he explained, and opened it on the grass at her feet. It contained a pair of grey worsted socks and two white handkerchiefs. One of the latter he handed up to her. "That'll have to do," he said.

She took it in a silence that had in it something of awe. She shook the generous expanse of linen out of its fold and got the clean whiff of ozone. "What lovely material!" she murmured through it, and smiled down at him. "I am going down to the river. You won't look, of course."

"I'll be busy cleaning the trout; but, if I looked itself, what harm?"

II

When Frances Mary got back up the brae from the river, Hugh was nowhere in sight, but a most deliciously tantalising odour came to her nostrils through the door of the bothy. She wisely followed her nose, sniffed frankly, and drew in a deep breath. "How fine I feel," she cried; "and how hungry!"

Hugh turned his head over shoulder from where he sat on his heels at the fireside. "You look fine too," he remarked; "and hunger is the fine sauce. Come away in." His face crinkled pleasantly. "I see you have taken your eyes out and polished them."

Frances Mary felt a queer little thrill of content. Under the pearl of her skin the clean blood of her came faintly but most delicately; her eyes surely did look freshly polished; and her damp hair curled over brow and ears. Hugh Forbes might well think at the moment that she was a darling girl besides having a darling name. She came close to his side with some new-found sense of companionship and looked over his shoulder. He had fitted the old gridiron over some crushed red peat, and the four trout were curling and browning on that martyr's bed. The packet of wet salt was drying-out close to the fire and he was grinding a pinch of it over the sizzling fish.

"That one and that are your two," he pointed out. "Any complaints have to be put in writing."

"I'll have the other two, I think."

"Very well so. And, besides, there are two biscuits and a skelb o' cheese for each of us. You'll have to take your drink for yourself this morning."

"And my knife and fork?" She was getting nice in her requirements.

"Fingers were made before forks, as my mother often told me. Tear that piece of paper in two, and I'll serve breakfast."

Frances Mary had no fault to find with that breakfast. Imitatively she sat aside on the table, one rounded leg swinging, and, imitatively but very daintily, she pinched the succulent white flesh between finger and thumb and consigned it pinch by pinch to its proper place. And like healthy young barbarians they made no small-talk.

She was giving her fingers a final and regretful touch of pink tongue-tip when, glancing through the small-paned window, she saw something that very nearly made her bite it. "Here they come!" she exclaimed.

"Where?" He darted his head so quickly that it touched hers and a curl tickled his cheek. He looked for the rescue-party on the near reach of the path.

"Not there—away beyond." She pointed, and he looked along her arm. The white path went out of sight round a horn of the glen and came again into view, perhaps a mile away, rounding another curve. And within that curve a tiny cavalcade was strung out. The two watchers narrowed their eyes and looked.

"Two ponies and two people—one a woman," noted Hugh.

"That will be Allison."

"Allison?"

"Yes. Allison Ayre. She has red hair, you know. The other is Vivian."

"Not—your brother?"

"No. I think that is Vivian." It must be Vivian. Since there were only two people, one had to be Vivian. Anything else was unthinkable.

The little cavalcade crawled out of sight into the hollow of the hill, and Hugh's eyes stared unwinking at the point of its disappearance. In twenty minutes or less it would again come into sight around that near curve—Stark and the red-haired one. Allison—Allsoon in the old tongue, Allsoon Ayre! A fine name too, but not holding the quality of Frances Mary. And with red hair! Ay, but when it came to the bit did he want red hair, or any other sort of hair? Was his boasted quest only a pose after all—something snatched out of dreams to keep dreams alive, a pretext that he could still hunger?

"They'll be here soon now," said Frances Mary. "We got on splendidly without them."

Hugh nodded. And they could do without them. Whatever might be said of red hair he had no desire at all to meet Stark—here or in hell. Big Tearlath Grant was the man he wanted to meet, and no one besides. And Tearlath was not there. Queer, that! Stark would have told him that Hugh Forbes was at Aunbeg. . . . Wait, now! He must think this out. He himself wanted to meet Tearlath alone, and Tearlath would want to meet him alone. A wise lad, Tearlath. He must be lying in the heather down there somewhere this very minute, waiting to jump out on him and give him a bear's hug and a tumble or two. . . . And then the two of them would sit on the grass and let their legs hang over, and get the feel of each other before going amongst strange people. And that was Tearlath.

III

Hugh Forbes blessed himself by way of grace after meat and reached for the black velour hat that was not nearly so new as it had been yesterday. He turned from the table and looked about the bare room. There was his ash-plant on the hearth, and there, on the chair, was his old coat whereon she had slept. The hat fell into place over an ear, the coat went over an arm and the ash-plant under it, and, without a glance or a word for Frances Mary, he went out the door into the brightening morn. She followed him slowly and wondered. What he called his luggage was lying on the grass where he had opened it, and this he bundled quickly and thrust in the side pocket of the burberry. The handkerchief that she had used and rinsed was lying over a tussock of heather, and he left it there.

"Are we going on to meet them?" she inquired.

"You might do that," he told her. She did not ask him to explain. She was a quiet girl and would not importune him. He had to admit that much now. He smiled at her. "Maybe I will climb back over Cairn Ban and never stop running till I get to a place I know that is a safe place. I couldn't be saying yet. Meantime I go my own road, and God be with the two of us, Frances Mary."

Without another word he turned the corner of the bothy and went marching up the side valley by the course of the little burn.

Frances Mary, some new speculation in her eye, limped to the corner and watched him go. His shoulders were thrown back and swayed rhythmically in time to the

72

peculiar, rolling, bow-legged swing of his legs from the hips. Some distance up he jumped the burn, his coat flapping, and, without a glance back, forged into the heather and disappeared round the flank of the knoll. And still Frances Mary stood gazing up the burn, and the speculation deepened in her eye. He would go his own road and let God be with the two of them. Apart, and was God with them? That was in God's power. And now he was gone on his own road. That road might twist and turn and lead him far, and at the end of it he might be surprised and she not be. And she not be. . . .

Frances Mary smiled a little wistfully. Then she limped across to the handkerchief, now almost dry, picked it up, and returned to the house.

CHAPTER VII

Her feet shall fall
Like thistle down
And crush his heart
Without one stoun.
O feet so white! O vein so blue!
To your fell purpose gently true.

I

Hugh Forbes lay on his back in the thick dry heather,
his coat under him, and stared up at the high, cloudless
morning sky. The sun was up now behind the eastern
ramparts, the chill was gone out of the air, and the
mountains were no longer savagely dead. They spaced
themselves out kindly and their high shoulders were in
the full day. The rocks on Cairn Ban, away up there,
glinted with orange, and the snow-bank on Ben a Mhuic
was flushed with pink. A hill-lark sprang up within a
hundred yards of him, singing its brave and lonely song,
and he watched it spiralling up and up into the blue.
When it was a mere speck his eyes left it for a bigger and
blacker speck that soared immensely high over the gut
of Loch Dhu. That would be a golden eagle, the first
he had seen. It soared as high as any kite of Syria: the
kites that with telescopic eyes had watched men die along
Jordan—where there was no peaceful camp-ground.
Maybe the eyes up there were watching him as he lay.
Every now and then the speck slid sideways like a bead
on a wire and then hung motionless. Presently it would
swoop like a thunderbolt, and heaven help some hare
crouching in the heather. How did Tennyson put it?
"The wrinkled sea beneath him crawls"—he got a sense

of the deeps of the air in that line—"and like a thunder-bolt he falls—close to the sun in lonely lands, clasping the crags with crooked hands." Was that it? He waited for that deadly swoop with interest, but it was slow in coming, and his eyes grew weary. He found himself looking through his lashes at a chain of minute trans-parent beads that floated down below his vision and then flitted up again. Some slight defect of sight that, but, of course, no sight was ever perfect. Couldn't be. . . .

He turned over on his face, his hands under his chin and his eyes looking through the twisted heather stems. When you looked at the heather low down like that, how like a forest it was! If one could forget comparisons! Between that immense bole and that one was not an inch but a hundred paces. . . . And now, in all truth, it was primeval forest, and he was gazing down far vistas between the huge trunks of strange trees. That insect crawling was a—a brontosaurus or a mastodon or something—no, a pterodactyl; and his own breath was a wind that made a hundred leagues of wood tremble. . . . The forest was gone now, and he was in the youth of the world, looking across a swollen and muddy river at a line of great, yellow-clay, green-crowned bluffs that had scaled down into the turgid water. He was very lonely and very much afraid, and the world was empty—empty—empty.

II

A hand on his shoulder waked him, and in his first waking he was glad to see Frances Mary sitting at his side in the heather. He that could smile smiled at her. "I was asleep, Frances Mary," he said simply.

"You were, Hugh," she said quietly, "though you did not deserve to sleep."

75

He twisted lithely and sat up. He was fully awake now and looked at her warily. "That is my name surely," he said. "Time you found it out."

Her smile was pitying and a little sombre. "I knew your name when the night was still young."

He took some time to grasp that. He might have known; but what the devil could he know about women? No use being surprised, anyway. He lifted his hand in salute. "Glad to meet you, Frances Mary."

She put out a hand and touched his arm. "What did you do to Vivian Stark last night?"

Wait, now! A sudden wallop in the wind like that was good for no man. What had he done to Vivian Stark last night? A little and then some, by dam'. Stark, the fool, must have told her; and there was no need to tell her, no reason in the world.

"You and he were fighting?"

That was a flaming lie, anyway. Fighting! A bit of a bustling match was not fighting. King of the castle only. "We were not, Frances Mary," he expostulated. He thrust out his broad strong hands, palm down. "Look! Not a mark on them."

"How did you break his collar-bone, then?"

"Blazes!" cried Hugh Forbes, and could say no more for a while. It was that last flying-mare—and no wonder! A broken collar-bone! That could not be argued away by any finesse of truth or lying. But could not a collar-bone be broken in a variety of ways? Coming down Cairn Ban, tripping over the edge of the path in the dark, flying from a catawampus—anything but the truth. That big fellow would be a stickler for the truth, and take credit for it. One small lie and all indignity and complications would be avoided. Two make a team, and a team could play or fight and please nobody but themselves—but three, and four, and five! What a splendid fine introduction he was having to Innismore! "Blast him!" said Hugh aloud.

"But why did you break his collar-bone? How?"

This persistent query was too much for him. Why did he break it? Great Jehoshaphat! Who started the manhandling before her eyes? Who would not talk? Who would be intolerant? Who— But what was the use of trying to explain? Naturally, she would see it from Stark's point of view, and . . . Suddenly he felt a little surge of heat go through him, and that steadied him. This man, when really angry, was anything but ebullient. He did no more than lean forward towards her and look at her, but the shock of those level eyes made her shrink.

"I did not set out to break his collar-bone, woman dear." His voice drawled deeply. "I am sorry I broke his collar-bone. It was his neck I was trying to break." He lifted his open hand before her eyes, and she drew back an inch, her eyes failing to focus on the spread fingers. "And look here, my fine partisan; you can tell that long man of yours that the next time he lays a finger on me I'll drive that hand through his breast-bone, and feed his pea-nut of a heart to a hound-pup."

"Oh!" said Frances Mary.

"Yes so. And to save you the trouble I'll tell him myself."

He was on his feet, lithe as a spring. But she was on hers just as quickly and without the aid of her hazel crook. Her hand checked him for a moment, and her voice brought him to a dead halt.

"He is not here at all," she cried.

He turned to her. "And his collar-bone?"

"That is broken—and I've just learned who broke it."

"You are a dangerous tow-headed devil," said Hugh

Forbes with complete conviction. Then another thought struck him eagerly. "Who were the two?——"

"Allison and Charles."

"Tearlath himself!" he cried, and this time her hand failed to check him. He was already ten strides away when her voice reached him.

"They are gone away again."

That halted him for a moment. "Where to?" he questioned over his shoulder.

" Back to Innismore—with the ponies."

"I'll soon overtake them"; and he was off again.

"Never!" she cried. "They are gone this hour."

He glanced eastward to the sun as he went. An hour or more surely. He could never do it this side of Innismore—and Frances Mary back there in the heather. What in thunder was in her mind, anyway? It might be worth inquiring into. It might, then—and Stark with a busted collar-bone. His first impetus died, but he had almost reached the burn before that impulse of curiosity, or inevitability, halted him. Even then he was slow to turn back. For a long and a long time he gazed at his toes, his face brooding and his mouth apurse. "Well, well, well!" he said at last and resignedly.

Frances Mary was standing where he had left her. Her back was turned to him and her head adroop; leaning on one foot, a knee turned in, and her fingers curving at the end of her long arms: something touchingly despondent in her attitude. And the austerely curving lines of her filled the eye.

"Damn her!" said Hugh Forbes, "she might as well have nothing on."

III

He came round her shoulder and faced her, "Let us make a fresh start, Frances Mary," he said quietly.

The delicate blood-flow had ebbed from her face, leaving it pale, but in her eyes was a dark glow hardly to be differentiated from obstinacy. "What brought you back?" she inquired coldly.

Hugh Forbes had no surprising answer ready. "Easy, easy," he placated, in a new rôle. "The referee has left the ring, and I'm still groggy. Would you mind explaining——"

"Certainly," she interrupted him firmly. "You got me into all this trouble, and I relied on you to get me out of it."

He sat down all in one piece, as if pole-axed. His head waggled loosely from side to side, and a glazed look came into his eyes. "You've got me going again," he expostulated. "Please be patient with me and sit down."

She looked down at him and smiled secretly, but she was perplexed too—and a little troubled. So this was the inexplicable Hugh Forbes. She knew who he was, of course, early in the night, but at the same time she had confidently made an estimate and a mind picture of him that—that would have to be revised drastically. And that was difficult. To think that she had been sorry for him in his degradation, and he licking his chops all the time! He had gone out the door like a small urchin, broken Vivian's collar-bone, and returned out of the night and as calm as the night. What had actually happened? How could Vivian, the great athlete, be mastered by this small man? Yet Vivian had had his collar-bone broken and had gone off down the glen. But then he had wanted to go down the glen—and he had not come back. Queerly enough she did not resent that broken collar-bone. Partisan though she might be, she realised that Vivian, having initiated strenuous action, had to abide by it. But she might have known that if this Hugh Forbes was the Aodh MacFirbis esteemed by her brother Charles, he would not stand many indignities without protest—and at the end his protest must have been chain lightning. The little thug! Grinning at her like an urchin, and some iron hardihood below the grin! Simply, she had failed to understand him, and would have to begin over again. And that troubled her and gave her a sense almost of foreboding—of the fateful, of the forbidden. For Frances Mary, sitting in the heather, had been watching Hugh Forbes as he lay asleep, his face turned aside on his forearms; and that sleeping face had been the face of a stranger. There was then no quirk at mouth corner, no wayward gleam in the eyes, no sardonic impishness. It was a strong, sombrely calm face, hiding all the deeps of the mind, telling her nothing, unknown to her, not knowing her. And then he had opened his eyes and smiled to her, and her heart had turned over in her breast. For that smile seemed to open for a moment a window into deep places —and she knew virginal fear.

And here he was now, giving her a fresh aspect—sitting cross-legged, his hands holding his shins, and in another moment he might do something astonishing. It behoved her, then, to hold on to the advantage she seemed to have gained. She sat down in front of him as women sit, her feet under her and an arm propped from the shoulder.

He looked at her cautiously from under his brows and made a mild suggestion. "If you would begin at the beginning——"

"Are you not Hugh Forbes?"

"I—well, I was sure of it a small while ago, but now . . ."

She resumed her catechism, and he replied with solemn nods. "You saw me at Croghanmoyle yesterday? You learned that we were climbing Cairn Ban? You

noted that I had the beginning of a sair blister? And
what did you do about it?"

He could not answer that last question with a nod.
"Nothing," he said, sarcastically regretful. "And wasn't
I the fool? I ought to have known that the female with
long legs was Frances Mary Grant in bad company,
and I ought to have taken her by one lug and clouted
the other lug, and drowned Bill Stark in the Croghanmoyle."

"You didn't do half badly later on. You tried to
break his neck, and you called me a damn'd little fool."

"Thank God for that much, anyway," said Hugh
Forbes heartily.

He was getting his wind and his tongue back, and it
was up to her to hit him another pile-driver. "Listen,
then. If I had not known that you were expected at
Innismore last evening I should not have made that
blister worse by hurrying the climb in order to be there
to look after you."—Dimly it came to his mind that she
was in no hurry at this bothy of Aunbeg.—"And if you
had not taken your silly short-cut and intruded on us at
the bothy, Vivian would have gone for a pony and all
would have been well. And if you had gone yourself
when you were asked, all would have been well. And
even after that, if you had refrained from breaking
collar-bones, all would have been not so bad. With
whom, then, does the responsibility lie?"

"With Hugh Forbes and be damn'd to him!" he cried
in his biggest voice.

"Keep it, then, till we get home to Innismore."

"Girl, dear," his voice was pleasant now, "your logic
has the force of a trip-hammer, though your premises
are away round the corner. Wait, now. Having ap-
portioned the blame and the responsibility and kindly
handed me the lot, will you come down to brass tacks

81

and explain how your brother Charles, my friend Tear-lath, who was here in this place, is here no longer?"

"Because he found no one here when he arrived."

He examined her from peeping knee to flaxen crown. "The diaphanous ghost that you are——"

"Nonsense! I hid too." But she did not tell him that she had not hidden till the rescue-party had appeared round the near curve of the glen, and until she, looking through the window, had seen that the man was not Vivian Stark.

"Well, that beats the devil," said Hugh solemnly, and he could think of nothing else to say. Fragments of thought and speculation were jumbling in his mind about the one clearly-grasped fact that she had stayed behind with him—and alone. But what had happened Tearlath to make him turn tail without search? He frowned. Tearlath would never have done that on him. What, then, had she done? And, heavens above! why did she do it?

She answered his thought. "I couldn't think of letting you run away from your responsibilities."

"And that's a fine fat lie. But never mind. 'Tis poor Tearlath that I'm troubled about. Failing he must be, and small wonder, with the sister he has in the family, or else would he not be wondering why he had not met us on the road up? Wouldn't he have cast about?——"

"No. I was hiding in the back place behind the peats and Charles and Allison came into the bothy and talked. 'We have missed them, Allison,' was what he said. 'They've gone the short-cut by the corrie of Ben Bhreac, and if we hurry we'll overtake them.'"

"Just so. And your other information?"

"Allison was so full of curiosity—she has red hair, you know. She would speculate on what had happened last night, and wanted Charles to tell her how he thought

Vivian had broken his clavicle. Charles did not know. 'Ask Vivian,' he told her. 'If Aodh Forbes did it, Aodh Forbes won't say.' But Aodh did."

"He did—the blame fool. And then they went off; and here we are."

There was silence then, Frances Mary watching Hugh, and Hugh contemplating his shoes. Frances Mary had nothing more to say, and Hugh, having a good deal to say, dared not say any of it.

After a time he got slowly to his feet, picked up his burberry and his ash-plant, and looked down at Frances Mary. "Let us make a start, then, in God's name," he said resignedly, and there was no smile on his face.

IV

They went back to the bothy together. Frances Mary was deeply silent, and now she felt strangely bleak and embarrassed. What she had done had been done on impulse—or what seemed impulse—sudden, impish, and not inappropriate in the circumstances. And now she was on the brink of regret. After all, the atmosphere of last night could not be lived in for ever. That was something special for the time and the place and the man— yes! the man, too. But now it was day, and the man had suddenly grown very quiet and aloof. And she could do nothing more to revive the old sib feeling.

He was indeed reserved and silent, but his mind had not yet withdrawn into its shell. With head down and eyes glancing round the curve of an arm he was watching very closely the progress Frances Mary was making. She was walking with only the barest trace of limp, but she leant heavily on her hazel crook, and he knew that no hazel staff cut by hands could help that limp over eight miles of hill track. Something he must do, and what could he do? Soft-soled, she could not walk shoe-less on granite gravel. He might cut the heel of that brogue away—a sort of sandal effect. It was too big for her and the hose too thin, and— Then he smiled again and, once more, the adequate, antic Hugh Forbes held the stage.

They got round to the front of the bothy, and Hugh noticed that the door was padlocked. "Charles locked me in," Frances Mary explained. "He said it was—oh!—silly of me to leave the door on the latch. I crawled head first through the window."

"I would like to see you at it," said Hugh whimsically. "Pity it wasn't smaller." He turned to her quickly and touched her arm lightly. "Wait now, Frances Mary, and let me have a look at that doubtful hoof." He dropped on one knee in front of her, and she slid forward a brown shoe. Her hands dropped to her sides and held her short skirts tight against her straight shins.

"Yes," he growled deeply, "that shoe is too big for you. Sevens you would take?"

"That is a five—and too new also."

He considered, head aside and a hand rubbing across his nutmeg-grater chin. Clean ankles she had—no spavins at any rate. He remembered seeing horse-copers running a hand down a filly's shins in the search for splints, but—she would kick his eye out at the very least. Better not try it, Hughie. Quickly he thrust out a hand, jerked loose the lace-tag, and sat back on a heel out of harm's way.

"How would you like to travel the last few miles on my back?" he questioned, looking up at her sternly; "your long legs trailing and you breathing in my ear?"

"I would bite it," she said firmly.

"Take off your shoe, then."

She looked at him steadily, and he smiled. "You have

84

laid the obligation on me," he reminded her, "and it is up to us to get to Innismore on our four feet." He gestured brusquely towards the shoe.

Without a word she turned and chose the tallest tussock of heather. She sat with her back to him and looked over her shoulder. "It is off, tyrant," she told him.

"And the stocking as well."

Her eyes widened at that order. "Must I?"

"It is a thundering sight easier for you than for me," he spoke savagely.

"Oh, very well!" She took some time to the business, and when it was done waited silently, and, when he came round to her shoulder, bent forward and hastily drew in that bare foot at the end of a shapely long leg.

Inexorably, his face grim, he came round to the front. "I must have a look at that heel," he told her. He carried his luggage in one hand, the grey worsted socks and the white linen handkerchief. "I won't bite you, God knows," he said fervently, "and that heel has to last out eight miles. Let me look at it, *aweenoch*."

"There you are, then." She thrust out her foot impulsively, toes and instep acurve, and her grey eyes were cold in a warm face. He took that foot in two finger-tips and turned it and his head sideways to get a look at the blistered heel. "Ouch! that ankle is not a universal joint," she warned him.

"Wo-wo-wo!" His voice had a deep croon. "The poor weeshy wee heel that's in it!" But 'tis fine healing you have, girl, and fine is the young blood."

"You are so extremely old yourself, of course."

"Sometimes I do be feeling very old," his brogue rolled musically. "And sometimes I do not be feeling old enough"—the muscle quirked at a mouth-corner—"same as now."

85

He laid the sole of that shapely foot against his uplifted knee, tore the linen handkerchief in three strips, and bandaged the heel with almost professional skill. The last time he had bandaged a foot had been in the cold eastern dawn after the night attack on Gaza. The hard hoof of a Kerryman, and not too clean. Blood and sand and the Kerryman smoking his last cigarette! There was no blood on his hands now, and the foot he ministered to was clean and white like milk, and the smooth fineness of it almost denied the sensation of touch. And there, too, as he had known, was that delicate blue vein aslant over the instep into the devastating curve of the ankle. And there were no fire blazes on the long shin of her as he had seen among the ancient, bare-legged women of the West, and, if he could see above the edge of that dress, there would be no calluses on the knee either— "not from saying your prayers, at any rate," he said aloud.

She must have followed his thoughts with uncanny closeness. "Sometimes I say them in bed," she murmured, "but I never forget."

He looked up, his forefinger pressed on the end of the bandage. "Don't you, now?"

"Not ever."

"That's damn nice, Frances Mary," he commended warmly. "Put your finger there, will you?" He turned one of the grey socks inside out, slipped it over her obediently bunched toes, and worked it gently over the bandaged heel. Then he fitted on the shoe, laced it firmly, and gave it a little tug to test the firmness of the fit. "Try that," he said with satisfaction.

She got to her feet, bent forward on her toes, stamped her heel on the ground, and "Splendid!" she cried. "I shan't have to bite your ear after all." Then and suddenly she swung to him, thrust out a hand with a heart-warming gesture, and there was warmth in her cheeks and in her eyes. "Thank you, Hugh; and please forgive me. I have been a bit of a beast."

"My fine girl!" His voice vibrated and his hand gripped firmly. "Sure you are your brother's sister after all."

"You could say no more. You see, I knew who you were early on, and you kept tempting me to find out all the things you could magic out of nothing—or out of your fine new hat—and I warn you the temptation still bides."

"The golden apples of the sun, the silver apples of the moon," murmured Hugh Forbes; and, aloud, "We are ready for the road now. Will you make the pace, Frances Mary?"

She peeped down at her long bare leg. "Perhaps you had better make the pace," she suggested.

He grinned at her. "The postmaster and myself back there at Croghanmoyle agreed that you had no splints, and if I keep about ten yards behind——"

"You'll keep one bare yard in front, Mr Forbes, and if you as much as glance over your shoulder I'll push you over the edge into the Abhain Ban."

"'Her feet beneath her petticoat, like little mice, stole in and out as if they feared the light.' Dear, oh dear! Oh! very well so! We'll be taking our time, watching the river run and the shadows flow, and betwixt and between we might be singing a marching tune. Are you ready? By the left—quick march! Left-right! Left-right! . . ."

CHAPTER VIII

The Love of man
For man most leal,
The loyalist love
That man may feel,
With nothing lost or nothing gained,
Is not the love by Fate ordained.

I

THE old house of Innismore is at the mouth of Glen Dhu, and the glen at that place no longer deserves the name black. It is a wide and a green glen, and the green breasts up the side of the hills and, like a sea, girdles the grey islands of limestone that outcrop hither and yon. Just outside the high wire fence of the deer forest the Abhain Ban makes a wide loop that encloses ten acres, and in the middle stands the house of smooth freestone, mellowed by years, with a portico under tall columns, a green shaven lawn in front, and trees in plenty: alders by the river, copper-beeches on the grass, silver birches on the lift of a brae, and a wood of black pine in the background where the north wind searches. The house looks due south up the first reach of the glen, and the great peaks that crowd in on Loch Dhu peep at it one behind the other. One long used to looking up the deep trough of the hills at the far towering summits calm in the sun, not changeful in any wind, austere under their white mantle, might acquire serenity and fortitude if he had the roots thereof in him; and if he had not, must hide behind a terrible patience, or die.

It was a sunny fine morning, and three people were on the lawn before the house, and, though a passing impatience was on them at the moment, serenity and fortitude had not failed to blossom and persist. Two of them sat side by side on a rustic seat that encircled the trunk of a wide-armed copper-beech, and the third stood, foot on the seat and elbow on knee. From under the cool dark sheen of the branches the spread of clipped lawn looked comfortable and sunny and, somehow, safe. Beyond the level of it a clump of shrubberies lapped an angle of a red-brick garden wall, and beyond that two tall white posts, supporting a swing bridge across the river, stood out against the lift of the brae beyond.

The two seated were ladies, one past middle age, with hair shining white, a gently lovely aquiline face and great limpid dark eyes; the other was young and red-haired. The third was a man, young and very big—all of six feet, with great shoulders dwarfing his height; his brown fine hair receded from a white dome of forehead, and his blue eyes crinkled engagingly; his strong short nose stood out above a mouth that might be a trifle loose if the chin had been weak, but was a wholly pleasant mouth in his face. A kindly, happy, placid man—only just now there was a humorous perplexity in his eyes. He was clothed in loosely-fitting brown homespun, and his trousers had not been pressed for at least two weeks.

"Did Allison and you have breakfast, Charles?" inquired the white-haired lady. The notable quality in her voice was its quietness, an apart, ruminative quality, as if she spoke out of some calm, secret place where thoughts engrossed her.

"Some, mother," said Charles Grant.

The red-haired Allison gave a silver derisive chuckle, and her voice was as flexible as a flute. "Some! And, besides, we ate all the sandwiches and drank all the coffee coming down from Aunbeg. Charles said it would be a pity to waste them, but I only got two sandwiches, Aunt Caroline—because I rode a pony."

"You drank most of the coffee, Red-head," Charles told her off-handedly. "I wonder," he speculated, "where these two devils are off to."

His mother did not look at him. Her lovely big-pupilled eyes gazed out over the lawn, but her ear was lifted towards him as if sensing the mood behind the voice. She smiled slowly. "They are all right," she said.

He looked down at her and paused. He accepted her words, not as a cheerful hope but as a statement of fact. His mother would know if things were not all right. She always did know. "But of course," he agreed. "Wherever Aodh is things are right—but interesting. What bothers me is that I cannot get a slant at what they are up to. You know they could have no grub with them."

"Which is the important factor, Charles, isn't it?" This was the red-haired girl, teasingly.

The silver-haired lady's smile deepened. "Listen!" she said. "Here they come now."

The two young people turned quick heads towards the white posts at the bridge. There was no one there, but from beyond came the sound of care-free singing: two voices raised in a fine song, the round contralto of a woman in her youth and the great roll of a man's baritone.

"Well, I'll be shot!" cried Charles Grant joyfully. "The infernal cheek of them!"

He slapped his thigh resoundingly, pivoted on his heel, and set out across the lawn at a full run. He did not run lumberingly, as heavy men run, but like a lad in a hurry, very fast and with the natural ease of a bird winging—like a Scots forward against devil-may-care

Irishmen—not the dour implacable rush with the Calcutta Cup at stake.

"David and Jonathan!" exclaimed the red-haired girl a trifle peevishly.

Aunt Caroline's eyelids flickered through a smile. "You go too, Allison."

"May as well have a look at Frances Mary," she agreed, and lifting slowly to her feet, Allison strolled easily across the lawn, while the white-haired woman, her ears set to listening, stared out across the valley and retired into her secret place of quiet.

Hugh Forbes came to the white posts at the end of the bridge and saw his great Tearlath Grant charging across the grass. "Feet! Feet!" he boomed and went out to stop that rush in a series of zigzag bounds, like a hard-bitten and indestructible full-back. And like two young bulls they met, rolled, and sat up side by side, an arm on each other's shoulder. Their hands patted each other and laughter was in their open mouths. The black velour hat was at their feet and it was flatter than any pancake.

"Blast!" cried Hugh Forbes; "I am always forgetting my good hat."

Tearlath reached forward and held it up at arm's length. "That's a hell of a nice hat, Aodh," he said, frank admiration in his tones.

Frances Mary, coming along the bridge behind Hugh, did not pause to watch the strange meeting of these two friends. She set foot on the path that went housewards by the side of the red-brick wall, and the dignity of her progress was the dignity of a queen. But within she felt no dignity. Suddenly, amongst her own folk, she felt only a consciousness of her long bare leg—her shameful, mile-long, short-socked limb that had to go striding, and in striding cried aloud for notice. She felt herself blush, and she felt her leg blush too, and that, of course, would make it look more ridiculous. Still, given luck and the concentration of the two men in each other, she might make the haven of the white porch a hundred yards away. She would sink into the ground if Vivian Stark——

"Hullo, Frances Mary!" cried the big cheerful voice of her brother. "How's the old limb?"

Frances Mary put the final poise of dignity into the carriage of head and shoulders. As a fact, Charles was only inquiring for the blistered heel and had not yet noticed the bare leg of her, but the inquiry naturally led his eyes thereto.

"Losh!" he exclaimed surprisedly. He stared open-eyed for a second or two, taking it all in, his mind infinite, comprehending in one flash reaches of time and incident. Then he leant over on Hugh, head thrown back, contorted face to the sky, his mouth open, and his great laughter filled the whole wide valley of the Abhain Ban.

Frances Mary retained her dignity, but she walked a little faster.

"My ribs," gasped her big brother. "Shortest sock —longest leg—ever I saw."

Allison Ayre, coming across the lawn, heard and saw that great laughter before she saw the cause of it and was herself infected to ripples and gurgles. And then, catching sight of Frances Mary burdened with that terrific dignity above a shameless leg, she crumpled down on the lawn, propped herself on her hands, arched her white throat backwards, and the peal of her mirth rose to heaven above Charles's.

Frances Mary dropped her dignity once and forever Furiously she bounded on to the grass and strode with fell purpose at the laughing girl. The red-haired one, still helpless, lifted feeble hands to protect herself, and was caught at the wrists and shaken so thoroughly that the red curls bobbed about her ears and her laughter died down into gurglings. Whereat Charles Grant bayed almost hysterically.

It was too much for Frances Mary. She turned tail, lifted up her light young feet, and ran like a hind for the harbourage of the white porch. As she went by the big copper-beech without checking she turned her head and called lightly. "All right, mother! They are only laughing at me. I'll get some breakfast for Hugh."

"For Hugh," whispered Caroline Grant, and that smile of hers flickered for a moment.

"There's action for you," said Charles in the calm of the typhoon, and Hugh Forbes thought it was full time to put a stop to this bellowing. He had no more than smiled through it all. What was there to laugh at, anyway? A great bit of a girl she was, tough as a gad, game as a pebble, and after a devil of a gruelling time she had come gallantly into camp, both feet on the ground and a song in her long throat. Ay, and couldn't the tom-boy run too!

He threw the big man's weight off his shoulder and jumped to his feet. "You great, soft, big, bellowing bull of Bashan!" he roared; "you never had a stem of sense and less you have now. I'll show you."

He caught his friend at the neck and big Charles Grant came to his feet willy-nilly. The girl sitting on the grass forty yards away stopped her laughter and watched the two swing each other playfully, and she, too, noted that this Hugh Forbes was no longer a small man. In action he was a wide squat figure on slightly

93

bowed towers of legs, and his speed and force were something not quite human. Charles, she knew, was immensely strong, but his strength seemed now to possess an inflexible quality that might snap, opposed to an indestructible gorilla-like toughness.

The battle was merely a playful one, and it stopped of its own accord. Charles rested a hand on his friend's shoulder and with the other he wiped his eyes. "The pleasantest morning I've had for a long time," he said. "I might have known, Aodh, that you'd arrive in a way of your own."

And there Hugh laughed. "Well, now!" he cried; "did you ever see the like of it, Tearlath? And wasn't it the hell of a short-cut? Did you get my luggage?"

"I did. The weight of that big steamer-trunk burst a tire, and that delayed me. I wasn't here when your wire came." He looked steady-eyed at his friend. "When I got back I found Viv Stark with a broken collar-bone."

"Do you tell me so?"

"I suppose you know?"

"Aren't you after telling me?"

Charles Grant knew his Hugh Forbes, and forbore to question more. Hugh would tell him in his own way and at his own time, by way of implication or comparison or admonition, never directly.

Hugh cocked an eye up at him. "A fellow might stand on himself," he suggested seriously. "I've seen you do it. Where is he now?"

"In bed. Oh, he's all right. His clavicle is not really broken, only cracked; and he'll be sound as ever in a week, the doctor says. It was getting the doctor up from Glenmart—" He stopped. These two men, who knew each other so well and in the ultimate hid nothing from each other, had a playfully futile habit of being secretive

94

with each other as a beginning. Later on it would come out that Charles and Allison had been up to Aunbeg and that Hugh was aware of it, but neither would give anything away in the simple game they were playing.

"I suppose," said Hugh sourly, "you never thought of going up the glen."

There was a gleam in his eye that warned Charles.

"You go to hell, Eiranach," he gave back pleasantly. "I wanted Frances Mary to turn your hair grey. How did you two get on?" He would not admit even to himself that he had been in no hurry up that glen; that some obscure urge, not all unselfish, intrigued him into giving his friend and his sister time to flavour each other. He wondered if they had, but hid his eagerness to know.

Hugh was sufficiently emphatic. "All right! That girl would be all right anywhere. Game as a pebble she is, and lifts to the height demanded—in spite of the brother she has."

"She is no' that bad, Frances Mary," her brother admitted complacently; and he felt, for no reason at all that he would recognise, a pleasant glow in himself.

And here Hugh squeezed his arm. "Tearlath," he whispered, "there is a girl sitting over there on the grass watching us, and I think she has red hair."

"Carrots, as ever was. That's Allison—Allison Ayre. Come and get acquainted. We'll have time enough for talk." He spoke in a carefully casual voice that made Hugh lift a cautious and speculative eye.

Charles was looking across at the red-haired girl. Blue are your eyes, Tearlath *avic*, and your sister's eyes are grey. But och and ochone! 'tis the same eyes you have all the same. Frank you were always, because frankness was in your soul, but woman, red-haired or black— or tow-headed either—is a reagent that is aye for clouding frankness. And why—and why? Ah, well! red hair is red hair, Tearlath, and has Fate set a board for us to play on? To hell with Fate, then!

III

Allison Ayre, leaning back on her hands, watched the two friends and listened to the deep murmur of their voices, and for once her blue eyes were a little sullen. She was looking upon the defeat of her sex, for she was looking upon a love that surpassed the love of woman. She felt barred out from something too big for her to know, and she experienced a curious feeling of futility. It was as if a small chill wind blew down the vistas of her life, her own secret life. It was as if her purpose in life had grown unattainable or—what was worse—if attained, might be as dry dust in the mouth.

The two men walked across the grass towards her and she rose with easy slowness and walked quietly to meet them. She might have stood still, but that was not her way. There was a firm stratum in this pleasantly soft girl, and she would not let any pique lessen the welcome that must be given to this much-talked-of stranger. As she walked forward she examined him frankly. What a complete contrast to big, fair, equable Charles! David and Jonathan! David and Goliath rather! But not in enmity. She saw now that Hugh was many inches the shorter and that he was as dark as any foreigner, with that blue-black chin—a broad chin, and not pointed like the Italian—and the crisp black hair. And the face in repose had a serious set that was somehow strong and at the same time wistful—and it could be a grim face too but for the beautiful dark eyes. She had not expected Hugh Forbes to look like that; she knew that he was not very big and that he was dark

96

in the hair, but she expected him to be and look quizzical, mobile, and unable to hide a national waywardness.

"A darling girl!" murmured Hugh Forbes at a mouth corner.

"Glad you think so," Charles murmured back.

Hugh Forbes could recognise a darling girl when he met one. And here was one, praise God. A chosen red was her hair, and that lovely skin would freckle nicely, given a fair chance and the sun ardent. She was not big; but one could never call her thin, plain unequivocal thin. Clean flesh on her cunningly wrought bones and her woman's figure not denied in the face of heaven! She walked slowly, but her feet did not trail. He had seen a well-trained boxer stroll out of his corner like that, nerve behind every muscle. Demure she was now and wholly unsmiling, but if that eye and that mouth meant anything they meant blitheness. A nice, softly made, vibrant, sweet, wicked morsel of a girl with a flavour like myrrh, and you could warm your hands at her. That was how she struck Hugh Forbes, and it was a good way.

Charles made them acquainted. "Allison, this is Hugh—Miss Ayre, Hugh." Hugh bowed with unusual dignity and Allison's little curtsy was daintily demure. For once Hugh Forbes found himself tongue-tied. Suddenly all his remembered posings and vapourings about red hair embarrassed him. He that was to be very ready and gallant felt as dull as water in a ditch. Scraps of phrases and openings that once seemed brilliant came into his mind and were rejected with dismay as sheer blatancies. In the end he said nothing. He even hesitated about his hand. Hadn't someone told him it was rudely out-of-date to pump-handle a lady's hand on introduction?

Allison Ayre, her own ready, discerning self, saw that

hesitating hand, and put forth her own frankly. "You gave us a busy and pleasant morning, Mr Forbes," she said smilingly, and soft dry palm met hard dry one.

"Sorry to be all the trouble, Miss Ayre," he rumbled, and could think of nothing else to say.

Charles, his own Tearlath, came to the rescue. "You've had enough of young quines this morning," he said slightingly. "Come and meet my mother, and then we'll feed you."

"I had my breakfast," Hugh told him.

"Daylight, cold water, and heather wine—I know. A plate of porridge and some rashers and eggs will rest well on that."

As they went across to the copper-beech Charles spoke in a low voice. "Mother does not see very well—I told you. In fact, she hardly sees at all."

Hugh nodded understandingly, but in his own mind he called Tearlath a liar. Blind that white gently-aquiline face might be, but there was another vision that did not depend on such an ordinary miracle as light, and that vision the blind had—some of them, and surely this woman. These lovely useless eyes set on him so uncannily might only see that he was a shade against a silver opaqueness, but, all the same, she looked into the drying marrow of his bones. Poor devil that he was! The warped dry soul of him no longer hungry! hiding itself behind poses and oddities and phrases. He had hidden it from all the world, but he could not hide it now. The moment she touched his hand she would have a vision before her mind; a sensation of colour he had read somewhere—and that vision would be his stripped soul.

Hugh Forbes shrank inside himself and knew fear. But always had he known fear, and always had it failed to cow him.

"Mother, this is Hugh," said Charles Grant soberly.

Hugh found his hand meeting the hand that so surely reached for his. And that small volition required courage. Holding hands, both were silent, and their faces were aware and unsmiling—as if this first meeting were an event of great importance and the time for make-believe, which is life mostly, had not yet supervened.

Allison Ayre, mystified at the silence and restraint, looked sideways at Charles. His face was eager as well as anxious. Tearlath understood, and the moment was an important one for him. Tearlath knew that his estimate, proved and proved again, might be a false one, but this wise, beautiful mother of his could not be mistaken. And then Caroline Grant smiled, and her watching son smiled too.

"I am very glad that at last you have come, Hugh," she said in that gentle silver voice of hers. "I was needing you."

"You are very kind to me, ma'am," he replied, and there was in the deep voice the least quaver. "There is not much harm in me, but 'tis my own harm I do mostly."

"I know that, Hugh; but I will not let you harm yourself here—if I can help it."

"There's my heart so for you, ma'am."

"Too big for me, boy, though you do not give me all of it. I will hold it for you—and later on——"

"Nothing that I could take, white lady."

And she smiled at him.

Allison Ayre was not even beginning to comprehend, and Charles himself had bogged down. The two speakers seemed to hold converse on some private plane of their own, and they still held hands.

And then came an interruption. A clear voice hailed

them, and the two hands quivered queerly and un-clasped. Frances Mary stood out under the porch and her long arm lifted and beckoned. She had changed to a flimsy morning dress, her legs were sheathed in sand-coloured silk hose, and on her feet were shining house-slippers.

"Come and have some more breakfast, Hugh," she called, and then laughed. "Not half as good as the first one"; and in a lower voice to herself she added, "biscuits and cheese—and fish instead of kisses."

"Great!" cried Charles. "She liked your heather wine, Aodh, and I could do with some more coffee. Come on, folk."

He and Allison moved off, but Hugh waited without a word. Caroline Grant rose smoothly to her feet, and, as surely as if she had sight, her hand found his arm. The two paced slowly across the lawn, and they were exactly of one height.

"I am very happy that you are here, Hugh," she said.

"I am not so happy myself, ma'am," he told her simply.

"I know. I am a very hard taskmaster—but I reward greatly."

And that was how Hugh Forbes came to Innismore.

CHAPTER IX

You spin your web
So still, so still:
No purr of wheel
In your dim mill.
But who dare break a single thread
That holds him sure, alive—and dead?

I

THE light from the tall, pink-shaded standard-lamp was softly diffused and did nothing to dispel the ghostliness of the twilight outside the windows. Out there the green of the lawn shimmered palely and the still bulks of the copper-beeches were cut out of black cardboard; the hills stringing southward up the glen were withdrawn grey shadows against a sky of unnamable green; and over all that wide landscape was a silence older than the oldest of the hills, with, lost in the middle of it, the voice of the Abhain Ban crooning to itself apart.

Inside the room there was a sense of safe comfort, of that long-established security that is the atmosphere of ancient and happy houses. It was a high, long room with curved ends, stucco walls faintly pink, and a deep frieze faintly stencilled. Three French windows, from ceiling to floor, gave on to a curve of stone steps above the lawn. Framed in a white marble mantelpiece that was embellished with curious insets of blue Wedgwood was an old polished steel fireplace, in which glowed a few birch logs. Now and then the birch hissed soothingly and a thin jet of blue smoke went up into the blackness under the marble. A tall pier glass, old prints and etchings hanging from a brass rail, a grand piano, a rosewood table with brass toes, a Chippendale bureau, a rosewood and tapestry fire-screen, damask-covered chairs and couches—such and such again made up the trappings of that big comfortable room.

The northern nights—even in July—hold a touch of shrewdness, and the six people were gathered loosely about the fireplace. Vivian Stark, one arm in a sling, was there, and, in his black and white, looked beautiful and distinguished—an indoor man perfectly at home in a gracious room like this. And yet, Allison Ayre, in a low chair farthest from the fire, examining the three men with a speculative eye, decided that Hugh Forbes had some innate distinction that the other two could not touch—something stronger in fibre than the conventional culture of Vivian Stark, something finer than the careless ease of Charles Grant. Charles sat at the end of a big couch, his legs at full stretch and his head over the padded back. Hugh sat at the other end, leaning aside on an elbow and talking quietly to Caroline Grant, who listened smilingly and touched finger-tip to finger-tip gently. Hugh was not in evening dress. A well-made, easy-fitting suit of dark worsted outlined his shapely shoulders, and his strong neck rose out of a soft silken collar. It was the aquiline repose of his face, white in that suffused light, that gave an impression of reserved strength and breeding not out of place anywhere.

Allison's eyes wandered back to the great recumbent figure at the couch end. All day her eyes had wandered back and forth between the two friends, and she had felt a little rebellious at being outside and looking on at something uniquely fine. From the first moment of their meeting she had sensed the great love these two men had for each other. Indeed, she had to sense it, for, in the presence of others, there was not much outward evidence. Away from each other she had noticed a certain vacant restlessness on them, and together, though they seldom looked at each other and often used playfully abusive terms of speech, they acquired a lazy serenity—as now.

Frances Mary had just come into the room. Shortly after dinner she had disappeared for half an hour, and had now slipped quietly back. She sat on the arm of Allison's chair, and her long slim body and long fine arm leant above the red hair. These two girls liked each other. Hugh Forbes recognised that—if one could be sure that any two girls ever liked each other as men liked each other! And, blast it! he liked them too. During the day he had conquered the restraint with the red-haired one—rather it had vanished. He had found her frank and full of a pleasant humour that had no pose in it. Only she had a tarnation bad habit of baiting Tearlath—almost vindictively—and old Tearlath bore it all dumbly or with the gruffness of an old bear. Poor old Tearlath!

Hugh looked at Frances Mary and wondered. Was this the amazon who sturdily brought her blistered heel down the glen behind him, the cave-woman who had drunk out of the spout of a kettle, licked her fingers, and crouched ahide behind the peats? In the harbourage of this quiet old room she looked slim and almost fragile. Her hair was smoothly fine and her eyes softly lustrous, and, in that mellow light, her mouth looked dark in a face exquisitely delicate. And that cunningly flimsy dress showed the long sorceress curves of her woman's arms and the perfect line from toe to knee-cap. A mighty dangerous bit of humanity, Hugh Forbes!—every whit as dangerous as that small, lovely, red-haired one whose blue eyes laughed and who emanated that queer compound of warmth and quizzicality.

Frances Mary looked across at Hugh and smiled to

him, and Hugh forgot to smile back. A girl smiling like that—a little intimate smile to recall pleasant secrets their very own—was no joke, by the Lord!—if she set out to be no joke. Let her turn her smile on Vivian— Bill Stark—and see if he could make a joke of it. It would please her surely to see the light of a new scrutiny in those eagle eyes. A cold-blooded fish he must be! Hugh turned his eyes on Stark where he leant against the piano, and found that Stark was looking at Frances Mary as if he had never before seen her. And Frances Mary had not looked at Stark at all, which was a new experience for that young man. He was used to finding Fred's eyes on him, and he was used to telling himself that he did not care for those grey orbs admiring him. And now she was looking and smiling at the little Irishman. Damn him! Vivian could not yet contemplate the small man with equanimity. Not yet had he fully considered their first meeting and its results—and its possibilities—yes—now its possibilities. Coming down the glen last night, with his shoulder hurting and embarrassment before him, he had decided to leave Innismore, but now he was not sure if he wanted to. He would like to put Forbes in his proper place, he told himself, but, besides that, he was aware that Forbes had introduced some new element that made a subtle change in his own reactions to life He did not like that, and, because of that, he did not like the small man.

II

Charles came out of a yawn and spoke. "Any of you people care for a rubber? I'm lazy myself."

"Go to bed, baby," chided Allison.

"Perhaps you should all go to bed," suggested Caroline Grant. "Do you play, Hugh?"

"A few games, ma'am—nap and spoil-five and slippery sam——"

Charles barked, "Ay, then! He'll teach you to play that simple game he calls spoil-five, and you'll find it an expensive education."

"I do wonder at you boys," said Allison, with a devastating maturity; and Charles gave her a withering blue eye that consigned her most clearly to a bad end. She grimaced at him and went on. "I have heard you two speak of your glorious experiences in the War, and they were all about horseplay and gambling."

"Not all," corrected Hugh mildly. "Some were about drink, and one or two about women."

"But not about war. When did you two meet, Mr Forbes?"

The two men turned to each other, and their minds converged back into the past and clicked to a point. "Do you mind, Tearlath?" Hugh's eyes were alight. And the two heads went over the back of the couch, and they laughed at the ceiling—a great gale of laughter —and Caroline Grant laughed gently with them.

"A pleasant morning, by glory!" said Hugh; "and it started in the trappings of dignity and discipline." He leant aside over the couch-end to Caroline Grant. "It was somewhere in the sand between Gaza and Jerusalem, ma'am, that I encountered the boy here."

"Could it be told, Hugh?"

"Some of it, ma'am. We were having a court-martial that morning. A Glasgow Irishman was after slicing the ear off a corporal with a trenching-tool, and, moreover, he said he was glad there was no one there to put it on again; but it wasn't for the blasphemy he was down on the charge-sheet. The orderly room was only a bell-tent, and the colonel sat in state on two ammunition-boxes—an old martinet of a dug-out he was, with a gift of tongues. I was by way of adjutant at the time, and the boy here orderly officer—the first time I had set eyes on him, he being fresh up from the lights of Cairo. Young he was, ma'am, young, young; and he taking his new duties very seriously, a frown on his brow, his back a ramrod, and his hands busy with his few papers. 'Devil the much fun we'll get out of this lad all the way frae Aberdeen,' was the thought in my head."

"I wasna frae Aberdeen," disclaimed Tearlath mildly, and added "Thank God!"

"I am," said Allison proudly.

"'Tis proud Aberdeen should be, O cluster o' nuts," said Hugh, not quizzically, but with a gentle warmth of tongue and eye that made the red-haired girl blush. He turned to Caroline Grant. "Well, ma'am, in comes the prisoner—and he was all the way from Garngad—between his guard, and there was the sergeant-major barking 'Shun!' and the colonel sitting on his boxes same as they were a throne, his hands on his thighs and his face darkening like the wrath-of-god as he listened to the bad news. 'Well, my man!' he blares at the end. 'Have you anything to say?'—'I have,' the other stops him sharp and hard. 'What?' roars the colonel.— 'That,' says the bold fellow, and kicks the two boxes out from below him. You would think, ma'am, it was the end of the world. The sergeant-major yelling 'Hould him,' and the guard wrestling and exploding, and the colonel entangled between the two boxes, his feet in the air and his voice coming up out of the sand like red-hot lava. And then I looked at Tearlath and Tearlath looked at me, and we knew each other till great Gabriel's trump. We did so. A glint of the eye, it might be, and nothing is hidden. We leant over on the tentpole and held each other, and the laugh we had split the canvas in two places. Oh, but it was the pleasant morning!" The two renewed their laughter.

"And then?" prompted Allison.

"The old boy wanted to court-martial the lot of us. But after a piece he cooled down, and everyone was happy. The men had a tale for their mates. We had our laugh and the beginnings of a friendship, and the colonel boasted that he had reached heights of language not before dreamt of."

"And was the prisoner happy too, Hugh?" inquired Caroline Grant mildly.

"The happiest of the lot, ma'am. He got his six months in clink back in Alexandria." He saw the widening of Frances Mary's eyes, and addressed her. "You see, Frances Mary, he was just back from a spell of six months in the same place—with a bed all to himself, fresh food and cool water, and a horde of black boys to smuggle him cigarettes. Working a trenching-tool under fire in hot sand! I ask you?"

"There you are," laughed Allison. "The War was only a joke to you two."

"I suppose it wasn't very serious in Palestine," said Vivian Stark.

"Johnny Turk was a richt bonny fechter," said Tearlath lazily.

"Did you ever fight a Turk, Hugh?" said Frances Mary smoothly; but Hugh was alive to the satiric hint that she regarded him as an inveterate fighter. And he was no fighter at all, as Heaven knew.

"Barring a few prisoners, Frances Mary," he answered her, "I never saw—but what am I saying? I nearly forgot that fellow."

Charles exploded. "I dare you to tell mother that one." he challenged.

"It was the other side of Jerusalem, ma'am, up Jordan

way, and, like a fool, I was doing a bit of an early morning scout. There had come a rumour that the German gunners had cleared out, and the same would be very pleasant news if we could be sure of it. I was thinking to myself how nice it would be to nobble a prisoner when his back was turned, and kept casting about till the hurrying Eastern dawn came about me before I knew. And there was I, standing by a rock, and there was Johnny Turk forty yards away, and we both looking at each other. A fine big lad he was. . . . It would be a pity to make such a fine lad a prisoner." He smiled at Frances Mary and was silent.

"What did you do?" she questioned.

"He ran, Frances Mary."

"And you?"

"I ran too."

"Did you catch him?"

"No, but he damn near caught me."

"You—you ran away?"

"Like a hare."

Frances Mary looked at Charles, and Charles bayed. Her eyes told him so plainly that she did not believe the small man. Already, then, she had formed the opinion that he was adequate to all occasions, and that pleased her brother. He nodded to her. "Like a hare, tow-top," he said in a calm. "I was there and saw him arrive, and he was spurting sparks out of Jordan rocks." Charles sat up and leant towards his mother. "The poor old dub," he explained, "had got within fifty yards of the main Turkish position, and he had to run—a case of die-dog-or-eat-the-hatchet. I'll wager he kept ahead of the bullets."

"I understand, of course," murmured Caroline Grant. "You make your reminiscences very interesting, Hugh." She paused, and went on, as if to herself. "I suppose it' is the only way to regard those terrible days—and be sane."

"Yes, ma'am. Seven years of war——"

"Four, was it not?" put in Stark.

"Oh that war! Any real fighting I ever saw came after that."

"In Ireland? Were you what is called a Black-and-Tan?"

"I would rather be the devil." There was warm conviction in the deep tones. But he said nothing about the Black-and-Tan war, or his part in it.

III

"I like listening to your voice, even when you swear, Hugh," said Caroline Grant. "You have the voice of a story-teller, and I think you sing too."

"He can, mother," said Frances Mary eagerly.

"Only come-all-yous, Frances Mary."

"Come-all-yous?"

"So they are called. Many of our best songs begin that way—like this:

> Come all you tender Christians
> And listen to my tale,
> And if you do you may be sure
> Your tears they will not fail . . ."

Though his voice was only above a murmur, he gave the words the queer devil-may-care lilt of the Irish ballad-singer at a fair, so that the listeners could not help sensing the up-thrown chin, the swagger of the shoulders, the hitch at the waist-band.

"Will you sing for me, Hugh?" requested Caroline Grant.

He was not accustomed to sing in company, nor did

he like to do so, but not for a moment did he think of refusing this lady's request.

He rolled to his feet, grimaced at Frances Mary, and moved across to the piano. Stark lounged away from the instrument and sat down beside the couch. Over it he could see the round fair crown of Charles's head and Frances Mary alean beyond.

"Sing that one you were teaching me coming down from Aunbeg this morning," Frances Mary requested.

"Very well. I don't wallop Wagner out of this, but I'll vamp a few chords to cover my faults. This, ma'am, is the song of a Donegal man who was sure his heart was broken—when everyone else knew fine it wasn't.

> And why did you say, then,
>   My eyes had gripped the heart o' you
> And thrilled all your drames when
>   The night came down on top o' you;
> That you couldn't ate a bite
>   With heart across inside o' you,
> And then up and lave me for a strange man of Clare?
>
> I'll sail the briny sea,
>   From China to Jerusalem,
> And the colleens that I see—
>   Faith! an' I'll make hares o' them.
> Ne'er a heart will be free
>   When I have had my way o' them—
> And then up and lave them like a strange man of Clare?"

His voice, while untrained, was wholly fresh and vibrant, and though it had great depth it had also an expressive flexibility.

"Lovely!" chuckled Caroline Grant. "I could see him watching the next pretty girl out of the corner of an eye."

"Here is another, now—and this is the real thing, if I could make you see it—a man singing with a sore heart and him brave.

The dawn and the dusk are the same,
  And wine it inspires me no longer.
To play at and fail at the game
  And be blithe I would need to be stronger
Than Finn or Cuchulain or Conal.

But maybe next year or next life
  The wine will have flavour and savour,
And beauty shall pierce like a knife,
  And in war would I laugh at a favour
From Finn or Cuchulain or Conal.

And again a love I may find
  Like the dusk of the dawn and the gloaming,
To take me and break me and grind,
  And set me again to the roaming
With Finn and Cuchulain and Conal."

That air came out of the deeps of life, and every note
vibrated. The voice died on the last long note and
silence lay deep on the room. Hugh got up from the
piano and walked softly to one of the long windows, and
Frances Mary came just as softly behind him, a thin
silken wrap in her hand.

"You would like to smoke, Hugh?"

"I would, Frances Mary," he murmured, without
turning.

"Come out on the lawn. Your pipe will keep away
any but the most reckless midge. Perhaps you'd like
your fine velour hat too?"

"Leave it have its rest, colleen. When you and I and
the velour hat forgather the velour hat has a bad time
of it."

IV

The four people left in the room remained silent, but
the silence was not constrained. They were near enough
each other in blood to remain silent when there was
nothing to say. Caroline Grant had withdrawn into her

own place of quiet and, as was her habit, touched finger-tips to finger-tips gently; Charles lay on the couch and looked at the high ceiling where the glow from the standard-lamp fell in a bright circle with the warm air tremoring across it; Allison, from her low chair, watched him with quizzical eyes and knew with her woman's intuition that he would like to be out on the lawn smoking with Hugh. Why he persisted in staying indoors was a puzzle to her, and her mind kept touching and starting away from one of two possible reasons.

Vivian Stark was the least patient of the four. His eyes would keep wandering to the window through which Frances Mary and Hugh had gone, and, in time, his patience snapped. "I'll have a last smoke," he excused himself, and went out on the lawn.

.The three left took no notice of his going and maintained their silence, but it was no longer such an easy silence. There was in it some touch of perverse purpose. Caroline Grant smiled secretly to herself, but she had no desire to interfere with the small stubborn game that these folks of hers were playing. Charles wanted a smoke under the trees, and he knew that Allison waited for him to suggest a stroll, but he told himself that he was perfectly comfortable as he was and he hoped that she was. Cosily snuggled in her chair, he could feel her presence. It gave him a pleasant feeling—a sort of sinking, anticipatory, not-to-be-long-contemplated feeling: it was better than fifty dusky beauties tied in a string. He would not go out on the lawn with her into the unsafe gloaming. That was a thing that could not be done any more— because she had red hair, and could be nothing to him. Out of a mind resolutely made up he warned himself not to play with fire. It was a good thing that, still heart-whole, he realised the danger. He had to be frank with himself—oh! immensely frank—and he knew that another step or two on a certain road and the flames might reach him. His friend, Aodh—Aodh MacFirbis—who had red hair as his ideal, must never get the least inkling that he, too, had come to admire the red curls on one small head. He knew his Aodh. If Aodh had the least inkling, Aodh, if necessary, would sacrifice his ideals —gay tongue hiding hurt. . . . And yet Aodh was out there now with Frances Mary. . . . Blow Stark, anyway!

It is possible that Allison, watching Charles, got fragments of his thoughts. She smiled a little wistfully, and after that she frowned, and her patience that should have outlasted the patience of man broke down into action. Without a word she gathered herself neatly and noiselessly out of her chair and moved in that rocking easy way of hers to one of the windows. For a moment or two she peered through the glass into the gathering dusk, and then turned the handle and stepped out on the stone steps above the lawn.

v

Vivian Stark saw the red of a cigarette glow and dull across by the big copper-beech, and paused to consider. Two nights ago he would not have hesitated: he would have strolled across the lawn or down to the bridge without a moment's consideration for anyone—and certainly not for Frances Mary. Now he had to decide that the bold course was the best, and that he must take the initiative in finding how the events of last night reacted. He lit a cigar with some difficulty and walked steady-purposed across the grass. His own purpose was so important to him that he failed to realise the actual littleness of it in the immensity of the gloaming. Everything was very quiet and withdrawn—queerly withdrawn and uncaring. This green-grey plot of grass was surely

113

only an island in a perilous vastness that was aware and did not care. The pinewood crowning the far slopes, black against the glowing north, looked like no wood that man dare dream of, and the murmur of the Abhain Ban, coming through layers of silence, came from a plane outside man's dimension.

The two who had halted in their strolling by the copper-beech saw the tall figure coming through the half-dark. Hugh bent to get it against the white of the house behind and saw that it was not Charles. "'Tisn't his other collar-bone that's troubling him?" he growled gloomily.

"Only the one you broke. How did you manage it?"

"Collar and elbow," he began technically. "Right foot six inches behind his right, right shoulder-point under his seventh rib——"

"Hush," warned Frances Mary.

"A fine night, Fred," said Vivian Stark carelessly.

"'Tis so, thank God," Hugh answered for her. To hear her misnamed Fred roused him strangely. "I was just telling Frances Mary the way I gave you that flying-mare last night."

"Oh, you little brute!" cried Frances Mary astonishedly and yet with a peculiar note of chagrined affection in her voice.

"So I am," he agreed brazenly; "but now we know where we are, and Mr Stark was at a disadvantage, not knowing that you knew."

"I don't mind," said Stark coldly, but he did not feel cold. The frankness of this little brute had shocked him, and, worse, had taken the initiative from him. "I don't mind if you broadcast your prowess, Forbes." It was unspeakably rotten that the little thug should blab to Fred.

"God forgive you for lying," said Forbes genially.

"Hugh! Hugh!" protested Frances Mary.

"All right, Frances Mary. Mr Stark does not like me, and I don't like Mr Stark; we make each other's neck hairs bristle. And what's the use of trying to hide what can't be hidden?"

All day Hugh had suffered Stark's intolerant eye, and had sought vainly in his mind for some ground on which they might exist together amongst decent folks. But he could not get hold of Stark's mentality behind its armour. Stark seemed entirely self-sufficient and would not let other people's discomfort affect his attitude. It would suit him finely to remain coldly inimical. And now, this very minute, Hugh had decided not to permit this cold enmity. A cold enmity was a cark of the soul leading to murder and hell's fire. Enmity, to be harmless, must be frank and lusty, the evil humours washed out by a decisive openness. There at last was the ground where the two could meet equally and let events mould their actions. And as far as Hugh Forbes could see there would be no need for any action at all, since they could have no common urge or interest that might set up friction.

The three were silent for a space, and two of them were uncomfortable. Stark did not trust himself to say anything, and Frances Mary knew how disturbingly frank the small man could be. She now saw that these two males would insist on disliking each other before the very Judgment Seat, and her duty was plainly to ward off anything too primitive. She sought hastily for some innocuous subject before Hugh could say something startling and irrevocable. Already she prided herself on knowing her Hugh Forbes, yet he surprised her by his deep and pleasant chuckle.

"Lord, the woman tempted me," he quoted ruminatively. "It was old Adam said that, and he has been sorely blamed for it. But a man must tell the truth to his Jehovah—though his Jehovah does not need to be told—and Adam did that with the perfection of simplicity: Lord, the woman tempted me."

"Who tempted you, Hugh?"

"No one, Frances Mary. I was only sort of contemplating the wicked old Eve that was in you when you tricked me this morning."

"There was really nothing to find out," said Frances Mary hastily.

"There was—and you made a mountain of it."

"Look here, Forbes," said Vivian Stark, boredom in his voice, "I don't understand what you're talking about, and it doesn't interest me. Anything that happened last night you can take credit for—if any credit is due to your—shall we say?—bar-room method. I don't mind." But though his voice was bored his cigar-end glowed hotly.

"Kind of you. You and I, faith! won't seek any credit from each other. It is Frances Mary's credit I am looking for."

"You were particularly prompt in looking for it," said Stark, too quickly for boredom.

"Wait, now. Let me get my bit of credit.—Frances Mary, I do not like fighting."

"God forgive you for lying," mimicked Frances Mary promptly.

"There, now! I deserved that. But I do not like fighting. I do not. All the world and Glounagrianaan know I'm a peaceable man."

He spoke with heartfelt seriousness, but yet Frances Mary chuckled irrepressibly, and at the same time understandingly. He was a peaceable man amongst his peers, indeed, but where he was would never be placidity.

"Oh, hell!" said Hugh desperately.

"Never mind, Hugh—I understand."

"And I want you to understand that I was not fighting last night. We had a bit of a wrestle down the path and Mr Stark hurt his shoulder. Then came the explanations that I should have made earlier—and that was all. Mr Stark has his grievance, I admit, but the thing was never serious."

"It was wholly unnecessary," said Stark.

"It was, then, but it was no bar-room rough-and-tumble. I didn't bite your ear for one thing——"

"I am glad it wasn't serious," put in Frances Mary hastily. "Please let it finish there."

"With all my heart," agreed Hugh.

But Vivian Stark said nothing. Frances Mary looked to him to say the peaceful word, but he would not unbend. He did not think it necessary. He would ignore Forbes as much as possible, but he would make no gesture.

Again Hugh chuckled. "He'll never love me, Frances Mary, and it can't be helped. But don't be minding; I'll be mighty careful. Faith! I'll have to be—for if it ever did come to a show-down, what chance would I have against height, weight, and reach?—Do you box, Mr Stark?"

"It does not matter," said Stark coldly. But there and then he was glad that he could box. He glanced down at the small man. If necessary . . . some day . . . if things grew impossible . . . height, weight, and reach. . . .

"Good night, Frances Mary." Hugh spoke out of the silence. "I am off in to have a palaver with Tearlath —and a drink, maybe." He turned away abruptly, and as abruptly turned back. "For Heaven's sake, girl," he said, urgency in his deep notes, "don't let him call you Fred. Your name is Frances Mary, and 'tis a darling name."

And then he was gone. And Frances Mary felt a strange surge of warmth, for her name was a darling one in the cadences of his rolling voice. And she was no longer so certain that Vivian Stark's aloof dignity was an admirable virtue.

VI

At the foot of the stone steps Hugh looked back. He saw the white of Frances Mary's dress below the black bulk of the copper-beech, and close by the red glow of Vivian Stark's cigar. He smiled his twisted smile. The blonde beast didn't seem to want to run away from Frances Mary—same as last night. Maybe he was learning something at last, and it was a good sign that he had in him the capacity to learn. If Hugh Forbes could manage it, his education would go on until he realised the precious texture of that grey-eyed one. And after that—well! Hugh Forbes could be going back to his green and sunny glen to teach his youthful clan that charity and humour and dreams counted in the Book of God, and that the new ideal of monied, full-bellied prosperity was abominable damnation. And sure! he could always dream of the red hair that was not lustrous for him—and sometimes too, but very carefully, of flaxen hair and grey eyes that warmed. And he could make-believe to have a fine lusty hunger in the poor dry bones of him. The poor dry bones of him!

He turned to the house, and found Allison Ayre looking down at him from the head of the stone steps before the French window.

Mother and son, within the softly-lighted room, heard the murmur of voices—Hugh's unmistakable rumble and Allison's silver pipe. Then came a care-free laugh and the voices receded. And in a little while another laugh came back.

"And that's fine," murmured Charles Grant. But why did that kindly face set into resolute lines?

Caroline Grant broke her silence. "I am very glad Hugh is here."

"Yes, mother."

"I suppose you two will be extremely busy?"

"A few stunts in view at any rate."

"Hugh and I will be busy too."

He turned his face to her and smiled. This mother of his could get anyone to do anything, but she was never busy. "You can get him to talk till the cows come home —if that is what you mean."

"No. There is something I must get him to do for me."

"He'll do it," said Charles, "or break a bone."

"Was he telling you of his encounter with Frances Mary and Vivian last night?"

"Not yet. It puzzles me—missing them at Aunbeg this morning—and he'll play that puzzle for a day or two."

"Frances Mary told me all about it."

"Of course." Her children told her things always. But there was one thing that Charles kept hidden. At least he did not speak of it, but he sometimes wondered if silence fooled his wise mother.

"She is so pleased with herself, and inclined to crow over you because she discovered Hugh for herself and exploited his resources. Already she thinks she understands him better than you do. I know she does not, Charles—and never will, no matter how well she comes to know him. Such simple pride I never saw, like a child retelling her first party, making a fairy story of it. He came to the bothy with nothing, just an old waterproof and an ash-plant, and a wonderful velour hat. A very remarkable hat! I got the impression that he produced unique—miraculous things out of it: biscuits, cheese, cigarettes. Nothing much really, but she was tired and very hungry—and not very happy—her chair uncomfortable and her foot aching—and, I think, she was alone in the bothy for some time, and the hours before her must have looked dreich. And he that had nothing kept adding surprise to surprise: made her bathe her foot, and upholstered the chair seat with heather-tips and his coat, and helped her to a drink out of the spout of an old tin kettle. For some reason which, I think, I can follow, he never said who he was, but she insists she guessed in the first hour. She would. Rouse her interest and there is not much you can hide from Frances Mary. And what pleased her most was that he called her a damn'd little fool."

Charles laughed. The soothing ripple of his mother's voice was very pleasant, and, as it was meant to, was taking his mind away from the folk who moved about or stood still out there on the lawn. "I have heard him say worse to a red-tab," he said. "Where did the two get to this morning?"

"They were not far away from you and Allison at Aunbeg. Hugh guddled trout for breakfast, and they had just finished it when they saw you two in the distance —a long way off. They took you for Vivian and— These two young men do not like each other, Charles."

"Viv Stark had better watch his step, then," said Charles with satisfaction. "Frances Mary didn't say how he hurt his shoulder?"

"No. I didn't ask. I look to you to keep the peace between the two, boy."

"Must I, mother?" The inquiry was regretful.

"Please. There is no need for—anything else, is there?"

"No-o-o." Beyond a natural antipathy, that Charles

understood, there should be no cause for quarrel between Stark and Aodh. Vivian took no interest in red hair, and Aodh—well! Aodh could hardly be expected to take interest in any other.

"Hugh apparently did not want to meet Vivian—again—so soon, and marched off into the heather, and then Frances Mary on a sudden impulse hid too. She was behind the peats in the back place when you were in the bothy."

"Listeners hear no good of themselves."

Caroline Grant said no more, but she had said enough to lead her son's mind to curious and interesting speculation. He could understand Aodh's excursion into the heather, but why had Frances Mary gone into hiding, and why had she remained hidden? She knew, of course she knew, that Aodh wanted to avoid only Stark and was eager to meet himself. Yet she remained in hiding—and with a blistered heel. Dashed odd, that! What could be in her mind? Frances Mary was no harum-scarum. She would never play an apparently silly trick without some distinct urge. . . . Ah, bah! Better not build on any such weak foundation. Frances Mary was out there on the lawn—probably with Stark. That should please Frances Mary—it would two nights ago. And old Aodh should be pleased too—he was with Allison away down towards the crooning water of the Abhain Ban. Charles Grant could not contemplate anyone being displeased in Allison's company. She had charm—charm—charm. . . . And so, without being aware of the insidious stealing in of the forbidden, he could see her down there at the bridge—could hear her silver chuckle, could see her laughing eyes in the half-dark, note the fine easy verve of her, feel in his every nerve the glamour that emanated from her, wave on wave, heart-switheringly. . . .

That night when Hugh Forbes went to his room, after a satisfactory palaver with Tearlath and at least one dram of the great Glenmart whisky, he noticed that his flannel trousers lay on the counterpane of the four-poster bed, and that they had been recently ironed and pressed. "Glory!" he exclaimed mildly, and lifted them to admire, and, admiring, he saw where the triangular rent at the knee had been mended by the most cunning needlework. Deft hands did that—long white hands with sensitive finger-tips—a thimble on a middle finger and no ring on any. And that's where you were early in the night, Frances Mary. Oh, darling name!

He held the garment high and continued to look at it with eyes that were intent yet unseeing, and into his face came that twisted smile that was not in the least happy. "Well, now! Well, now! Well, now!" His tone deepened and deepened below any throb of drum, and in it was something infinitely sombre and sternly resigned.

CHAPTER X

Slow flow the days
In mood serene,
But far and deep
There twists unseen
A current sure that knows its sea
And seeks it in the heart of thee.

I

HUGH FORBES came to Innismore in his own way and
set the eddies moving in quiet lives. He was one of those
rare individuals who give life a fresh orientation, make
dull motive insurgent, set up vibrations that penetrate
the armour of inaction. He aroused a mood of expectancy, a flurry of interest, a quickening of speculation.
At least three people looked to him as the resolver of
Fate, the agent of some final purpose, the breaker of the
shackles of circumstance. Something had to happen
with Hugh Forbes taking an interest in things. And
then—and then, nothing wonderful happened. Three
whole weeks went by and the old inertia that had weighed
down the urges of youth seemed still to hold sway.
Though hearts beat warmly, no hearts bled. Worse
still, no noses bled. For though life can occasionally
dispense with the bleeding heart it moves very dully
without an occasional bleeding nose. There will be at
least one before the end, with the help of God—as Hugh
Forbes himself might say.

Nothing happened—nothing that can be tangibly
displayed—and yet, perhaps everything that mattered
happened in that quiet three weeks. Here, on the edge
of the wilderness, were five young people and a wise

123

woman set on the same board and being gently man-
œuvred by destiny towards the decisive move in the game
of life. In the quietly sliding days, in the slow-descending
evenings, in the gloaming that never darkened, thoughts
and emotions crossed and touched and went on and
curved back and moulded feelings into shapes of per-
manency. And at the end came the demand for action,
when the two most important people definitely decided
how they themselves felt and how everyone else ought to
feel. And then one of the two acted, and the other spoke
a few quiet words.

II

Charles Grant and Hugh Forbes had, for many months,
looked forward to these few weeks as particularly and
completely their very own. They were to be something
apart and splendid, and nothing and no one was to be
considered while the two did exactly what the two
planned. And yet, from the very first hour that Hugh
had set foot in the glen, other people and things claimed
consideration—a whole world of consideration: Frances
Mary and Vivian Stark and red-haired Allison Ayre,
and Caroline Grant above all—and the problems they
set. Hugh and Charles had their holiday certainly, but
it was never the holiday of their anticipations. It could
never be that, of course, in heaven or on earth, but, so
much admitted, it was not the holiday it should have
been—two care-free men in open country with no secret
speculations to cloud intimacy. They fished—oh, but
they fished!—from Glendhu right down to the Spey,
and, once or twice, tried a little harmless but pleasant
poaching. They climbed; they camped out in the
heather beneath the naked stars, and in the cold dawn
revived their blood by a plunge in Loch Dhu; they
wandered over the wide policies of Innismore, the thirty

thousand acres of fenced-in deer forest, the sheep-runs in the lower valley, the big home-farm along the haughs of the river; and always they talked; but never was there full peace of mind between them. Their love for each other had not diminished, but now a much less admirable and more urgent love had entangled them in its tentacles. More than once in these fine days Charles silently cursed all women—without particularising any woman—and if at any time he forgot, Hugh faithfully remembered. Women, indeed, would have had a bad time if these curses fell—and it is probably a pity that some of them did not.

They did no shooting yet, but Charles promised three days amongst the grouse and then a glorious week of deer-stalking before Hugh's return to duty. All the other things they did were only time-passers to tide over to that great week. Charles was very proud of his deer forest and his method of running it. It was his unmixed pleasure, where his other pursuits were mostly duties. He pursued farming and forestry extensively and for profit, but his deer forest cost him money. At that, he was not more than moderately well off, and if he had cared to consider the forest from an economic standpoint it would have secured him a bigger income than all his other activities combined. That would have entailed letting, and letting was the last thing he dared do. For Charles Grant was that type of laird once common amongst the Gael, but now all too rare in the Highlands. He was chief of his sept and was responsible to his sept. His few privileges bore their unshirkable duties, and he had many duties that were without any privileges at all. But the deer forest was his very own. There he and his friends—mostly his own tenants—shot some stags in August–September and a good few hinds in November; but the sport was not the main purpose of the forest.

That was to provide a refuge where the grand animals might survive, not a preserve for the pampering of game beasts for slaughter. What shooting was done was necessary to maintain a healthy stock, and incidentally it was the sport at its finest, without any of the modern amenities of certain arm-chair preserves where killing is the only thrill and costs a fortune. Steady tramping, steep climbing, hard stalking, pitting reason against instinct and getting or losing the quarry one has carefully chosen and no other—that was the sport as practised by Charles Grant and his friends. And though he preserved his deer very closely he did not deny the public access to his grand mountains. Within his wire fences the law of trespass did not run.

It was only natural that, in their wanderings over ben and corrie, in glen and valley, Charles should endeavour to initiate his friend into some of the mysteries of the great sport. At first Hugh was inclined to scoff. "Bah!" he exclaimed, "there is nothing to it but its expense and rarity. Look! there's a bunch o' beasts up there and a big head amongst them—and good cover between. Up that fold in the heather and who is going to miss a sitter at a hundred yards?" There was only the very gentlest drift of air, and Charles had to wet a finger to get the airt of it. Then he smiled. "Right!" he said; "let us get within a hundred yards." But when, at eight hundred, they lifted heads for a peep the deer were already on the move. "They've winded us, son," said Charles with satisfaction. "Try pressing them, and see their pace for the sanctuary."—"Let them go to hell," snapped Hugh.—"And remember," admonished Charles, "that you cannot stalk a stag down-wind in any sort of cover."

The very next day, with a breeze blowing up-hill, Charles brought Hugh sliding down a brae with the deer

126

in full sight, made him crawl painfully on his stomach over and between rough hummocks, cursed him into stillness when the quarry lifted an inquiring head, and at last halted him at two hundred and fifty yards. "We'll get no nearer," Charles told him. "Can you see that stag's ears?" Hugh could not. "Then we are too far away. Never pull trigger till you can see an ear twitch, and then sight for a hundred and fifty, low, and six inches behind the forearm."

And one evening, with the sun pouring orange across the heather, and a side-wind blowing, they did a work-manlike stalk to within eighty yards of a royal stag, and could clearly distinguish his brilliant black-ringed eye. "Could you hit that fellow?" whispered Charles. Hugh, lying flat between two tussocks, lifted cautiously on an elbow, looked along imaginary sights, and clicked his tongue. "My meat," he whispered.—"Good," said Charles. "And remember, he is the first one that gave you an even chance."

At the end of ten days, then, Hugh had some practice and many maxims: never hurry, never shoot when winded, never use a rock rest, stalk your damnedest when deer are lying down, shoot low down-hill, rush a deer that drops to the shot, pursue a maimed beast to hell and high-water. And so on.

III

But in all those ten days there was never full peace of mind between the two. And because of a red-haired woman. For had not Hugh, in all the time that Charles had known him, idealised some dream-maiden with red hair, and was not such a one alive in Allison Ayre? That she was an ideal come alive Charles was perfectly satis-fied, and dared anyone deny it. Therefore his friend

Aodh must be given full opportunity to appreciate her and be appreciated by her. And Hugh, nothing loath, accepted every opportunity, and appreciated and was appreciated. Anyone with half an eye could see that Allison Ayre and Hugh Forbes liked each other, and so Tearlath, sure that the liking was blossoming into something warmer, nodded his big, fair, foolish head—and set his Scots jaw dourly. If love was not there friendship was, with frankness and gaiety and a good deal of understanding. Her blue eyes sparkled to Hugh, the silver pipe of her voice deepened for him, intimate little remarks went back and forth between them; walking together, they made a picture that was a blend of contrast and unity—a contrast in colouring and a unity in the abounding verve subtly controlled and subtly manifest. Charles should have been highly pleased; at any rate he tried to make it plain that he was, and patiently told himself that he was. He looked for no gratitude. He hoped some folk would offer him some so that he could direct them to their exact destination. He got none. Instead, Allison treated him outrageously, twitting him, making fun at his expense, laughing at and not with him. And he, like a dignified Newfoundland pup, ignored her when he could and played up ponderously when he could not. Sometimes he was gruff, and once or twice discovered a fine salt savour in being rude—and was repaid with interest.

The two men, then, did not monopolise each other's company. The days were long, the evenings longer, and, in the state of mind that held sway, much was sought to be done to evade time. There were fishing picnics down the valley and camping-out picnics up the glen, motor runs to the sea and the golf at Lossiemouth, a visit to the Highland Games across the watershed in the Dee valley, and, of course, there was tennis on the lawn—and a quietly vindictive game called croquet. And in the gloaming there were cards and music and talk—and thoughts. Altogether a rather intense holiday-making, instead of a quiet and sane drifting. Indeed Woman did deserve her cursing.

IV

Frances Mary saw a good deal of Hugh Forbes too, quite as much of him as did her brother and Allison She made it her business to do so. Had she not discovered that small dark man for herself, and was it not her duty and her pleasure to cultivate her knowledge? Hugh understood her interest. He was as certain as daylight that he understood. He smiled wisely and told himself that the girl was learning sense and acquiring her technique. Sure, all the world knew that the quickest way into the grasp of a man's arms was not by throwing oneself into them; that way, the arms let one drop, and one bumped the nose of one's susceptibilities. This present method of divided interest might bring a long, blonde lad to his knees in quick time: already there were evidences of a slight wobble. And Hugh Forbes would play the game too and be damn'd to him. Who the thundering blazes was Bill Stark anyhow to reserve to himself the power of saying ay or no to a girl like Frances Mary? Frances Mary and Hugh Forbes, playing the old, tiresome, hellish game together, would drive Stark by his own urgent impulses to the jumping-off place —and, if necessary, Hugh would kick him in the pants into immolation. "Don't let anybody hurt nobody," said specimen Jones—but wouldn't it be great if he bumped his nose at the bottom? Alas! there was little fear of that, if the look in a grey eye meant anything.

During the day Frances Mary was a tall, long-legged,

tomboyish sort of person, and Hugh treated her as an equal, without any consideration for sex and its short-comings. There was certainly no trace of sentiment in their relations. He abused her with remarkable but friendly adjectives when necessary, and called ruthlessly on her staying powers on occasion. And she seemed to like the abuse and the ruthlessness. She was game as a pebble, tough as a withy, careless as a boy, contempt-uous of assistance—an easy companion on any road. She could talk or be silent as the mood suited, and, better, she had a reserve of her own that demanded neither speech nor silence.

One day, when the others had gone down to have a look at the golf finals at Lossiemouth, the two went up the glen to Aunbeg bothy and tried to recapture that something they had found there for the first time. They took biscuits and cheese as a ration, and nothing else. Barefooted they paddled in the burn, guddled brown trout and cooked them over peat, crawled through long-stemmed heather close to a herd of hind, came on a twelve-inch viper sunning itself near a whin bush and did not kill, and, in the nick of time, saved a young rabbit from a brown stoat—or, rather, Frances Mary did the saving. Hugh said he agreed with Hudson that it was impertinent to interfere, as well as useless; that the rabbit was as good as dead, anyhow, since the brown fellow would come back and get him, in spite of the devil and Frances Mary. And in the lazy, still, sunny after-noon they sat near each other on dry tussocks and con-templated the mountains and the sky. They were both hill-folk, and they had that very wonderful aptitude of hill-folk for sitting still, the eyes slowly wandering, and the mind almost completely detached from thought or dream. The soft air drifted by them, the cloud shadows flowed over them; they were part of the hills, and their gaze did not fail to focus into the blue deeps. Their eyes lazily traced the line of Cairn Ban towering into the sky, and they swept that line up to the gates of heaven, a colossal miracle of a mountain dominating mysterious hollow lands. They contemplated the lessening snow-field on the northern face of Ben a Mhuic and realised the abiding horror of whiteness. They watched an eagle soar and glide and at last swoop, and imagined the zoom of his pinions. And for a long and a long time they said no word. Hugh it was who spoke first. He did not want to speak. He could have sat there till time and tide were done—and Frances Mary sitting there too—but something so keenly poignant entered his soul that he dared not be silent any longer.

"Would you like to live away from the hills, Frances Mary?"

"I think I would die," said Frances Mary simply; and after a long pause she added, "You live in the hills too?"

"I do." The silence settled down and cut off the context before he put his next question. "Where does Bill Stark live?"

"Edinburgh."

"A fine town, they say."

"The only town in the world——"

"That's Dublin, say the Dublin people. How would you like to live in Edinburgh—or Dublin?"

"I suppose one could learn to live anywhere," she replied tonelessly.

"A mess of lentils—how does it go? I mind reading it somewhere."

"The Bible. But if it were only the mess of lentils!"

After that they were silent. And in the evening they went home.

But indoors, when the soft light of the hooded lamp

131

fused with the silver glimmer of the gloaming, Frances Mary was mysteriously transformed into a lovely slender shaft of young womanhood, robed fittingly, mannered entrancingly, dowered with sex that was not bold but subtle. And Hugh Forbes treated her accordingly. In his dark clothes, silken-shirted, freshly-shaved, his face calmly strong, poise in every line of him, he displayed an old-world courtliness. To Frances Mary, the lovely young virgin, he was the knight out of his armour. In the touch of his hand, in the glance of his eye, in the cadences of his rich voice, was a courtesy that approached almost to tenderness. But Frances Mary knew, better than anyone could tell her, how detached and selfless was that courtesy. And sometimes it gave her a sinking stoun at heart.

v

Charles William Vivian Stark had altered too in his relations with Frances Mary. Their positions were very nearly reversed. He was no longer condescendingly frank, no longer treated her as a cousin and a somehow-to-be-borne-but-occasionally-useful nuisance. His attitude of you-are-in-the-way-but-I-want-you-to-be-in-the-way had changed into a direct cultivation of her company. Where before he made a semblance of avoiding her, he now sought her out. And in return she treated him exactly as an attractive, worldly-wise, self-confident young beauty would treat a not-quite-to-be-despised admirer. Hugh Forbes smiled a little twistedly. Her manipulation of Vivian reminded him of an Irish horse-jobber getting a colt to display his paces: she hit him and held him. And Hugh allowed himself to be rather shamelessly used to give Vivian an appreciation of her freedom and her desirability. That he was being so used was very clear to Hugh, but Vivian was not at all sure, and there was heat behind the cold eye that occasionally contemplated the small man. Between the two men was a precarious neutrality, depending largely on the way they ignored each other. Charles Grant saw to it that they were never alone together, and in company Hugh was careful not to make things uncomfortable for people that he liked.

Stark's shoulder was now mended and his arm out of its sling. In the privacy of his own room he exercised it judiciously and shadow-boxed with his reflection in the long pier glass.

VI

That wise, still-faced woman, Caroline Grant, went about her own affairs and seemed to have forgotten all about that task she had promised to set Hugh. She gave no sign, but no doubt she sensed all the currents of thought and feeling that eddied around her, and sensed anxiously that this was the time of all times for her two children. In the evenings in the drawing-room, where once she had talked readily, she was now mostly silent, yet kept the talk, with its underplay, briskly going. She smiled, and touched finger-tip to finger-tip, and looked through wall and world out of her beautiful blind eyes, and no cadence of any voice was lost on her.

Hugh Forbes was the only one she talked freely to, but only when they were alone, and even then Hugh did the larger share of the talking—mostly about himself and his pursuits and ideals. It would seem as if she were keen to understand his manner of life and his outlook, and he, in turn, seemed anxious that she should fully understand. At the end of three weeks she must have had a clear mind-picture of Glounagrianaan and the folk that lived therein, and the things they did and did not do. Oh, Glounagrianaan! that widest, sunniest trough of all the valleys raying out from the Four Churches, green with short grass, grey with limestone, alive with the sound of birds singing and water cascading down the wide aprons! Serene hollow below high hills of heather where sheep were dotted like pale brown stones —with low white houses strung along a winding grey road, the little town at the mouth of the glen, and Hugh's school near by, and, beyond, the sea lifting to the horizon!

"Strange that you are a teacher, Hugh!" mused Caroline Grant. "In the old days you would have led a clan."

"'Tis what I am making—a clan to lead, ma'am," he told her quaintly.

"A clan to lead, Hugh?"

"Surely, ma'am. A few of us have a notion that Ireland is in a bad way, with wrong ideals out of the mouth of prosperity mongers, and the only remedy, as we see it, is to get hold of the young."

"And what do you teach them, Hugh?"

"First, the things I have to, and after—it would be hard to tell you—and maybe I am not too sure, myself. But in sanguine moments, on a sunny morning or late at night over a drink with a friend, I do be boasting that any boy who stays with me to the age of eighteen will never be content in a city, and 'some of them will never be content out of Glounagrianaan."

"Is that good for them?"

"Good?"

"Will it make them any happier?"

"No, ma'am. All we seek is to make them think, and thinking pierces to the bone. 'Tis how I—and better men—are making our clan—gathering and scattering and holding it too; and in good time, it could be, that clan will arise and drive the huckster and the shopkeeper out of Ireland."

"But are we not the shopkeepers, Hugh?"

"Dublin is full of them too, dear lady."

"Dublin of the Intelligentsia?"

"The very place. You, here in your Innismore, could name ten Dublin men of note that most of the Dublin people never heard of. The man that counts most in Dublin is a bright boy who has the trick of making two or ten thousand a year on the Christian principle of grinding the faces of the poor, goes to his duty or his lodge regularly, and hasn't the time or inclination to read a book."

"Are you not too hard on them?"

"I'll be harder yet, with the help of God," said the real Hugh Forbes in his deepest voice.

CHAPTER XI

His task is set.
In secret ways
His subtle mind
That task essays,
And still the woman smiles and smiles
And on him twists her deepest wiles.

I

HUGH FORBES had two days at the grouse, and found the sport not nearly so exciting as keeping rooks off a field of young turnip. But then the latter is not quite a sport, and it is exciting to the point of madness, manslaughter, and suicide. One has to be out with the dawn to discover that the rooks are out earlier, and that they play their dangerous game of touch-and-go as cleverly and interestedly as any other biped—ay, and so successfully that usually the farmer has to resow his field. A man has been known to kick his hat and his dog and his male servant after the rooks have had their morning's sport with him.

Early grouse-shooting on a well-stocked moor means a steady walking up behind the dogs and the bringing down of easy-rising bulky black objects—or the missing of them if one is a disastrously bad shot. Hugh had pursued grouse on moors where the coveys were scattered and wary as hawks, and, after a long day's stiff walking and hard stalking, had been boastfully proud of a three-brace bag. After two days on the moors of Innismore he did not care any more for easy slaughter.

Vivian Stark, accompanied by Frances Mary, went out on the third morning for a beat across the lower moors.

Charles would not permit any gun-fire in the vicinity of the deer-forest during the next two days. Charles himself stayed at home, and was busy in the gun-room all the morning with Wullie Mack, his head-stalker, a red-headed young Banffshire man. Hugh, at the last moment, decided to stay at home too, and so made Frances Mary frown. He said he did not want to shoot, but did not add that he did not care to be out with Stark, or that it was time he gave up playing third. He pottered about the gun-room with Charles and Wullie, ran his eye along the sights of a ·450 Ballard & Moore, asked a variety of fool questions, was told to go to blazes out of that, and drifted into the brick-walled garden, where he found Allison Ayre eating over-ripe blackcurrants, and joined in the occupation.

"He is a bear, that fellow," he grumbled.

"He is," agreed Allison.

"Who?"

"That fellow, of course."

"Exactly. He'll come to a bad end, and marry a woman with red hair."

"I'd like to see him try it," she cried, a snap in her voice.

"Would you, then?"

Some touch of wise sarcasm in that query made her flush. "I don't love you one bit, Hugh Forbes."

"You do so—you do so," he said comfortably, and she threw a currant at him.

II

In the afternoon the two men, reclining side by side in long chairs, lazed on the sunniest part of the lawn, companionably silent, feet at full stretch, Hugh's no-longer-new velour hat shading his eyes and a white

137

handkerchief draping the dome of Tearlath's head. Hugh's eyes were shut, but he was not yet asleep, and before the approaching drowsiness could close in he felt other eyes watching him. He opened a chink of his own under the brim of his hat, and saw Allison Ayre. Leaning forward on her hands, she sat over there on the seat that circled the copper-beech, and if she were a little nearer he could observe in her eyes the small discontent that was always there when they looked on this David and this Jonathan.

"Are you asleep, Tearlath?" he asked quietly.

"I am. Shut up, will you!" replied that man grumpily.

"There's a nice girl over beyond looking at us."

Tearlath tilted back his head and his eyes looked along his nose under the handkerchief. He grunted. "A red-headed monkey."

"You damn'd old bear! You know, Tearlath, I like that girl."

Again Tearlath grunted.

"But I do."

"Oh, hell! The world knows that," said Tearlath desperately. "Since the year of our Lord, 1916, I have never seen a pretty girl with red hair—or an ugly one for that matter—without thinking that the mighty sultan Abu Aodh MacFirbis Ali would like her in his carrot-topped hareem."

"A bear! that's what you are. That particular girl over there—Allison—she is a nice girl, and I like her."

"Have you told her so?"

"No, but I am going to tell her now." Hugh gathered in his legs and lifted to his feet, and the velour hat jerked itself into place over an ear.

Tearlath lifted a corner of the handkerchief and looked

up sideways. "It is time you were serious, Aodh," he admonished soberly.

"That is what I am this minute. You lie there on your back and watch me."

"Will I so? I am going to sleep. If you two start skirling I'll run you out of there."

Hugh strolled across the lawn, and Charles settled down comfortably, his head tilted and the handkerchief hiding his eyes. Yet if those eyes looked down his nose they could see what was to be seen. Perhaps he slept

III

Allison smiled up at Hugh and with a little gesture of the hand and movement of knee invited him to sit. Instead, he took a step back and examined her critically.

"She is red-headed enough," he decided, "but I'll bet a sovereign she is no monkey."

Allison looked across at prostrate Charles. "I know where you can get a big chimpanzee," she said. "Sit down here and be nice to me, Hugh."

He lifted a hand. "Wait now, Allsoon Ayre. I am going to talk business, and I'll start by sitting at a safe distance."

For an instant a startled look came into the blue eyes, and Hugh did not fail to catch it. "Heart o' gold," he muttered, and sat down a yard away. He lifted a knee, clasped his hands over it, and looked straight ahead.

"Do you own such a thing as a male parent, young woman?" he asked suddenly.

"And a female one forby—in Aberdeen as ever was, young man."

"Pity 'tisn't in Glounagrianaan they live."

"Perhaps—but why?"

"I would be sending a friend of mine across to say a word or two to the decent people."

"I am sure any friend of yours would be welcome," said Allison, mystified but fencing. "But why not come yourself—you'd be so much more interesting?"

"That's not the technique demanded by custom. Your fond parents would find my friend's talk interesting enough, and yourself would be listening with your two dainty ears—and your mouth as well."

"Tell me, please?"

"Amn't I telling you? My friend would be taken into the parlour, and you would be sitting over in the corner, demure and coy—two adjectives you don't deserve. My friend would not be taking much notice of you, but he would be observing to himself the shame of a fine young woman reading John Buchan or Annie S. Swan instead of darning socks."

"But I would be darning socks. I have three hard-footed brothers, besides two young sisters."

"A terrible lot of ye in it," said Hugh gloomily. "With a clan like that, hard put to it would your parents be to gather a fortune for their daughters—a tocher, you call it."

"Would a tocher be essential?"

"It would in Glounagrianaan. Wait now. Your father and my friend would have a drink or maybe two, and, your mother putting in a word, they would talk of the weather and the crops and the drop in cattle, and, after a piece, the name of Hugh Forbes would be drawn down, sort of casually-on-purpose. Hugh Forbes! Yes, your father had heard of him—a decent boy, but with a poor way-of-living. A poor way-of-living doesn't mean a moral poverty, you must know, but a small share of the world's goods. Your wise old devil of a father wouldn't be giving anything away in the game in hand and my friend would be ready with his counter. 'A poor way-of-living! The tidiest in all Glounagrianaan or the five valleys round it, Mr Ayre. Six hundred a year and a pension at the back of it, a free house with a dining-room, a drawing-room, and four bedrooms—and a bathroom, bedad; but that should not be held against him, for seldom he uses it. And above and besides there are a sound-hearted sixty acres of arable land in the hollow and the sheep-run on all Barnaquilla Hill.'—'Glad am I to hear it,' says your father, 'and if 'tis so—and I don't doubt it—he is a man to be looked to and sought after. I haven't heard—.'—'It is that he is hard to please, the same Hugh,' says my friend in a hurry, 'and will have decent connections or none. Offers enough have come his way this Shrove and the last. And now, Mr Ayre, as his friend and yours—and here's your very good health— I was just by way of thinking that it was time that your daughter, Allsoon here, was settled in life. There is no better family than your own, and everyone knows you're snug.'—'She is young,' says your father, 'thirty come——'"

"You wretch! Twenty-four——"

"Let it be. I have been abridging shamelessly and cutting out the finesse, but you'll have a sort of a kind of a notion of the proceedings, Allsoon—and the trend of them?"

"I have, Hugh. Most exciting too. And what do you think my father would have to say?"

"What would he have to say, Allsoon?"

Allsoon considered that, her eyes alive with intelligence and impishness. "My father would be very direct at the end, as is his way," she said deliberately. "He would say, 'Allison can cook and bake and make and mend— and mind, and doing all those, what right has any man to seek the tocher he'll no' get from me?'"

"Do you tell me your father would say that?"

"His very words."

"I was afraid it would come to that. A great pity—
a great pity!"

"And would your friend have anything more to say?"
Allison continued to play the game, sure that it was no
more than that.

"Devil the word. He would finish the last of the
whisky and come away. Ochonaree! but it would be
hard on you, Allsoon."

"And on poor Hugh Forbes too."

"You I was thinking of and age coming on you."
He looked sideways at her. He was getting close to where
he was wanting now. "Of course there is a way out,"
he said darkly. "You could marry an old man and have
him dead in a year."

"A year is a long time."

"There's a fellow that makes me tired I would like
you to try your hand on."

"How does he make you tired, Hugh?"

"The same way that you make me tired, you darned
little red-head," said Hugh hotly. "But wait, now.
Look at him, the veiled Touareg, lying over there like a
log. The trouble that fellow is to me no one knows.
When he takes a thing into his head—" He shook his
own head sadly, and Allison saw that at last he was
serious.

"Poor Hugh!" she murmured, a warm light in her
eye. "How fond of him you are!"

"And couldn't we two do something for him? You've
heard me at the match-making, Allison, and I'm not a
dumb-bell at it. Suppose—just for a bit of fun—we open
negotiations with him." He leant forward and lifted a
stentorian voice. "Tearlath! Tearlath! come here."

Allison started to her feet and her face was aflame.

"Hugh Forbes," she sibilated tensely, "if you say one word I'll—I'll——"

"What will you do, Allsoon?"

She pointed a finger between his eyes. "I'll tell Frances Mary how madly in love with her you are."

His mouth opened and shut with a click. "Oh! you little monkey," he said warmly.

Tearlath had jerked away the shielding handkerchief and was coming across the lawn, a smile on his face and his teeth clenched. Allison took half a dozen quick strides towards the house and looked over her shoulder at Hugh. "I warn you," she threatened fiercely. "If you don't promise not to say a single word—" She lifted a finger, and there was no doubt as to the force of her intention. Then she turned and ran for the white porch.

Hugh jumped to his feet. "Allsoon—Allsoon!" he shouted. "I promise." From under the long columns she waved to him and her red curls shook satirically. His stentorian bellow in reply filled the glen. "You damned, red-headed little monkey!"

Charles Grant could not follow these proceedings to any conclusion. He could understand Allison hurrying off like that—a sudden shyness driving her. But no successful wooer would call his dear one a name so whole-heartedly vituperous. And yet—! Aodh was capable of saying outrageous things in the most sacred moments. "Have I to congratulate you, Hugh?" he inquired, steady-voiced.

Hugh slumped gloomily on the seat and looked at his friend disgustedly. "You have," he said grimly. "You have so, you pachydermatous rhinoceros."

"Perhaps you had better tell me why?" suggested Charles mildly.

"On a dam' narrow escape."

Charles sat down and sighed resignedly. "No use expecting seriousness from a cross-grained Irish bog-trotter."

"I am serious—serious as a judge, you Hielan' bodach! I set out to make dead-sure of a thing I knew already and to do something that has to be done. And did I do it?"

"What was that, Aodh?"

"Go to blazes!" Hugh cursed him warmly and started up and away across the lawn towards the white posts of the bridge. "You are a terrible great trouble to me, Tearlath Grant," he shouted over his shoulder.

"Go to blazes yourself," shouted back the foundering Charles.

IV

Hugh met Caroline Grant walking slowly and surely on the path up from the Abhain Ban. She knew him before he spoke.

"What is worrying you now, Hugh?" she questioned gently.

"That big son of yours, ma'am," he replied sadly.

She nodded her silver head. "I know. Perhaps I should not have placed the burden on you, but what could a poor blind woman do?—I was so helpless. How are you going to do it, Hugh?"

"God knows, ma'am. Can I do it at all—why wouldn't you ask me that?"

"Because you will do it—and earn your reward."

"Reward enough! And, anyway, there is no reward for me ever again on top o' earth."

Caroline Grant smiled at him. "You are very young that think yourself so old," she said calmly. "Give me your arm now and let us go walking, and you'll tell me some more about your Glounagrianaan."

Her hand was on his sleeve and he touched it lightly

with his strong fingers. "I have told you everything—truth and dream—about that place, and I am dry as a bone, Caroline Grant," he said firmly. "Be good to me now, and let me go a walk up the glen by myself and think this hellish thing out."

She patted his arm. "That will be best, Hugh. It will not be long now."

CHAPTER XII

Out of the Past
  Some nameless sin
    Ye might have heired
    This pain to win.
And yet! And yet! It well may be
That God stores up your ecstasy.

I

BUT Hugh Forbes did not go up the glen. If his mind had not been wholly concerned with its problem he would, indeed, by an effort of will, have turned his footsteps up the river-side; but for a time he was really not aware of his surroundings, and some inward volition set his face down the valley. And down there, somewhere in the moors rolling back from the river, Frances Mary and Vivian Stark were busy grouse driving.

He went on down past the lower bridge leading to the home farm, crossed the wide haughs where sleek, polled Angus beasts grazed, skirted fields where oats and barley were in ear, and so came amongst the scattered birch-trees edging the sweeping contours of heather. His feet were on a well-defined path, his hands deep in his pockets, and his head sunk on his breast. After a time he halted, wide-legged, in the middle of the path and filled a pipe. He did it instinctively, his eyes staring at the ground and not at his fingers slowly pressing the tobacco home. Then he went on, his head wreathed in smoke and his teeth chewing the pipe-stem.

Tearlath Grant was in love with Allison Ayre—and well he might be. Hugh was as sure of that as he was that Frances Mary loved Bill Stark. And to-day he had made sure that Allison cared for Tearlath. But they would not be brought together, and they must be brought together. That was his problem. Tearlath had taken it into his head that Allison Ayre and Hugh Forbes were meant for each other, and one might as well hit him with an iron mallet as try to remove that notion. Allison herself could see that, and it made her mad and wicked and rude and obdurate—and a vindictive little devil. But there must be some way of righting things. There must—there must—and Caroline Grant looked to him to find it. Thank God, he had no problem of his own. Next week he could be going back to Glounagrianaan, there to live his life of subdued effort, and there to bide till his bones were blown dust. Never again would he leave that glen, and why—oh, why had he ever left it? . . . He found himself humming an old air between his teeth:

> The wandering men of Baravais
>   Go far away from Rem,
> Their feet on all the winding ways,
>   Their keels on plain of sea,
> Till the hollow homing hunger murmur dimly,
>   "What seek ye?"

He went on walking and thinking; the moors, serene and changeless, closed round him; the sun reddened the waxing purple of the heather; and a bodyless wind went carelessly by him. There are days like that in spring and autumn when the wind seems to come out of a far pale sky between the pinions of white cloud floating, and they are days that touch a man's heart with sadness, for they seem to hold some serene secret of their own related to an eternal nothingness.

He might have gone right down to distant Balwhinnie if nothing had come to interrupt his thoughts, but something did come. The path had lifted on a heathery bluff, and he was half-way round the curve of it when a clear halloo brought his mind out of its well. He stopped dead, and his head came out of his breast with a start. His pipe jerked out of his teeth, and he caught it as it fell.

"Hell!" he swore shortly. "How'd I get here?" and his eyes sought the river-bank thirty yards down the gentle slope.

Down there by the water sat Frances Mary and Vivian Stark, and Frances Mary was beckoning him with an imperious hand.

Vivian Stark's arm was round her waist.

II

Vivian and Frances Mary had found the shooting dull. At any rate the man had. Frances Mary did not shoot at all, nor did she stay in the butts with Vivian. She wanted exercise, she said, and, besides, she did not care for shooting, so she changed places with one of the keepers and shared the beating sturdily with the other. And she did not shirk her work. Her long legs had the heather step to perfection, her wind was good, and her lightness and her litheness aided by a trained eye took her over doubtful ground safely. The waiting Vivian, his shoulder against the peat wall of the butt, could see her, a point of colour, away out on the purple-washed brown of the moor, and very often watched that speck, bright in the sun, dull under a passing shadow, when his eyes should have been on the low-flying birds.

Vivian was disturbed in his mind. He was compelled to contemplate the possibility that his power over Frances Mary was slipping or had slipped. He remembered how, last year, she had insisted on acting as loader for him in the butts, and how apologetically she used to accept his half-playful cousinly abuse for fumbling in moments of tense shooting. But within the last few weeks she had calmly claimed independence and equality—and superiority too, for she no longer sought favours, but rather yielded them. Only this morning he had had to persuade her to come out with him, and her acceptance had been ill-favoured enough. Suddenly she had claimed the prerogative of her sex—the right to ignore, to demand, to condescend, to snub. And it all dated from that night at Aunbeg and the incoming of that blasted Forbes fellow. It could not go on. It simply could not go on. Stark realised that now, for he realised that Frances Mary meant a good deal to him, and that, though he had not been aware of it, she had always meant a good deal to him. He had been a fool not to make sure of her before his seeming coldness turned her to look for warmth elsewhere; but surely it was not yet too late? He could not readily contemplate anyone or anything that he had ever held slipping from his hold.

And so the shooting was dull, and Vivian called a halt early. Immediately after lunch on the sunny side of a knoll, he sent the keepers home with the bag, dogs, and guns, and suggested that Frances Mary and he get to Innismore round by the river-valley. Frances Mary casually agreed, and the two went off side by side.

All the way across to the river Vivian was detachedly silent—as was, indeed, his habit. But Frances Mary was silent too. Stark noted that, and he did not forget the old days when she used to do most of the talking and try so patiently to get him to respond. It was that silence and all it connoted that made him finally resolve to recover his dominion—or at least to find out exactly where he stood with her. And so, when they got down to the path, he took the first opportunity to strike down to the river-bank and call a halt.

The river had here narrowed into a deep pool between

shelving ledges, and the far bank, vividly green and out-cropped with limestone, rose steeply to a knoll crowned with birches. On the near side the heather sloped down to the overhanging brink of the pool, and, as they approached, Frances Mary touched Vivian's arm. "There are some big fish in this pool," she said. "Don't let them see you till I have a peep." She crouched in that lissome way of hers, slipped forward through the heather, lay full length on the yielding stems, and cautiously slipped a head over the edge of the bank. She looked directly down into an eight-foot pool with slabs of rock jutting out below the surface, and the water was so limpid that she could clearly discern the gouged-out bottom. Three-quarters way down two big black-backed salmon lay side by side, head to the current, flukes slowly winnowing, and their polished noses looking exactly like the metallic prow of a torpedo. As one of them turned on its side for a moment she saw the upturned under-jaw of the male fish. "They are here," she said in a low voice. "Come and have a look—careful, now."

Vivian was standing looking down at her, and his eyes were no longer cold. The long lithe body of her and her lovely tapering legs filled the eye. This girl was no longer his cousin. A dominant surge went through him. Here was life at last and all he wanted of life. He threw himself down by her side, his shoulder touching hers, and his head close by hers.

That sudden appearing head frightened the fish. A lightning flirt of black and silver and they were there no longer. "I warned you," cried Frances Mary hotly, and turned a vexed face towards him. The warmth in the eyes close to her own astonished her, and her lips fell a little open. And then Vivian Stark threw a strong arm over her shoulders and kissed her full on the mouth.

"Oh!" gasped Frances Mary, and, with remarkable

150

vigour, twisted away from that holding arm and sat up. Vivian sat up with her, and his arm went round her waist. "Don't be silly," she cried, straining away.

"We've been playing at cousins long enough, Fred," he said coolly.

Frances Mary was no fool. Vivian had occasionally kissed her in a cousinly, careless fashion, but she recognised the quality of this last kiss. She felt her heart beating. She knew that she was at a disadvantage, and for days now she had determined to maintain the advantage that she knew she had acquired. But Vivian was once again dominant. She did not quite know how she regarded him. A month ago she worshipped him for his physical beauty, but recently she had been more interested in his mental qualities, and she was not sure if she cared for them so much—or at all. She liked him, but also she was a little vexed at having shown her liking so patently in the past. And it was only in the last few weeks that she realised how patent it had been. She had set out to remedy that, and she had even told herself that she would not mind if Vivian did declare himself, with the time and place her own choosing. And she had decided how she would act—putting him off tantalisingly, not quite refusing, not quite yielding, emphasising her freedom to choose. But now she had felt Vivian's possessive kiss and was feeling the constraint of his arm, and she found she could not have her own way so easily. She had lost the initiative, and Vivian was growing dominant in a way that frightened her. And then, looking over his shoulder as she strained away, she saw Hugh Forbes come round the curve of the path.

"Here is Hugh," she said calmly enough. "Don't be silly, Vivian."

"Blast him!" snapped Vivian, but his arm tightened.

And then Frances Mary hallooed. She saw Hugh's check and start, and saw him catch his pipe as it fell, and then he was staring down at her. She beckoned, but he made no move. "Come down here," she cried imperiously. "I want you." And obediently he stepped into the heather and came slowly down the slope, his hands in his pockets, shoulders hunched, and no expression on his face.

Vivian Stark swore savagely and jumped to his feet. Frances Mary remained seated, her legs over the edge of the bank.

III

Stark was savagely angry. He really saw red. The blood had drained from his face and his aquiline nose was white as chalk, his eyes blazed. A minute ago he had given Frances Mary the kiss of passion, and had felt the fine brutal thrill of male power as his arm tightened. He had her, and now he had lost her, and it was the small man's fault. Well, by Heaven! he would see this thing to a finish right now. All his resentment, long gathered, boiled over; all his imaginings and desires came to a point. The only thing Forbes finally accepted was brute force. Well, he'd let him have the chance of accepting—or clearing out. He took a slow stride forward and called out, "Where are you going, Forbes?"

> "'Where are you going?' says Fainne an Laoi;
>   'Where are you going?' says everyone o' them.

Hugh sang the old comic, ironic Gaelic air quaintly. "Cork, if you please."

"I don't like your company," said Stark calmly. "Suppose you get out of here."

Hugh stopped dead ten yards away. "My! Oh

my!" he exclaimed mildly. He saw the flare of battle in Stark's face, and looked past him to Frances Mary. She leant sideways on one arm, and there was abundance of colour in her face and a fine light in her eyes. "Frances Mary called me," he said reasonably.

"I don't care who called you. Get out."

The small man's nostrils expanded, and a little leaping flame came behind his eyes. But his voice was deep and steady. "Wait now! I'm a peaceful man, and I'll go if Frances Mary wants me to go." Hugh Forbes would be damned if he could understand this conduct, but he would hate getting to grips with the man who had had his arm round Frances Mary.

Frances Mary answered promptly. "Please yourself, Hugh."

Frances Mary was a woman. She did not like brawling, but if brawling would serve her purpose she would abide it. She saw that things had come to a final show-down between these two men, and that all her future was deeply concerned in it. And she had to remain neutral. If she had told Hugh to stay, he would stay, and she would be directly responsible for what followed—and it would tell her nothing. But if Hugh had sufficient interest in her he would stay without being asked, and Vivian had better look to himself. She forgot to take into account the fact that Hugh had seen Stark's arm around her.

"Please yourself, Forbes," said Stark, sneeringly bitter; "but you'll go." He was working himself up to the point of devastating action. "You've been hanging round Fred for a fortnight, and we all know what you want. Well, I won't have you hanging round. Are you going?"

Stark's words made the small man flinch—not the flinch of fear, but the flinch where raw nerves are wrenched. Now it has come, Frances Mary. Hugh will tell him to go to hell, and throw him in the river. Oh, Hugh! Hugh! why don't you tell him to go to hell? If you do care one bit for that girl sitting there you will not stand that. Now is the test, Hugh.

But Hugh Forbes, standing up there on the path, had seen her waist encircled by Vivian Stark's arm, and the memory stayed with him. It hurt him physically. There was something so elementally opposed in the two men that dislike amounted almost to nausea. But, having seen that waist encircled by that arm, what action could he take? He could not understand Stark. Some fellows might go berserk when interrupted in their love-making —and Stark disliked him desperately. But that was no reason why Hugh Forbes should throw him neck and crop into the river, or have his own nose squashed. Frances Mary would not like it. She had told him to please himself, and instead he would please her.

Stark took a stride towards him, and Hugh lifted a hand. "Right!" he said; "I am going," and without a look at Frances Mary he turned and strode up the slope. But half-way up he turned his head over his shoulder and called to her. "I am a peaceful man, Frances Mary." He lifted his black hat and turned away. And then and suddenly he dashed that poor hat in the heather and kicked it before him to the path. And if Frances Mary could have seen his face she would have seen a blindness of fury and despair. But the day went its way uncaring, and all round him blew the thin serene wind that was careless of all fury and all despair.

But in time Hugh's mood dulled too, and he soothed himself with his old tune:

> Baravais is lonely by the Marshes of the Rem,
>> With redshank calling weary
>> And the plover's pain,
> The high, eerie, shaken whistle of the curlew
>> Calling rain.

CHAPTER XIII

A whispered word,
  And man was bold
To wrest from God
  What God would hold—
To love, to lose, to dream, to know,
To choose his Hell—and there to go.

I

NEXT day no shot was fired in all the wide policies of
Innismore—unless some poacher was daring enough to
try and slip a stag out through the wire fences. The
grouse shooting was no longer of any interest, and
Charles Grant had ordained a day of peace and stillness
before the stalking season began.

That last day before the season was the day of the local
games down the valley at Glenmart, and Charles, as
Chairman of the Games Committee, had to be present—
could not fail to be present. Hugh and the two girls
went with him. Caroline Grant, as usual, stayed at home
in her island of quiet; and Vivian Stark, who, for the
first time in his life, had a perplexed and self-doubting
look in his eye, refused to be one of the party.

"Keep out of the forest, then," Charles told him
shortly.

"Certainly. I've some letters to write." Stark
hesitated, and went on, "By the way, I can give
you only a day or two amongst the stags."

"Indeed," said Charles dryly, noting the condescen-
sion. "Anything wrong?"

"No. I'll probably run across to Norway."

"More fool you!" said the brief Charles, but he

155

wondered why his cousin should so suddenly forsake the great sport and cut his visit short by a fortnight. He was a keen and excellent stalker, too, and a good shot. Charles looked at his sister, but his sister was entirely self-possessed. She was quiet enough this morning, but then she was always quiet, and she resolutely kept her mouth from drooping at the corners. But if he had looked closely into her eyes he might have noticed the washen-out weariness of them.

Hugh had not heard the exchange with Vivian. He was himself a bit gloomy and distrait to-day. Going down the valley in the early afternoon, he sat in the front of the car with Charles, his hands deep in his pockets, his shoulders far down on the back-rest, and one of his great silences heavy on him.

"What are you thinking about, black fellow?" Charles inquired.

"You," he answered shortly.

Charles looked at him quickly. He didn't doubt that reply, and it made him uncomfortable. Hugh had an uncanny capacity for thought-reading. "I'll give you cause to think of your own shortcomings before the day is done," the big man retorted. "You're entered for the shot-putting—the sixteen-pound one."

"Are you by way of being the local champion?"

"I'm supposed to be no' that bad," Charles admitted complacently.

Hugh sniffed. "I needn't worry," he growled, and went back to his gloomy cogitations.

But down in the level haugh by the swift-flowing burn of Mart, Hugh, like the true Gael, peeled off his gloom and became one of the crowd. And a fine crowd it was. Very few from the outside world were there, but all the wide and narrow valleys from Mortlach to Glendhu were fully represented. Old bearded men, who talked of

hots that had been pushed and hammers that had been
hrown, were there; and middle-aged men, with red
noustaches, who realised with hidden dismay that their
day was done and the time not come for boasting; and
young men, clean-shaven, who knew that their grand-
fathers were "dom leears"—and all with healthy,
weather-tanned faces, wind-washed eyes, and shoulders
hat were thick and massive rather than supple. And
coveys of the gentle sex were there too, but mostly
young, well-shod, clean-limbed, silken-hosed, head-
cropped, and entirely modern. And they all knew
each other and were friendly and cheerful—and occasionally broad. The crowd was not big enough and it
was too familiar to demand a strict keeping of the ring.
The folk drifted about and concentrated, and made room
for the different competitions, or went in and out of the
refreshment places as occasion demanded. Friends
met and talked and laughed and moved away. Maidens
gathered and looked at each other and whispered, and
presently slipped off with the chosen swain. And always
he old men insisted.

Down by the stream was a big marquee with a boarded
floor, now used for teas and innocuous refreshments, but
later in the evening and well into the night to be used for
dancing—and very modern dancing too, sprinkled
sparsely with eightsome reels. Scattered round about
were numerous smaller tents for various purposes, and
one special tent for the committee, much resorted to by
the members and their friends, since it contained an array
of soda-water siphons and a number of demijohns of the
famous Glenmart whisky.

The valley here opened out its wide arms and the
horizon took a wide sweep. From the green of the fertile
river bottoms the moors rolled southwards in immense
low curves and the purple of them was finely contrasted

with the dark foliage of pine and the brighter green o
larch. Northwards big Ben Shinnoch lifted its granit
cowl atilt, and between it and the steep battlegrounc
of Corryhow the narrow gut of Glen Breisach slope
down to the distant grey of the firth. Near by the game
field the tower of an old Roman Catholic church peepec
above a clump of deciduous trees, and away to the wes
the pagoda-like kiln ventilators and steep warehous
roofs of the famous distillery looked over a swell of green
From a round chimney-stalk a dying plume of smok
waved in the gentle breeze that held a pleasant tang o
pine, heather, malt, feints, and spent wash.

Charles introduced Hugh to the committee, mostl
farmers and distillery officials, and he was made welcome
"Forbes!" said one. "A name we ken. Their countr
is up above by Tomintoul."

"That's the honest branch of the clan," Tearlatl
ioked. "This lad is out of a place called Glounagrianaan
somewhere in Ireland. He thinks he's good at the ligh
stone, and I've entered him for it."

"Surely, surely, laird! I'se warrant he'll putt
bonny stane."

These were the polite men of the glens, who woul
not say the impolite thing to a stranger and the laird'
friend, but "fit hell's chance had the wee laddie, gui
showders an' a', against a noted putter like Laird Grant?'

"He's good," the laird told them, sensing their thought
"I have seen him put a round stone across Jordan water.'

"He'll be that," they agreed; "and a drap o' the ra
Glenmart will make him nane the waur."

II

It was a busy afternoon for Charles, and he left Hug
and the two girls to their own devices. There were foo

158

races for the men and one eighty-yard sprint for the lassies; jumps broad and high, and a pole vault; the light and heavy hammer throwing, the heavy shot, and tossing the caber. Tearlath won the heavy shot easily enough, but was well beaten at the caber by a thick-shouldered, mighty-thighed young brewer from the distillery. Hugh had never seen such power as this man displayed in the thrust of a leg and shoulder. And there was fling and jig dancing, and a Highland schottische for couples. Hugh enjoyed the fling with its graceful foot-work, fine shoulder carriage, and the restrained hand gestures, but what was called the Irish jig astonished him.

"Do you dance this, Hugh?" Allison inquired.

"I can dance a bit of an Irish jig, Allsoon, but that up on the platform is not one. If an Irishman tried that in Ireland he'd be like the traveller in Stevenson's fable—buried at the dawn."

"What's wrong with it?"

"Nothing, but 'tisn't Irish. See the lad hopping around and waving his arms and wielding what is called a shillelagh. Irish traditional dancing has rules strict as chess. A man dances with his feet only, and from the hips up he is as rigid as stone, and the inner concentration is so great that his face is like a stone too. Never mind. I could talk a lot about it—but I'll maybe show you sometime."

Frances Mary looked at him quickly. He would show Allison sometime—and perhaps he hoped to have a long time in which to show her. Well, it was none of her business.

The event that pleased Hugh most was the tug-of-war. It was the event of the afternoon, and brought out the old Gaelic devil in these men, usually so restrained and almost subdued. The finalists were a team of distillery hands and one of the pick of Charles's estate workers, and every man on the ground was a partisan, a judge, a referee, an umpire, a protester, and a defendant. The shouts and skirls went to the tops of the highest hills, and for fifteen minutes the clansmen were again alive and again ready to draw dirk if any were handy. Each team had won a pull on change-over, and the third and final one was full of tenseness. As Charles, the official referee, held the rope, a hand on each side of the middle ribbon, and called on the teams to take the strain, a silence, almost dangerous, settled down on the packed crowd. That first dead strain held for ten seconds, and then one side, at a signal from its crouching captain, made its effort. The other captain threw his hand out, palm downwards, and his team like one man yielded cannily from the hips, and swinging like a crew of trained oarsmen, brought the rope back to dead centre. And there they strained and waited for the next signal, and the crowd strained with them. And then the rope, that had been in use for many years, broke, and the teams fell apart on their shoulders. For two seconds there was silence, and then a great gale of laughter relieved the tension. And Charles Grant, that wise Highland man, at that psychological moment, declared a draw. Everyone was satisfied, more particularly the teams, every panting individual of which was dead-sure that he had the pull of victory in his last gallus-button, but was glad not to be called on to produce it.

Hugh enjoyed it all. He and the two girls moved about and drifted apart in the crowd, met again, laughed, and again drifted apart. He noticed that Frances Mary was responsible for most of these driftings. She met friends and stopped to chat, leaving Hugh and Allison together; but Allison, as if impishly aware that Frances Mary wanted to drop them, waited for her, and Hugh, moving a few yards by himself, got lost in the crowd.

Sometime in the afternoon, shortly before the shot-putting, Hugh, moving about by himself, discovered in a quiet corner behind the big marquee a game that he had never seen before, though it is a game hundreds of years old. In isolated country-places, both in Britain and America, worn-out horse-shoes are often the implements employed; in its fully developed form the game is called quoits. An iron ring, seven pounds or so in weight and about nine inches in diameter, is lobbed at an iron pin fixed upright in the ground some eighteen yards away, the object being to circle the pin or get nearer it than one's opponent. The score is kept much as in bowls or curling. Taking into account weight, shape, and distance, Hugh realised that the game called for a fine partnership of hand and eye. A tall, clean-faced man in plus-fours was pitching a practice round by himself in masterly fashion, and Hugh admired the soaring curve the quoit made, the strict angle it maintained to its own flight, and the smoothness with which it bit into the earthen "hob" close to the pin. "Running 'em on a string," he remarked aloud.

"A gey guid pitcher, Mr Lewis!" spoke a voice at his shoulder. "D'ye ken the quoits, Mr Forbes?"

Hugh turned to recognise Wullie Mack, the red-haired head stalker. Hugh and Wullie were already good friends.

"No, Wullie. Never saw it before. Quoits? It could be a good game."

"It's a' that." He walked up to the pitching score and returned with a quoit. He explained the shape of it, back and front, and showed the one and only grip for right pitching. Hugh hefted it in his hand, and swung it once or twice to get the feel of it.

"Man," said Wullie, "ye'd sune hae the knack
Come awa' up and I'll show ye a bit heave. Mind, I'l
no' be great at it the day."

Wullie was in fact a master of the game, but attention
to his duties in the committee tent had resulted in a
slight disaffection between hand and eye. The man in
plus-fours had finished pitching and was lighting a pipe
as the two approached.

"Mr Lewis," introduced Wullie, "this is Mr Forbes
the laird's freen'.—Mr Lewis," he told Hugh, "is the
officer yont the still."

"Glad to know you, Mr Forbes," acknowledged Lewis
"Do you play this thing?"

"No, no!" laughed Hugh. "I was admiring the
way you were stringing beads, and Wullie, I can see, is
a zealot."

"Wullie knows."

"Does he, then?" said Wullie, stepping to the mark
"Fit are ye daein' with thae twa-three pins I'm seein'?"

"The middle one is real, Wullie."

Wullie stood a trifle swayingly, feet close together,
lifted the ring at arm's length, and looked through it at
the distant pin. Then, with an easy, knee-bending
swing, he delivered the quoit, that soared up into its
ordained arc and plunked edge-on into the hob, six
inches to the right of the pin.

"Gosh!" he exclaimed, "I aimed for the wrang ane."

"A nice shot to get inside it," said Lewis. "Try it
Mr Forbes!"

"If I knock anybody's eye out, say I'm an orphan."

Hugh picked up a quoit and stepped to the mark. Al
his life he had been using muscle control in his nation's
games, from pitch-and-toss to shot-putting, and this new
game came naturally to him, as it does to all country
men. That first effort was too low in trajectory and the

162

quoit soared flatly, but the line was as straight as a string. The iron ring shaved the top of the pin, met earth a foot beyond, and slid a yard.

"A bittie higher and she'd be a ringer," commended Wullie.

His second shot was higher, but wide; his third shot still higher, but short; and his fourth went edge-in close outside Wullie's.

"An' noo we'll hae a bit game to oorselves," said Wullie complacently. "Hi, Sanny, come owre here." Sanny was the big man who had beaten Charles at the caber.—"He's in gey guid form," hinted Wullie.

"Ay, is he," agreed Sanny. "No' every day I'll beat Chairlie Grant."

"Sanny'll no' be as clever at this as heftin' the bit stick, but he'll be daein' to mak' weight."

"Oh, I'll play, I'll play," agreed Sanny. "Mr Lewis and mysel'!"

They were in the middle of their second game, and Hugh was getting familiar with the right shibboleths, when Charles came in a hurry looking for him.

"Come along, Aodh—the light shot is on.—Hullo, Lewis!"

"Go 'way," said Hugh. "I'm busy."

"But I've entered you. Are you afraid of shaming your Glounagrianaan?"

"No, but I've that peg down there on a string——"

"We'll be dune in a wee whilie, laird," spoke up Wullie.

Charles laughed. "Oh, very well! Bring him along when you're ready. I'll try to thin down the crowd meantime."

Hugh and his partner succeeded in winning that second game. While the others were bending over the last head big Sanny Menzies stood back, swaying a little on his

163

heels, but swaying lightly for so big a man. Had he heard Laird Grant say that this small dark Irishman was for puttin' the stane? There was no' a man in the glens to beat the laird at it—an' that was well known. What about this laddie? The Irish were aye good at stane and hammer. He looked at him with interest. "Dom!" he muttered. "He's neat, but he's wee—nae weight till him ahint the stane; and I've seen the laird draw inch after inch out of himself to break a body's heart." He walked down the pitch to the others.

"Are ye for the putting, Mr Forbes?" he asked.

"I s'pose I must. The laird, as you call him, has entered me."

"Then he knew you were good," said Lewis wisely.

"Ay so!" agreed Wullie Mack. "An' anither thing, he wouldna enter him if he kent he had nae chance of winnin'."

"Gosh!" said Sanny. "An' that's a fac'." He looked at Hugh with new interest. "I'm thinkin'—I'm just thinkin'." He turned to Wullie. "I jalouse you'll be for backin' your laird?" he half-queried.

"I could be backin' the laird's freen the day," said Wullie.

"Guid for you. Ye ken it heartens a body to have a tail ahint him."

"Right!" agreed Lewis. "I'll check the tape, and you two can look after the shot and the circle."

Hugh laughed. "I am in your hands," he said; "but don't bet on me. I'm only fair to middlin', and doubt if I could touch Tearlath at his best."

"A sma' bet would do nae harm among freens," said Sanny. "Come awa', noo."

Hugh wasn't worrying an atom about the contest. He knew he could putt respectably, and he never could take games seriously. It was all fun, and winning or losing did not matter if one played the game heartily. His three backers, however, behaved with due pomp, Sanny parading in front and Lewis and Wullie on either hand of their champion. The whole crowd was watching the putting—a close pack behind the seven-foot ring tailing out in wide wings as far as the limit of the throw —and Sanny forged a way through it like a snow-plough. "Room, chiels!" he cried. "Ye'll be seein' something in a meenit."

Charles Grant, coatless and bare-armed, in the inner circle, laughed. "I knew you'd gather your tail, Aodh," he said; "and a traitor among them." He looked at Wullie.

Wullie was eloquent to fit the occasion. "Laird or no laird, I'm for backin' the laird's freen. I hae ne'er seen him as much as bool a stane, but I hae half-a-croon that says he can; and let any o' ye cover it if ye're no' feeart." He stared with humorous truculence at his fellow committee members.

And that started the fun.

IV

The competition had reached an interesting stage. It was not run under the modern games rules of confining each competitor to three putts, but under the ancient and leisurely custom of allowing each three putts to beat a better putt. Charles and two others were left in, and Charles, without unduly exerting himself, had laid down a nice stone with twelve inches to spare. A stocky bearded man had failed twice to reach it, and was now making his desperate final effort. The shot certainly dunted ground an inch in front of Charles's mark, but the putter had burned the front mark with a toe, and the judge quietly said, "Out." The second man shook his head as he came to the mark. He knew his distance, and he knew he was beaten. None of his efforts reached his own best.

"Your turn, Mr Forbes," said the judge.

Hugh stepped forward and grinned at his Tearlath. "Shame me before the world, would you?" he made believe to growl. "I'll show you." He jerked off his tweed jacket, and Wullie took it out of his hand. "And mind my good hat too, Wullie." Sanny Menzies and Lewis walked ceremoniously down the pitch; Lewis stayed down there, and Sanny picked up the iron ball, that looked small and light in his great hand, and walked back with it. Hugh waited, and all eyes watched him, a small, dark-haired, bloodless-faced lad in white shirt and loose flannel trousers. Odd how his shoulders seem to have widened with his jacket off! . . . Handy but small! and how could he expect to beat the thew and force of Chairlie Grant? Hugh himself was not expecting to do that. This was only a game, and he wondered if the Scots took their games seriously—as the English did. These fellows looked mighty serious, at any rate—and yet! Probably they were only hiding their smiles at the little bow-legged devil pitted against the big man of the glen. . . . He looked along the grass to where the shot had made brown dunts and judged the distance with a practised eye. He could just about make that, and neither shame himself nor make Tearlath sorry. Ah! there was red-haired Allsoon nicely flushed and happy-looking—and thundering proud she would be of the big man in her heart. She might well be. And there was Frances Mary close at hand. Good old Frances Mary! A darling name and a darling girl! And he knew that she liked him in spite of everything. He wouldn't like to hurt Frances Mary—and he would avoid doing it in spite of the devil and Bill Stark. Frances Mary was looking at him anxiously. She would not like to see him badly beaten, even by her brother. Well, she wouldn't either, by dam'! He smiled at her, and she smiled back.

"Remember Glounagrianaan," she called to him.

"Up Glounagrianaan!" said Hugh, and there was bugle in his tone.

"Up Glounagrianaan!" cried Wullie Mack. "We'll no' forget that."

Sanny dropped the shot into Hugh's hand, and the hand sank under it as if it weighed a ton. "Wow, Sanny! What am I to do with it?"

"Gie it a bit heave, laddie—and let's back to oor game."

Charles Grant laughed happily. He had complete confidence in this small man's prowess, and here was his chance to prove that prowess. "Hurry up, Aodh," he urged. "We have a long programme. Take your three putts, and we'll get going."

Hugh hefted the ball in his hand, threw it a foot in the air, and caught it in his finger-tips with a little twirl. "See that, now," said Wullie. "A wee bit rubber ba'." Wullie recognised the muscle behind that easy throw and catch.

The moment he balanced for the putt the experienced ones knew that the small man was a master of the art. He threw his weight back on his right foot, set square inside the back mark, his right knee was a spring, his left toe patted the ground with a dancer's touch. He raised the shot above his head, and dropped it back again. His unbuttoned shirt-sleeve slipped up his arm, showing the transparent white of the inner forearm and the film of black hair outside. And once more men noticed that he no longer looked small as he poised. Rather was he force carried conveniently.

And then he exploded. Two short, sharp, springy hops, a timed pivot on to his right foot just inside the front mark, and the black ball went soaring from a piston-like drive that seemed full of ease.

Lewis and an umpire bent over the mark. "Take your second," called the umpire.

Sanny walked back slowly with the ball in his great hand, peace on his face. "Daein' fine, laddie. A matter o' fower inches, and the laird 'll hae to let out a link."

Hugh took his second putt, and the umpires after a look put the tape to it. "Level with the best—take a third."

Here and there a man craned forward. The wee man could putt, by gosh! The laird wouldna hae it that easy, after a'.

"Come away, Eiranach," urged the laird. "I am cold in my shirt-sleeves."

"I 'll warm up in a minute, big boy. Take a look at this one." And this one had a lead of three inches.

And Tearlath, no longer under wraps, regained the lead by a further three at his first attempt. There was a murmur and a stir amongst the crowd. This was good putting—the best putting seen in the glen since the War. The men still had confidence in the laird, but they were no longer dead-sure. Neither was the laird.

The contest now became very interesting. They were both in good form, but were not specially trained, and so, each doing his best—one with sheer weight behind the ball, the other with concentrated force skilfully applied from the heel up—they were able to draw inch after inch out of latent reserves. Half an inch, an inch, there was never more separating them, and a second putt was often called for. The crisis came at last. Hugh succeeded in timing pivot and thrust so perfectly that the flying ball touched ground at the exact limit of parabola and gave him a lead of four inches. And when a man is fully extended four inches are hard to come by.

"Thunder!" said Tearlath ruefully. "I knew you were good, but not that good."

"Beat that, avic," said Hugh, "and I'll have to take a bite out of the ball."

Tearlath tried twice, and failed. Indeed, he failed to reach his own best. He was just beginning to tire, and an elbow sinew warned him that an old strain was beginning to twist it. He had another effort in him and no more. He took the shot in his hand for the third time and stood looking down between the lines of people. When it came to the pinch he did not want to be beaten. Aodh had shown his prowess, and no one could now smile at the little man's presumption. That was all Charles wanted. To be beaten in his own bailiwick by a smaller man stung him. He had no trace of resentment, but he would like to win—just. And every man there, except three perhaps, wanted him to win. Slowly he drew all his forces close, and his clan, all around him, helped him with their minds. The vibrations could be felt. His third throw proved that Charles did feel them. It was a supremely satisfactory effort. He felt the shot go sweetly, and for a moment he balanced precariously inside the front mark. And everyone shouted hugely. Gosh! this was the finest putting the glen had ever seen.

Charles had a lead of six inches.

Hugh stood in the circle, his shoulders adroop, his hands in his pockets, his legs wide and a little forward at the knees—a wholly relaxed attitude. His dark-lashed, dark eyes were on the ground and a small smile quirked about his mouth. Wullie Mack knew his champion was beaten, and he stood at his shoulder to comfort him. "Man, ye're a gran' putter, but—but the laird is hard to beat." Lewis and Sanny Menzies walked up the pitch and stood in front of him. "Great work, Forbes," commended Lewis. "I thought you had him. I lay there's not another inch in Grant."

"Nor half an inch," said Charles, reaching for his jacket. "That elbow of mine is gone again." He was suddenly a bit sorry for old Aodh. "Can you do it, son?"

Sanny Menzies stood in front of Hugh and threw the black ball lightly from hand to hand.

Hugh Forbes was not paying any attention to anything that was said to him. He knew that he was beaten and he did not care. He was thinking of Allison Ayre's face. He had been watching Allison for some time, and she was a partisan if ever there was one. Murder! she did want Tearlath to win. Her well-fleshed little muscles must have ached with effort; exultation and doubt must have flowed over her in turn. And at the end she had shouted with the others and clapped her hands. And probably she was now a trifle ashamed, and hoping that no one—and especially Tearlath—had noticed. Well let her have her little victory and welcome. She deserved it, did little Allsoon. He lifted his eyes and smiled cheerfully. "Sorry to lose your money, boys. I'm down to the dregs."

Sanny Menzies never stopped tossing the ball under his nose.

And then a voice close by spoke to him. It was low pitched, but it had in it the whinny of a bugle, the shrill peal of pipes, the ululation of taunt and bitterness and pride.

"Glounagrianaan! Grianaan! Grianaan!"

"Thunder o' God!" said Hugh Forbes, and his head went up. That was Frances Mary. Their eyes met. He had never seen Frances Mary look like that. A flame seemed to flow from her to him. A woman of old time sending heroes to glory or death! Poor hero that he was! What was in him to answer that voice, those eyes, that pride? His nostrils expanded. He caught the shot as it curved in the air, and gestured with his left hand for room.

His toe touched ground just once. Then step—step—pivot—thrust. And no one there needed to ask the result.

There was a moment's silence, and then four voices lifted together in a slogan new to Glenmart, that had heard many slogans.

"Up Glounagrianaan!" And Frances Mary's voice carried the top note. After that followed the general and generous applause. And a black, but not new, velour hat sailed into the air and dropped amongst the crowd.

"'Tis ruined forever now, Wullie Mack," lamented Hugh Forbes.

Tearlath threw an arm over Aodh's shoulder and laughed. "I knew you had that link somewhere—but blow Frances Mary!"

"Amen!" agreed Hugh.

"Laird," said Sanny Menzies, "it wis a chain. We'll gang noo and dae the richt thing by oorselves."

"You will not," said the laird. "Not yet. First we'll give the ladies some tea."

Frances Mary came up to Hugh, slipping on his old jacket. "Some day, Hugh," she said, a strange wistfulness in her voice, "I'll call on your reserves and find only empty silence."

He replied in the same tone. "That day I will be dead, girl dear—and that is the final and finest resource of all." His tone changed marvellously. "I wish to God you'd behave yourself, Frances Mary."

"I wish I knew how, you little brute," said Frances Mary.

CHAPTER XIV

O Love! O Love!
That you should be
So kind, so kind,
And not for me!
That I should know your heart so true,
And all my life wear bitter rue!

I

FRANCES MARY and Hugh lingered over tea in the big marquee. Charles had drunk three cups and hurried away to the completion of his duties, and in a little while Allison, only too aware of Hugh's satiric eye, had slipped away too. Frances Mary, who, somehow, did not want to be alone with Hugh, had risen from her chair and suggested following, when he reached out a hand and touched her arm. "I am wanting a word with you, Frances Mary," he said, "and this is as good a place as any."

She hesitated, looked round her, and sat down. "I suppose it is," she agreed.

It was public enough, at any rate, but no one attempted to interrupt them. They had a small table to themselves, far back in the marquee, and folks, crowding in for tea, seeing the two leaning across to each other, gave them plenty of room. No one would be that rude as to intrude on the bonnie lass, Frances Mary, and the swack Irish laddie—but fit micht they be saying tiv each other, the craturs?

Hugh moved his cup out of the way, leant his elbows on the table, smoked a cigarette, and occasionally flicked ashes into the tea dregs. Frances Mary leant forward

172

oo, her forearms crossed beneath her breast. The evening sun, shining through the canvas overhead, made a yellowish, diffused, rather pleasant glow all round them. And they talked.

"Frances Mary," began Hugh, "that big brother of yours is a great trouble to me."

Frances Mary wholly failed to see whereto this beginning led, and she wanted time to consider it. "He was a little while ago—out there," she said, "but surely not now."

"Now and yesterday and the day before—and tomorrow as well. He is pig-headed, if you want to know—and so is his sister, for that matter."

"Yes, Hugh. And am I a trouble to you too?"

"You will be if you keep on interrupting. Wait, now. This is it. Tearlath is in love with Allsoon Ayre. You know that?"

"How do you know?"

"God give me patience! I say, do you know that?"

"I suppose I do—pig-head yourself. But why should it trouble you whether he is or not? All is fair in love—and shot-putting—if a woman has red hair."

"So it is—so it is. But listen. Allsoon is in love with Tearlath as well. Do you know that?"

Frances Mary did not answer at once, and Hugh looked at her steadily, smoke trickling from his nostrils. She felt the blood come into her face, and blurted suddenly, "I do not."

"You blushing liar."

Frances Mary stirred restlessly. He was uncanny. She looked away and back again. "Even so, Hugh. She is not the only red-haired girl in the world."

"There are not any nicer."

"What can we do about it—nothing?"

173

"Faith, we'll have to," he said, firmly impulsive.

She looked at him in perplexity and wonder. We—the two of them had to do something! What did h mean? She thought she knew him, the strength belov the waywardness, the kindness behind the bluntness the gloom underlying the blitheness, and the resilienc underlying all—except, perhaps, a sensitiveness that onl) she knew of. And now, was he refusing to accept facts his own coolly stated? Charles loved Allison and Alliso) cared for Charles. Probably he was right, and yet h had no intention of leaving the field. He was going t do something about it, and what could he do? N doubt he could do something—he had it in him to d something wholly surprising and adequate. And sh was to help him. The irony of it. . . .

Hugh, watching her, smiled his crooked smile. Th poor transparent blonde bit of a girl, that couldn't kee) her thoughts hidden behind her eyes! "Wait now Frances Mary," he advised. "Don't be buck-jumpin) to conclusions. Tearlath, as I said, is obstinate. Fron something I might have said once—or maybe twice— he has taken it into the round head of him that my min is set on a red-haired girl——"

Frances Mary could not help that small mellow bark "How silly of him! I have not heard you declar it to high heaven more than ten, or maybe eleven times."

"And couldn't I be doing it eleven more times and i no more than a foolish dream? Can't you let me dream? He leant forward and threatened her cryptically. " warn you that, waking up, I might see your hair a tow."

"Tow as ever was, Hugh. Go on." She had he opportunity there and missed it.

"Big Tearlath thinks—knows—is dead absolutel

sure that I must have a girl and she with red hair, and he's twice as certain that Allsoon is that one. He has that embedded in his mind beyond the reach of a pickaxe. He would have, of course. Therefore I must have every chance with Allison, and that's all there is to it. If he as much as suspected that my fancy—but never mind. There's Tearlath for you."

"That is Tearlath," agreed Frances Mary.

"But Tearlath—and others as well—cannot hide any feeling that goes deep, and you and I, Frances Mary, need only to look at Tearlath and he looking at Allison to see that she is the very apple of his eye. My poor Tearlath! Lucky Tearlath!"

The delicate colour again tinged Frances Mary's cheeks, but Hugh was not looking, and she did not look at Hugh. "You are very wise," she said, but not agreeably.

"Wise—wise—wise!" He mocked himself sombrely. "I'll have time enough to be wise. Listen to me. Tearlath has an iron-hard rein on himself—and so has Allsoon. I guessed how it was with her early on; yesterday I made sure; and to-day there can be no doubt. Hsh! I tell you I know, and there's no use talking. She is very proud, that small one, and she is wise too. She can read Tearlath, and she is angry with him to the point of biting his nose off—and he hasn't much of a nose to spare at that. She hides her feelings behind mockery and playfulness. The thing can't go on." He tapped a finger on the cloth. "The job before us, Frances Mary, is to get these two into each other's arms—and be damn'd to them."

II

Frances Mary looked at him, and there was a soft light in her eyes and a surprised wistfulness in her smile.

"I might have known, Hugh. I might have known. But then you always surprise me—always—always."

"The surprise I could give you—" He stopped.

Frances Mary traced a line on the table-cloth. "Would you always keep on surprising me, Hugh?"

He would, by the Great Lord God! He would give her the moon for an Abernethy biscuit, and clip the edges of the sun for a comb for her hair, and make the stars jealous of the grey shine of her eyes. "I would have you hungry for ever, longlegs," he said deep-voiced.

"Lose hunger and you lose God. You said that once, and I think I now understand what you meant. . . . I suppose I would have no surprises——"

"My dear, you'll have surprises where they are due. Keep them for that and pay attention to what I am saying. In a week I am going back to Glounagrianaan, and in a week Allsoon is going back to her own place, and I must get herself and Tearlath to an understanding before I go."

"Why must you?"

"Because it is the task your mother has set me."

That reply wholly satisfied Frances Mary. What Caroline Grant ordained was not to be questioned by those who loved her—not even by Hugh Forbes. "My wise mother," she murmured. "And what very stupid children she has got!"

Hugh gave her his satiric eye. "To be sure," he agreed briefly, and went on. "For days now I have been thinking high and hard and back and fore how to strip the armour off them. It has to be done suddenly—and through the medium of some imagined crisis and risk—there is no other way. Well, girl, I am going to take a chance to-morrow, and you are to help me. You know the arrangements?"

"I have heard Charles and you speak of them."

"In the early morning Tearlath and I try a stalk on the Glen Sealig ground, and you and Allison come up with the lunch pony to Aunbeg. In the evening Bill Stark is trying the flank of Cairn Ban—he'll be out of it. You know how Tearlath has been training me for a fortnight on the Ben Bhreac ground. I know the whole of it like the palm of my hand, and he is letting me do the evening stalk there with only one gillie and one pony. Listen. Between now and then you are to arrange that yourself and Allison do that stalk with me."

She considered that. "Yes, Hugh. I shall like that stalk, and it should not be difficult to inveigle Allison. But why? You don't expect to get a head with us two scrambling after you?"

"No, then—but that's neither here nor there. Sometime in the evening, when I give you the nod, you'll get tired of scrambling up corries and sliding down screes, and you'll politely tell me to go to hell—and you'll trot away home down the glen."

"Oh dear! And I already beginning to look forward to seeing you miss a sitter. All right! All right! I shall tell you where to go. And then?"

"Allison will stay. That can be managed, and luck or no luck I'll draw the stalk out till getting on for dark. Then on the trek homewards I'll lose Allison good and hard."

"Ah! But the gillie—and the pony?"

"You know the short-cut by the corrie of Ben Bhreac? Allsoon and I will take that and send the gillie by the glen track. He'll get home in due course, but Allsoon and I will not. Listen again. You will then put it into Tearlath's mind that we are lost—lost—lost. I leave it to you to emphasise how desperately lost we are."

"And that will set him searching for you. But remember, Charles is a hillman, and he'll find you without much trouble. He has a quick knack of working out the wrong turnings. He has done it in winter with the snow drifting and a man lost on Cairn Ban."

"We'll be lost long enough to serve. And that is all."

Frances Mary looked at him long and carefully. "Is that all you are going to tell me?"

"There is no more to tell you."

"There is, but you will not tell it. Do you think it will be safe to have Allison lost in the little hills behind Ben Bhreac? If she gets as far as the Moss of Torran it will not be in the least safe."

"I'll never be far away. Like a weasel stalks a rabbit will I stalk her. Will you do your part—will you?"

Frances Mary did not hesitate. "I will," she said shortly. She knew that he could be trusted in the final issue.

"I knew I could rely on you, Frances Mary," he said warmly. He flicked her brown fine hand playfully with a middle finger. "I would rely on you with the last thread of my life at stake." But there was nothing playful in that deep voice.

"Thank you, Hugh. And then you are going back to your Glounagrianaan?"

"I am. My work will be done," he grinned at her. "Unless you'd like me to help you at your job."

"And what is that?"

He shrugged his shoulders. "You are a quick learner, and your job is coming easy to you."

She gave him a swift glance that had hurt in it. Alas! there was no task for her—no task that could be fulfilled outside dreams. Hopeless! And yet she was driven once

178

again to prove how hopeless would be that task. "You know," she said smilingly, "how I spent yesterday on the moors with Vivian?"

He nodded and barely kept from frowning. Of course he knew, and what was the use of opening up that subject?

"He proposed to me—you saw?"

"Time for him," said Hugh carelessly. But he felt his face twitch, and hid his feelings under speech. "Not very likely that Bill Stark and you will come to see me at Glounagrianaan?"

"If you invite me," she said, steady-voiced, "I will come to see you in Glounagrianaan."

"If ye come, ye will be made welcome." He used the plural carefully.

Frances Mary Grant, Highland woman, could not go on. She was too sensitive and too proud. "You are a selfish brute," she finished warmly, "and you are bent on keeping your glen to yourself."

He was. To himself he would keep it. It was a green glen and a sunny glen, and there was no spot in it that was yet grey with poignant memories. Let her once set foot in that glen and leave it, and there would be grey shadows in the sun, and a sigh in running water, and all fine music would have an overtone that only he could hear. Enough of this! He lifted to his feet without looking at her. "Wullie Mack has been peeping in at me on and off this time past, and I am now going to pitch quoits with him. Are you coming?"

She did not answer or look up. She gave a small gesture of dismissal, cupped her chin in her hands, and looked within her own mind. Grey vista after grey vista in that young life! And then she saw her mother's face, and it smiled at her. "Oh, mother—mother!"

Hugh looked back from the flap of the marquee and noted her stillness. Dreaming she was—and fine dreaming, no doubt. He would remember that still pose, and he would dream too—for dreams would be all that he would ever have.

CHAPTER XV

If man might play
  This simplest game
With open heart
  And tongue the same,
No woman's power his power could mar.
Lord of all the things that are.

I

THIS is not a chronicle of deer-stalking, but a deer shall
be stalked all the same, and a little blood—and not all
the heart's blood of the hart—shall dye the heather.

Nothing need be said of the morning stalk, which was a
failure owing to a flaw of wind from a gut in the hills
carrying the man-scent to the stags, that forthwith drifted
across to the sanctuary. Hugh Forbes, with the back of
his neck sun-scorched, had plenty to say; but Charles
Grant was happy enough in having proved that the game
was not so very easy after all. And nothing need be said
of Vivian Stark's more successful evening stalk on Cairn
Ban. Vivian, on the string of fate, will be slid into place
in due time.

In the afternoon the whole party met at Aunbeg bothy
and had a good lunch and a long laze. Then Vivian
moved off up the glen with a stalker, two gillies, and a
pony; and, after a further period of talk and smoke,
the others drifted down the glen. There was no hurry.
Charles and Hugh went ahead, shoulder to shoulder, and
Charles was telling Hugh exactly where he was to look
for a stag, how he was to get there in the eye of the wind,
and what he was to do when he got there. "Leave it to
Wullie Mack," was his final advice.

"Will I, begob? I'll listen to him with great care, and then go off and shoot that stag according to the sense God has given me."

"And you'll come home empty-handed."

"And can't I blame Wullie Mack for that too——?"

"And those two jades behind us. Frances Mary knows how to stalk, of course, but if Allison gets that carrot-top over a skyline——"

"The deer will take it for a new sun, and come up to see. I tell you, boy, I might be watching the sun of that hair myself, instead of a poor devil of a stag."

The imp in Hugh could not help pricking his friend. Charles went silent. And then Hugh was sorry. "'Twill be a grand day, to-morrow, Tearlath boy," he said.

Tearlath looked at the sky. "We are in for a good spell," he agreed.

"It might rain to-morrow and snow as well, but it will be a grand day all the same."

Tearlath was no fool. He put his own meaning to that. "In that case," he proposed, "I may as well take Frances Mary back to Innismore."

"Leave that girl alone." Hugh spoke shortly, having made his friend's case worse.

They went down the glen a couple of miles, and there, where the tributary Glen Bhreac came in at a slant from the north, the party split up. Charles, with the gillies and all the ponies except one, kept to the main track for Innismore; and Hugh, Frances Mary, Allison, and Wullie Mack turned their faces to the hills. Charles never looked back, and Hugh stood gazing after him, doubt and brooding in his eye. You are hard hit, Tearlath son, and you have a loyal heart—and a head of solid ivory. And someone is going to make a bloody fool of himself.

"Big-noise, we await your orders," said Allison with mock deference at his shoulder.

"A big noise—that's all I am," he said sombrely. "But my rank and file have duties, nevertheless."

"To obey?"

"And be silent."

"Never," both girls cried together.

"I suppose that is asking too much. If ye can't be silent, be as silent as ye can. Let us be going now, and with the help o' God and Wullie Mack we'll be lucky."

II

They skirted round the wide base of Ben Bhreac on a negotiable path. This was a short cut to Innismore, but a corrie in the neck of the hills made it impossible for ponies, and, as Hugh knew, Wullie Mack would have to retrace his steps, later in the evening, to the main glen. The sun was now well on in its westering. It poured its light slantwise down the slopes of the hills, and the tall clumps of old heather cast long streaks of shadow. And there seemed to be nothing on all the hills but sun and shadow. Wullie Mack could not mark down a single stag. Every now and then he and Hugh, leaving the girls holding the pony, crawled to the brow of a contour and, lying on their breasts, raked the further slopes with the glasses. Nothing! Nothing but sunlight and shadow and granite rocks jutting out of the heather —mighty sweeps of hill slumbering emptily and unchangeably!

"The beasts know," said Hugh. "Probably keep a calendar of their own."

But Wullie Mack was quietly confident. "I hae it in my marrow that I'll blood ye the day yet," he said. "The beasties are no' far awa', and we'll hae a look at

183

them onyway—and come upsides with them too, I'se warran'."

They went on another half-mile till they came to a hollow in the hills where the path swung to the right. "We are comin' to the placie noo," said Wullie.

"The Drum o' Sgor Luadh!" remarked Frances Mary.

"Just that, Miss Frances Mary. We'll leave the shelt here, and hae a keek—the fower o' us—ower the knowie yonder."

He tethered the pony to a stone, and the four climbed the knowie. They did the last few yards, Wullie leading, on their hands and knees. While Wullie peeped over for a reconnoitring look, the others remained well below the skyline and looked at the pattern of hob-nails on his boot soles. Then Wullie's hand came behind him and he beckoned with a finger. Hugh, holding his rifle carefully, crawled to his side, and Frances Mary and Allison came level. The four lay on their breasts on the dry cushion of heather, looked down a short slope and then up the great mile-wide sweep of the first ridge of Sgor Luadh. And there was nothing to see but purpling heather and grey boulders and, beyond, the cold eastern face of the big mountain, its northern rim lit with orange.

"Div ye see them?" whispered Wullie, though there was no need to whisper.

Hugh looked at him and followed his eye. Away up near the crown of the ridge he saw a great rock splashed white with quartz, and a heather sea all round it—and nothing else.

"I see them," said Frances Mary, the hill-maid. "They are lying down."

Hugh lifted on his elbows and extended the telescope.

"Pit it on the bald stane," directed Wullie. "Noo to the left and a little bit doon—about there."

"Ah!" breathed Hugh and steadied the glass. "One —two—three—four. Yes! taking their ease. One— two—and that's a good head—and him scratching his rump. Take a look, Allsoon."

Allison had not yet picked out the deer, and Hugh, his shoulder to hers, held the glass till she found her focus. First the great white plain of the sky swept across the ground of the glass, then the blurred image of the mountain-head reeled dizzily, and then the white splashed rock came sharply focused. She steadied on that and moved the glass cautiously downwards, and at once the stags seemed to leap close to her. She could see the light tips of their antlers, the movements of their eyes, the still pose of their heads, till the big hart threw back its plumed neck and scratched a rump with a sur-royal.

"Lovely!" she murmured. "Why, they are looking at me!"

"They are the big part of a mile fra here," Wullie assured her. "We are safe eneuch—for all they hae the wind o' us."

"You are in for a long stalk, Hugh," Frances Mary told him.

Wullie Mack looked narrow-eyed at the sun, low down beyond the shoulder of Sgor Luadh. "They'll be gettin' up to feed in half an hoor or a bittie less," he considered, "and like as not, they'll drift this airt and get oor wind; but there's a chance, tae, they'll work round the showder to where the heather was burned the spring afore last. You'll hae to get in ahint them, Mr Forbes—a guid bit stalk, as Miss Frances Mary says."

"Can I get in ahint 'em in time?"

"An we hurry. You mind the neuk o' a glen we passed half a mile back—that's the road—richt up to the corrie at the neck, and climbin' it you'll be in the

fauld o' the ridge to the left o' that humploch o' stane.
The beasts micht be oot o' range by then, but it maun
be tried, Mr Forbes, if ye'll be takin' the only chance
that's in it."

"We'll try it," said Hugh decisively. "Say, Wullie,
supposing I had the luck of your auld Clootie, how near
could you get the pony?"

Wullie glanced at the contour of the slopes. "Within
a quarter of a mile o' that bald stane onywey."

"Right. I am going to do this stalk on my own——"

"Oh, Hugh!" protested Allison. "Mayn't I come?"

"To be sure," agreed Hugh; "but Wullie will stay
here with the pony."

Allison looked aside at Frances Mary, and Frances
Mary looked over Allison's head at Hugh. One of his
eyelids flickered, and he gave the faintest side-nod in the
direction of distant Innismore. She gave him the pink,
vindictive tip of her tongue for a moment. "I am fine
and comfortable where I am," she proclaimed. "I'll stay
and watch that big hart go bounding when you miss
him."

"Ye'll hae to hurry," warned Wullie.

Hugh, still lying flat, hauled himself back from the
brow of the ridge and drew his rifle after him. Allison
imitated his movement, and Wullie Mack said, "That's
the wey," commendingly. Below the brow they got
crouchingly to their feet, and Hugh threw a final word
over his shoulder. "Put up a prayer or two, Wullie.—
Frances Mary, if you won't pray for us, don't pray for
the stag."

III

An hour's strenuous going and they were at the foot
of the corrie in the neck of the ridge. Light-footed Allison
had been no drag on the pace, and Hugh was breathing

quite as deeply as she was at the end of that hour. Hugh was of the true hill-man type. Distance or pitch made absolutely no impression on the enduring sinew of him. A mile on city pavements might tire him, but in the hills he had never knowingly to call on his reserves. Frances Mary was like that too, he knew, and now Allison was showing the same metal. He was glad of that, in view of what he contemplated for her. "You are a gran' bit of a lassichie, as Wullie Mack would say," he praised her in a whisper.

"Thank you," she whispered smilingly. "I am ready to climb when you are."

"Gosh! I couldn't hit a dead elephant at this minute. But come on."

The corrie was not difficult. The rock was firm in spite of harsh weathering, and no loose stones went slithering and bounding behind them. There was only the slight scrape of brogues on boulder edges, and an occasional small clink as the butt of the carefully held rifle touched stone. Ten yards from the top Hugh gestured with his hand, and Allison was glad to flatten to the rock and pant. She watched him crawl to the sharp crenellated rim above, lift a cautious head, and push his rifle in front of him. Then he drew himself over the brink and she saw the soles of his shoes disappear. She crept up to just below the rim and waited, and in less than two minutes his head and one shoulder appeared above her. He nodded his head, and his eyes were bright with interest. He reached her a hand, helped her over the edge, and put his mouth to her ear. "They are there," he whispered, "and almost in range. Come, and maybe the red flame of your hair will draw them. My! what a neat bit of an ear you have."

"You are making it tickle," she grimaced, shaking a forefinger.

Above the rim of the corrie was a short bare stretch, curving over quickly to the slope beyond. On the skyline long-stemmed heather straggled thinly on either side of a big lichened stone lying aslant, and the butt of Hugh's rifle shone dully amongst the twisted stalks close to it. The two stalkers crept up, and Allison got her first close look at the stags from the left flank of the stone. Hugh, at the other side, was already sprawled out flat as a frog, his shoulder to the butt of the ·450—a Ballard & Moore with a flat trajectory up to two hundred yards. The stags—they could see only three—were below them, and moving at an angle across their front. They were not feeding seriously, merely nibbling here and there as they drifted towards their own particular feeding-ground. The big hart with the fine head was in the lead, and he was already within range—but not a safe range. Hugh could just discern the flick of his ears, and estimated two hundred yards.

Allison lay still and watched and waited—and admired the grand beast. For a second or two she hoped he was a doomed beast, but, having time to appreciate him—his grace, the nobility of his head, the perfect slenderness of his limbs, the rich brown of his hide—she was beginning not to care—almost to hope . . . But whatever was Hugh doing at the other side of the stone? Lift your red head, Allison, and see the stag go bounding. No. She could never do that.

Hugh had no qualms. That stag was fair game, and he would bring him down and he could. He would not be hurried either. He was still a bit winded—he felt his heart thudding against the ground—and he was glad of the chance to get hand and eye steady. Carefully he looked left and right and made his calculations. On the slant the deer were moving the big hart would come within a hundred yards at the nearest point, and Hugh

auged that spot by a tussock of heather. At that point
e would let him have it, and not before—unless he had
o. He settled himself down, breathed deeply and easily,
an his left hand out under the rifle barrel, snuggled the
utt into his shoulder and looked along the sights.
Probably he could hit him now—this instant—but no!
What was that Tearlath had impressed on him? Leave
the head alone except when your stag is lying and at an
wkward angle. Six inches behind the forearm! There
—no! lower—lower still for a down-hill shot. AH-H!

At that instant the stag, still one hundred and fifty
ards away, threw up its royal head and looked directly
t him. Hugh knew why. For a long time there had
een no appreciable drift of air one way or another, and
ow he felt the smallest cold breath move in the short
airs at the.back of his neck. And next instant the
tag's head was in the air. Winded, by the Lord!

Hugh had, perhaps, four seconds in which to act.
And he acted. He looked along the sights at the brown
de just above the body line, held with all the steadiness
hat God had given him, and pressed steadily on the
rigger. The smack of the shot roared amongst the rocks.
Allison started and bit her tongue. And the stag fled.

A frightened deer usually starts off with one tremendous bound, but this one did not. From a standing
art it went off in a dead run, the undignified, furious
crambling run of a small and angry terrier.

"Missed him," cried Allison.

"I have," agreed Hugh, dreadfully calm.

And then, and without warning, the stag went over
a a clean somersault, his hindquarters lifted and dropped,
nd he collapsed on his side. His legs did not even give
ne final kick.

"Missed him!" cried Hugh. "Have I so?"

He got slowly to his feet, and Allison came round the

stone to meet him. "I was on the other side a whol
minute, Hugh, but I do congratulate you."

They shook hands warmly. And a fine clear hallo
came all the way up the slope to them, and, looking, the
saw a white head-band waving.

"There's old Frances Mary," said Hugh with satis
faction.

"I bet she's glad too," said Allison.

"That girl would be." Hugh knew that much, a
any rate.

CHAPTER XVI

The thing you do
For other's weal
May in the doing
Your own fate seal;
But should Doom strike above the guard,
The game is played—and that's reward.

I

In half an hour Wullie Mack, striding long and smoothly,
arrived on the scene. He was pleased and even excited,
and examined the dead stag with admiration. "A sound
job, Mr Forbes! A sound job o' work, by dom, as ever
I kent. And when I blood ye, ye 'll be a stalker to richts.
Losh! I was swearin' hale moufu's—an' Miss Frances
Mary listenin'—when the breeze died on us and me
kennin' the fluffs and by-blaws up oot the corrie. Sure's
death, my hert coupit owre when the lad here up and
off. And then I heard the dunt o' the shot."

"I thought I had missed him too."

"I didn't, then. I kent fine he was dead on his feet."

"Is Frances Mary waiting down below, Wullie?"
inquired Allison.

"No, Miss Allison; she's awa hame."

"Oh," said Hugh, "the great hurry she was in!"

"She wasna keen on facin' the brae," Wullie explained,
"an' wi' the sink o' sun it got gey nippy. She bid me
say she was movin' off in front." And to himself he added,
"An' twa's company onywey, and oor Frances Mary is
nae sae blate."

Allison Ayre smiled, but not happily. Poor Frances
Mary! Surely she could not be suffering a twinge of

191

jealousy? That was not like Frances Mary. Oh, Frances Mary, Frances Mary! Are you in this twisted mesh too?

Allison moved a little away and looked down at her toes in the heather—and there was no smile on her face now. Everything was so hopelessly perplexing, with everyone at cross purposes and hiding their feelings. Charles Grant—Charles, and this small dark man of Ireland, and Vivian Stark, and Frances Mary—and herself too—moving in cross currents—and nothing smooth anywhere. What was Aunt Caroline doing? Aunt Caroline knew, and she herself knew too. But what could she do! Nothing! Nothing! Only wait and give no sign.

And there, on that darkening hill-side, she felt for the first time the weight of life on her—the first real touch of hopelessness—that first touch of futility and dreichness which is no more than the passing of youth. She was in tune with the gloaming and the wilderness. For now the sun was down, away down behind the hills, and a wan light lay evenly on that upheaved and barren land. The mountains, stark against the pale glow of the sky, took on a strange entity of their own—a still and brooding entity, remote but not unaware, not concerned with life, yet opposed to all life, serene too in their own certainty, but now, at this moment, denying serenity to all things wherein life stirred. And the valleys that slowly darkened were weighed down by silence.

She shrugged her shoulders at last and lifted her head. "We had better hurry," she called.

Hugh and Wullie were busy over the stag. "Ready in two minutes, Allsoon," Hugh called back.

In half an hour they had the gralloched burden of the stag on the pony's back, and in half that time again they were back in the hollow of the valley. There they

alled a halt for a few minutes, and had warm coffee out
of a thermos flask and the last of the sandwiches. Hugh
pressed Allison to one sandwich more than her share
and told her that coffee was what she needed. He had
noticed the droop in those lips where no droop should be,
and knew the devastating effect of the gloaming on that
blithe spirit. "Courage, comrade! the devil is dead,"
he murmured, his fingers patting her shoulder with the
lightest touch; and she looked at him and smiled understandingly. "I do like you, Hugh," she whispered.
But how long would she keep liking him? He shook his
head sadly and turned to the stalker. "The long road
for you, Wullie," he said.

"An' something to show at the hinner end. Are ye
or the back o' the Ben? Ye ken the road, Mr Forbes?"

"Been over the corrie two or three times with Tear-
ath."

"Fine that. It'll save ye an hoor, but I micht be close
on yer heels come Innismore, and ye can be telling the
laird that his best head is off the groun'—a warrantable
hart and a bit to spare. I'll take the rifle, Mr Forbes."

"Which path did Frances Mary take?" Allison
inquired.

"The short-cuttie, Miss Allison."

"Come on, then, Hugh. She may be waiting for us
in the glen." Little Allison did not want to make Frances
Mary suffer more than she had to.

II

The two made good time up the valley. It trended
upwards before them at an easy gradient, and, even in
the lessening light, the path winding in and out among
the heather clumps was easily followed. Hugh took the
lead at a steady hill-man pace, and for once remained

silent. His head was downcast, his hands deep in his
pockets, and he seemed to be lifting himself along with
a forward thrust of each shoulder in turn.

At long last he had become the prey of gloom and
doubt. Now, at the approach of the critical moment,
he was not in the least enamoured with the plan he had
worked out. It was a damn silly plan, he informed
himself, and nothing would come of it but his own discomfiture. Not that he minded that, but it might only
make things worse for all of them. Well, he could draw
out of it within the next five minutes and no one would
know—except Frances Mary. And Frances Mary would
laugh at him. She would do worse. She would find
that he had come to the bottom of his resources. Wait
now. This thing had to be considered apart from his
own vanity, and he could suffer laughter and despisal if
he had to. This whole plan of his was no more than a
forlorn hope, and there was no great risk in it. Discomfort certainly, but not risk! A night on the moor
in August could not possibly hurt a hardy slip like
Allison—given careful stalking. And it would be a long
night too. Not a chance in ten of Tearlath finding her
before the dawn. The cold and desolating dawn
Allison—poor little Allsoon, game as she was, would be
terribly sorry for herself by then—pride gone, vexation
wiped out, all her guards down. And Tearlath would
be in a hell of a state too. He would so! And the only
thing Tearlath might do would be to give Aodh Forbes
hell's own pile-driver. And Aodh Forbes might deserve
it. Ah well! sure that would be a fine excuse for making
straight back for Glounagrianaan. Why did he ever
leave his own glen? Ought he not have known the
splendour of anticipation and the bitterness of realisation
Bitterness! no need for that. He had experienced what
he would not now be without, and he had his own work

to do in Ireland. He would do it too, by Heaven!—and he could do without red hair or tow hair, or any other sort of hair, till hell froze over. And he would have to do without the old dreams too, and curb his small affectations and poses and vapourings. . . .

He was striding along the outside of the path where it edged round a few feet of downward slope and, by some chance, his left foot tripped against a clump of heather. He stumbled, failed to get his hands out of his pockets in time, managed a neat tumble on the curve of a shoulder, rolled over, and brought up at the foot of the slope. "Well, now!" he exclaimed in mild surprise; and then hotly, "The devil damn it!"

Allison gurgled in that infectious fashion of hers, and it was a fateful gurgle for her. Hugh from his seat among the stalks of old heather looked up at her with a dark and calculating eye, and in his mind Fate pointed a finger. "What are you doing, Allsoon?"

"Laughing, Hugh."

"And why are you doing that, my fine girl?"

"You turned such a very nimble somersault, and you have such an entertaining way of swearing."

"Laugh away then, *mo cailin deas*, and God be good to you—and to me too. Some tempt Fate with laughter and some with tears, and for a reason of its own Fate has twisted my ankle."

"Oh, Hugh! I am sorry," cried the gentle Allison, all at once solicitous. "Is it very bad?"

"I don't know yet. 'Tisn't the first time it has failed me, that ankle." He turned over on his face, pulled himself up to the edge of the path, and got gingerly on one leg. He grimaced as the other foot touched ground.

Allison leant to him, all anxiety. "Will it carry you, Hugh?"

He smiled at her his pleasant and wistful smile. "We'll

195

be seeing." He took a few limping steps. "Not so bad—not so bad at all." He bent and rubbed his ankle briskly.

"Look," cried Allison. "If I hurry back I can overtake Wullie and get the pony here."

Hugh considered that, stamping his foot gingerly and wrinkling his nose. "No," he decided. "There'll be no need, I think, and as a matter of fact we'll get to him quicker by going ahead. We'll see how I manage, anyway, girl."

"Let me help you, then." She went on the outer side of the path. "Take my shoulder," she ordered with decision, and nothing loath, he put his arm across that firm little prop. She in turn slipped an arm round his waist and, thus welded together, they made progress towards the corrie. He did not lean heavily. Just heavily enough to apprise her that she was indispensable.

III

So they went for ten minutes. They had still a half-hour of half-light before them, but with the sky clear of cloud and the stars beginning to show, they knew that the night would be very little darker than it was now.

"A fine prop you'd be for a man all his days," murmured Hugh, music in his deep brogue.

"Isn't it a pity for me?" she murmured back imitatively.

"What is?"

"That I have no tocher."

"Ah! indeed and indeed! With red hair it is required. It isn't that you haven't a good deal. Brains to burn and a kind heart, a quirk of humour and the very devil of a temper, and that dour Scots pride behind all, but—ah! and ah again! that your hands be empty."

"I hold you with one of them this instant."

196

"You do so—and another you hold with the twiddle of a little finger."

Allison said nothing to that, but Hugh felt her shoulder slacken under his arm.

"Amn't I the dam' fool, Allsoon?" he said gloomily; "and I'll be a bigger fool yet."

"You are as wise as a woman in some ways, Hugh, but you are foolish too."

"As a woman. And now we know it."

They came round the sharp curve in the path and brought up below the corrie in the neck of the pass. It was not a particularly steep corrie, nor was it a long one, but it was a very cataract of stones. Hugh lifted his arm off Allison's shoulder, and she loosed her clasp. He threw back his head and examined the pitch above them, and then wiped his brow under the back-throw of his velour hat, and, strangely enough, his brow needed wiping—and his heart went away down into his boots. It was the critical moment and he hated facing it. He shook his solemn head, but at the same time clenched his teeth, and the gloom in his voice Allison put down to physical, not mental, stress.

"I am afraid I can't make it, old girl," he said.

"Poor Hugh! That ankle must hurt dreadfully."

He turned and sat on a square boss of stone, and looked up at her dumbly. And Allison rose to the occasion briskly. "I will hurry on and meet Wullie. Up over here and straight on, isn't it?"

He shook his head. "Not quite, but the road is easy to follow. I suppose it is the only thing to do. Listen now, Allsoon. You can't go wrong for half a mile—the path is there for you—and then you come to where the valley forks. You'll be inclined to take the fork to the right, because the path is bit deep, but it is only a deer track that after a while twists back and up. Take the fork to the left, and that'll bring you where you have to be. The left, remember." He gestured firmly in that direction.

"To the left—I'll remember. Can the pony reach the head of this corrie from the other side?"

"It can—easily."

"Then I'm off. You'll be all right, Hugh?"

"Right as rain. I'll smoke a pipe, and might manage to crawl up to meet you." But, if he only knew, his next smoke was a long way off.

Without another word Allison turned and began to climb. Hugh watched her for a little, and then called to her, "Don't be vexed with me, Allsoon. I'm doing the best I can."

"Silly!" she threw back.

"And say, Allsoon, don't forget the dam' fool I am."

She waved her hand, laughed down at him, and went on climbing. A neat and handy climber she was, that small one, not trusting too much to her feet, making sure of her hand-grips, barely touching the stones with light toes; and the easy verve of her, some quality not so much of the body as of the mind, a poise and quickness that was lithe yet resolute. No wonder that she was loved. He loved her himself in a way—and could only thank God that he did not love her more—as if that could help him. A girl like that should be able to solve her own problems. Perhaps she was doing it her own way . . . and here he was acting mighty Jove for her, bent on plucking her out of her own chaste armour—like a periwinkle on a pin. Pure unadulterated cheek! And now he would have to see it through. . . . That rough brown she was wearing would not be so easy to pick out against the heather, but those light stockings would. And he would have to be careful as any cat, swift as a hawk's pinion, silent as an owl's wing, thinner than any shadow—too many things for any man.

He looked at the ground frowningly, and was not in the least confident. And suddenly the folly and futility of his hare-brained scheme came home to him with a shock. Simply he could not go on with it—and there was yet time to stop it. Let him stop it then, in God's name. He lifted a quick head to the corrie. Allison had just disappeared over the top. A shout might reach her—would indeed reach her—but somehow he did not want to shout. Still, he could easily overtake her. He started to his feet and took two quick strides forward, and there was no trace of limp in either. . . .

"Hullo, Forbes," said a voice behind him.

CHAPTER XVII

Out of the brute
Have we evolved.
To rule by mind
Have we resolved.
But if you want to soothe your woes,
Go meet your foe and blood his nose.

I

HUGH stopped dead, but did not turn round. A tiger, a wolf, or a dog would have done that, but this man's physical reactions were based deeper than mere instinct. He was one of the few who have evolved beyond instinct, while still using it. He stood stock-still while one might count three slowly, and his face became a smooth mask —inscrutable, and yet, in some way, indomitable. And then he turned leisurely and looked calm-eyed at Charles William Vivian Stark, who looked not calmly but only coldly at Hugh Forbes.

Hugh, in some detached compartment of his mind, admired the workmanlike appearance of Stark in his two-peaked deer-stalker, leather-bound homespun, and pigskin anklets. His big-calved legs carried his body with ease—almost too much ease. A light rifle was under one arm. Altogether a formidable figure.

And then some queer antipathy of race lifted a sullen head. Was it God or the devil sent this man here? An instrument of some providence to show the finger-snap worth of all Hugh Forbes's planning! Well, he, Hugh Forbes, would be hanged, drawn, quartered, judged, and damned before he'd accept this instrument. Whatever he might do of his own volition—ah! and what was he about to do of his own volition? Hugh Forbes smiled quizzically. "I think it was God sent you after all," he said aloud.

Stark looked at him puzzledly. "Anything wrong?"

"No," said Hugh. "I was only feeling lonely. Sit down and talk to me."

"Don't be a silly ass," snapped Stark ill-temperedly. "I am going on." He stepped past Hugh and faced the corrie.

"A great hurry you're in," protested Hugh mildly. "Wait till I fill this pipe and I'll be with you." In fact Hugh was thinking furiously. He must detain Stark for at least five minutes, until Allison had taken the left fork of the valley. But, even if he succeeded in that, Stark had complicated things. He would get to Innismore before Frances Mary could unsettle Tearlath's mind, and then—anything might happen. If only the long fellow could be persuaded to go round by the glen, and thus waste another hour! Hugh drew pipe and pouch from pocket.

Stark hesitated only for a moment. There was no longer any need to be considerate and restrained with this Irishman, to refrain from expressing his feelings by words—or by deeds if necessary. It gave him a warm and lusty glow to be able to express himself adequately. And yet, though the inner restraint was gone, the training of his caste still held, and there was no trace of heat in the spoken word. "I don't care for your company, Forbes."

"Had any luck?"

"A fairish head. I'm going on." He turned away.

"Know the road?"

Stark did not deign to answer.

"The great Bugaboo has his lair up there. You'd better watch out."

"So had you," said the other grimly.

Stark had his foot on the first boulder, and Hugh was improvising wildly.

"Up there's the wilderness full of wolves where he loves to lie and—and crack the bones of overgrown whelps." His deep voice mangled Tennyson's words impressively.

Stark brought his foot back to the ground and turned. "Is that meant for me?"

"Something I read somewhere——"

"I should advise you to be careful."

"That is the very thing I am."

Stark contemplated the small man, and some inner voice whispered prudence. Was the little brute baiting him and urging him on to the point of violence? His eyes glanced past Hugh at the darkening valley. Forbes had been stalking, but probably had sent his gillie by the glen. They were alone here. A day or two ago the Irishman had gone off with his tail between his legs, but then Frances Mary had been present. And now they were in the darkening and brutal wilderness, and Forbes seemed to be making a dead set at him. The little thug was capable of anything. He was small, but Stark had already felt the rending quality of his grapple. Some inner desire of avoiding trouble evinced itself. Stark looked and said nothing. Two dogs, stiff-legged for fight—no more, no less!

"Let you and me make a bargain, big man," Hugh proposed suddenly.

"Bargain? About what?"

"Wait now! You don't like me. You regard me as a hell of a nuisance—an interloper. Well, if you will go round the safe way by the glen I promise to leave Innismore to-morrow and trouble you no more." This was direct enough, surely, Hugh considered.

But Vivian Stark simply and naturally could not understand what Forbes was driving at—and bargains were no longer any use to him. "You can go to blazes if you like," he said, "and stop your fooling. I don't want any trouble with you." And that was half a lie only.

Again Stark turned, and this time both feet were on the lowermost boulder, when a sudden twitch at his coat-tail very nearly brought him on his back. He staggered, recovered his balance with a mighty effort, and sprang to one side. When he faced round the rifle barrel was held across his breast as a guard. That inner prudence still warned him to avoid the bear-like hug of this callous and inexplicable little thug.

But Hugh Forbes showed no inclination for handgrips. All that Hugh wanted was time—just a little more time. He had thrust his pipe and pouch into a pocket and had stepped to a safe distance, intoed and alert, his strong legs slightly bent at the knees. The two looked warily at each other through the gloom.

"You are trying to pick a quarrel, Forbes," said Stark in forced calm.

"I only want you to be reasonable," replied Hugh placatingly.

This was maddening. Reason! from a man so utterly unreasonable.

"You want one of your beer-house brawls."

"I do not."

The sincerity of the reply precipitated the trouble. If Hugh had been patently pugnacious it is possible that Vivian's prudence might have called once again on his dignity. But—well! the Vikings never went berserk in the face of indomitable defiance, only where they suspected fear and looked for inferiority. Stark saw red; but he did not actually lose his head. He saw before him a small man in a withdrawn attitude of defence, and he hated that small man. And he felt within him a surge of force and knew his own strength and skill—his great height and weight and reach. The time was come to deal with his enemy. "Very well, Forbes! If you must have it——"

Hugh shook his head desperately. "Have sense, man."

Stark leisurely propped his rifle against a rock, placed his deer-stalker on the muzzle, buttoned the lower button of his jacket, and, hands coming on guard, took a boxer's stride forward. "If you will have it——"

"O God!" cried Hugh Forbes in pure dismay, and he backed away. "Take any road—any dam' road you please, but don't start this."

Which only made Stark the more determined. Any road he pleased! Yes, after he had dealt with the cur. "Put up your hands." He took a quick stride forward.

And Hugh Forbes turned and ran—shamelessly turned and bolted down the valley like a rabbit. And Stark, at last gone berserk, pursued him.

II

It certainly looked as if Hugh Forbes did not want to fight. Great my Lord! why should he fight? There was nothing Stark could take from him, and nothing, any longer, that he could take from Stark. And what would Frances Mary say and do if he beat up this swank, blonde man of hers? Strange how the thought of Frances Mary swayed him. He must avoid hurting her. He had only been playing for time, and the time was past now. Stark could no longer overtake Allison, and it was full time he himself was on her trail. If he could keep dodging the big fellow until he made him see how ridiculous the thing was the trouble would fizzle out and

Stark take himself away. Let them play this game of hare and hound, then. But a big, blonde, angry man cannot so easily be made a pawn in any game.

Hugh heard Stark's footsteps pounding down the path behind him, slowed down till they were close to his heels, swerved sharply, and took a flying spring down the few feet of slope to the level of the valley. But in landing his heels slipped on the edge of a tussock and he came down sitting. He was on his feet in an instant, but already Stark was on him, and, before he could dodge his head into his shoulders, the little man received what he himself would call a side-winder that rolled him over and over in the heather.

He came to his hands and knees and shook his black head. His fine velour hat was gone and, for the time, forgotten. That was a humdinger of a wallop—and more where it came from. Two more like that—and good-night, everybody. He looked sidewards and upwards at Stark, and Stark was ready for him at a handy distance.

"Go away out of that," urged Hugh. "I'm done with you."

"I am not done with you. Get up."

This was most damnable. The big fellow had taken the bit in his teeth and would insist on blood and bones, teeth and flying hair. And there was no time to waste either. Allison was away down to the wrong turning, and here was he with a head singing. Something had to be done and quickly. Get close in, Hughie, cross-buttock him, and fall on top. Two falls like that and you might wind the big fellow for five minutes—and five minutes would give you time to climb the corrie and get away. Now!

Like a vibrant spring he came off the ground and launched himself forward.

But Vivian Stark was ready for him. Vivian no longer underestimated this small man. He knew that, at close quarters, in spite of his own weight and strength, the small man had some terrific and rending force; and that he must use all his weight and reach and skill to keep that force at arm's length. Now, poised and ready, he saw that flying leap, took a pace backwards, handed Hugh off with a stiff left arm, and whipped his right across savagely. And once again Hugh found himself flat amongst the heather stems.

Down there in the hollow of the valley was a patch of grey grass, islanded thinly by tussocks of heather, and towards this Stark edged. Here he would have room for footwork and be able to avoid that gorilla-hug he had cause to remember. Devastating as he felt, he was again cool and wary and icily determined to deal out a thorough and abasing punishment. And after that anyone—anyone that cared—could make a battered idol of the little brute. He, Vivian Stark, would show that he too possessed resources and prowess worthy of admiration—and fear. Yes! Fear. A hot spark leaped across his sight.

Poor Hugh Forbes was not cool or wary at all—and in a crisis, too, where coolness and wariness were the only weapons for him. Remembering Allison Ayre going down the wrong turn of the valley into all the queer lost hills beyond, with the treacherous Moss of Torran in the hinterland, he grew furiously bent on boring in to close quarters and, with luck, breaking another collar-bone. And he found it woefully hard to get to close quarters. Yet he kept trying.

There were none there to see that great battle—except one counts a big, brownish-white owl that went on silent wing down the valley and back again. It was a battle worth seeing too, but probably the owl did not appreciate that. Two foolish bipeds circling round each other, awkward-footed amongst the clumps, and flapping at each other futilely! So it must appear to the owl. There were no clutching talons, no rending beaks, no flying feathers. In the beginning, certainly, the squat biped seemed to be looking for a claw-hold, but when the owl returned, after many minutes, he had given up that commendable endeavour, and was no more than circling away from the big biped's flappings and flapping back aimlessly.

Yes. After painful minutes Hugh Forbes was no longer thinking of getting on Allison's trail. He hadn't time. He was too busy saving himself from an early and complete demolition, too intent on husbanding his waning reserves; in fact, too near defeat to think of anything. It had come to that, and it went further.

III

It was, indeed, a great and long-drawn-out battle, fast, and then resolute, and after that grim, and in the end going back to primal savagery—as battles will go without the restraint of rules and onlookers. And in that final phase the issue was decided by some little basic thread of toughness—apart from will—that twists somewhere in the mystic recesses of race. For unless a man has a steely confidence and, when the confidence is gone, a natural and unconscious resolution, it is terribly wearing on mind and body to see one's enemy take his hiding and take his hiding, and grow cooler and more cunning and indomitable and indestructible. A black-browed, aquiline-faced, broad-jawed man, that came and came and came again.

And, once again, in action, Hugh Forbes, no longer small, was a squat powerful figure with long arms. It was that first futile five minutes that told on him, and that he never recovered from right to the end. No man of his weight could stand up to the punishment he then received and not feel the worse of it. But once he realised that he could not overwhelm Stark, and that he was simply boring into destruction, he changed his method, dropped his head behind a protecting shoulder, and slowly repaid his account. And the big owl went away in disgust.

Oh! but the small man was weak now—winded and dizzy and wanting to be sick. But there was no giving in, and those bowed towers of legs bore him up finely. Licked he might be, but as long as those good legs bore him, and his senses remained with him, he would just keep pegging away. Keep at it, Hughie. You've still a little of your tenth wind left, and your footwork is as neat as a reel. The big fellow has a wicked right, but one saw it coming. Get your head down, and give up making long reaches for handsome face—you have already gashed a knuckle against a front tooth. Ah! He doesn't care for body blows. Hit him in the slats, advised Mr Dooley. There's that, and there's that—and there's his jaw for you at last.

Stark staggered, and Hugh piled in, and the big man clinched to save himself. And the end had about come. The smaller man twisted a shoulder inwards, got his hip leverage, and Stark went over in a savage cross-buttock and had the wind driven out of him under one hundred and sixty pounds of bone and muscle. Pity the big owl was not there to see that.

Hugh was on his feet at once. "Get up," he ordered, and Stark obeyed. That was foolish of him, but already he was being dominated. Had he taken a longish count he might still have come out victor, for the small man was the more spent of the two.

Hugh got close in now, and got home left and right

with the last of his strength. Stark crumpled and lay flat.

"Get up." Stark stayed where he was, and Hugh, swaying over him, touched him with an urgent and contemptuous toe. "Get up. You won't? There's your road." He pointed a stiff arm down the valley and again used his toe. "Get up and go."

Stark staggered to his feet and went without a word. Even now he was stronger on his legs than his conqueror, but the basic streak had worn down to yellow, and all fight was out of him. And the victor, upheld only by some indomitable and heroic spark, swayed on wide-planted feet and gazed after him.

CHAPTER XVIII

Splendid it is
  That men there be
In time of stress
  Strong as the sea;
When beaten, most formidable,
Facing Death, indomitable.

I

HUGH FORBES was winded and sickish and dizzy, and he could not remember clearly what it was all about. Where was he, and what was he doing, and what had he to do? He had been struggling dourly and timelessly in some fury of arms and blows, and now there was a great quiet. The northern night with its wan glimmer, self-evolved, was about him, and the weight of it hushed all the hollow lands and hilly lands. There was blood on his chin and on his brow, and his breathing hurt him. He rubbed the back of his neck with that old gesture of his, and he swayed on his wide-planted feet as he looked at the grey ground. There was something black lying at his feet—blacker than a heather tussock. Glory! was that his good hat? Carefully he bent and picked it up, and stared ruefully at the flat squash of it.

"Always you get the worst of it," he addressed it, smiling twistedly. But it had not got so much the worst of it this time. He punched it into shape and smoothed the fur of it. A good hat all the same, and, do what you like, it still remained a hat. Frances Mary used to laugh at that. She had a nice way of laughing, Frances Mary. Ah, Frances Mary! you will not laugh to-morrow. If her blonde man had a sound rib to him it was no fault of

210

Hugh Forbes! What was wrong with the world at all that Bill Stark and himself must be always taking a wallop at each other? What was the trouble this time? What—? And then he remembered. "Saints of Glory!" he groaned. "Allison! my poor Allsoon."

His hat came down over an ear, and he went in a staggering gallop round the corner to the corrie. The heather dragged at his feet, and once he came down on his hands and knees, but was up again on the instant. At the foot of the corrie he came on Stark's deer-stalker, cocked at a rakish angle on the muzzle of the rifle, and, to him, hours seemed to have elapsed since it was placed there. Actually not more than twenty minutes had elapsed. But they were minutes packed to overflowing. He saluted that rakish hat, and turned to climb.

He surmounted the corrie without resting, and it called on all his hardihood. Somehow it had steepened into a mile-high pitch, and it tried time and again to buck him off on to the ugly rocks at the bottom. But he did it, and at last saw the valley running away in front of him. The hills opened out grey and wan, and the sweeping curves of their summits were dark against a star-scattered deep sky; and those high dark curves looked nearer than the toneless glimmer of the slopes close at hand.

Hugh went the down-grade of the valley at a slow trot —a dogged trot, but it was the best pace in him, and his heavily drawn breath went in front—and every breath hurt him. He wanted to be sick. He wanted to lie in the dry heather and let Mother Earth send her healing currents through him. He wanted to let all his senses go in one grand long swoon in which, with luck, he might cease forever, and be done forever with grey life and dry thought and the urge of ideals that were of no use any more—no damn'd use any more. But, instead, he drove himself forward ruthlessly, and, in time, came to the fork of the valley. He made a brief but weary gesture of farewell to the right-hand path, and without pause continued his heavy-footed lope into the left branch.

He was going uphill now and the going was rougher, but he kept on steadily, and in less than a mile the valley opened and shallowed and lost itself in a welter of low brown knowes. And there he halted and lifted his voice in a long halloo, throwing back his head and letting his great baritone voice roll along the slopes. He listened for a reply, but there was only silence. Above the thin hissing of the blood in his ears there was merely the abiding silence of the wilderness, aloof and appallingly serene. "You have us in your web, you still brute," he cried aloud to it; "but I'll run up a thread and down a thread, in spite of all your spiders."

And he went on.

II

Very soon he discovered that he had lost himself. One knowe was the same as another, and there were multitudes of them. They seemed to grow up all round him and twist his footsteps hither and yon; they seemed to lift before him as a barrier. But persistently he kept moving down and across the twisted threads of that web, sometimes at a dog-trot and sometimes at a hurrying walk, and very often with a lurch and a stagger as the heather tangled his hurrying feet. And occasionally he fell. And ever and again his great voice cut through the layer of silence, and the silence closed in on it like water slashed with a dagger.

The one persistent purpose in his mind was to keep going amongst these tangled wildernesses till he found Allison. Beyond that he had no clear thought. He had been hit hard and often and every sinew and nerve demanded surcease, but some fibre in mind and body—

indeed almost apart from mind and body—kept him at his task.

Once he splashed through water running stilly amongst rushes, and, having gone on a few yards, turned back to it. He lay down on his breast, removed his hat, dipped his head deep in and moved it back and forth in the cool fluid. The cold of it stung brow and chin, but the shock of it helped him. His face still adrip, he sucked in a mouthful, and finding it fresh, took a deep drink. And then he was beautifully sick, and that helped him too.

But he never found Allison. Perhaps the big whitish-brown owl winging silently over the low knowe tops saw, with its wide-open and brilliant eyes, the two lost ones making their meaningless pattern along the valley bottoms, drawing near, moving apart, crossing each other's tracks, but at no time getting within hailing distance. Perhaps there was no owl there to see, for no owl hooted. And yet Hugh the Gael—or the Firbolg—or the Pict—knew that something watched sardonically—something that had no entity, no name—and no pity. Something that did not care.

In time—a long time it seemed—he won clear of that tumbled land of knowes and found himself on the edge of a dark plain, so wide that the half-dark of the night shrouded the lift of the hills beyond it. He knew that this was the Moss of Torran, and that in daylight this darkness of it would be the bright green of treacherous swamp. On its soggy margin he halted, and his voice pealed out over the levels. Not even an echo replied. He shook his head fiercely and wiped a hand over his damp brow and hair. He must get rid of this fuzzy brain-haze and think.

Wait now! Allison would never venture far on that treacherous surface. The girl had sense, and if she did set foot in it, would discover the treachery in a few yards and edge out again. She must still be back there amongst the hummocks, and there, in the dry heather, much harm could not come to her. But sometime in the night, beyond a doubt, she would wander out on this wan shore, and that was the eventuality to watch for. His duty plainly was to patrol this edge of the moss and let a yell out of him occasionally. That thing he would do till the slow coming of the dawn, till time and tides were done, till hell froze over, till the devil grew envious of Hugh Forbes's hell. And there and then he started his patrol and his regular hallooing.

III

It was an hour later that he had an answer to his calling. He stopped dead and threw up his head. "That's Frances Mary," he said. He would know that bugle note anywhere—dead or alive. He did not answer back, but there was no need.

Two figures appeared round the dim flank of a knoll and came charging down on him. Frances Mary was one. The other—big and bare-headed—was Charles Grant. Hugh blinked his eyes and looked again. Two only! Frances Mary and Tearlath. Allison Ayre would have to be thinner than air—God! thinner than air— her spirit hovering round them, her body, where? . . . He pulled himself together then as a soldier pulls himself up in front of a firing squad—head erect and hands clenched at his sides.

They slowed as they came nearer. Indeed, Frances Mary lagged, but Tearlath came directly to him after his own direct fashion. "Where is Allison, Aodh?" The question was quietly put.

"I have lost her, Tearlath." And that voice was quiet too.

"Where?" A fine ear might catch the grate.

"Back there." Let Tearlath strike him now. One good blow would finish him, and they could drop him in a peat hole and he would not rot till Judgment Day.

But Tearlath did not strike him. Wise Tearlath! Tearlath knew. He only placed a gentle hand on the stiffly held shoulder and bent to look into his friend's eyes. "You and I are a couple of damn'd fools, Aodh," he said almost softly. Hugh's shoulder trembled under his hand.

God is good, and He pushes no man too hard. At that moment a clear high call came out of the knolls close behind them.

"Allison!" It was Tearlath cried that word, and he put a whole world of relief and joy into it, and the cheering yell with which he followed it could be heard at Innismore. Some said that it was. And then, as once before, he lifted up his feet and ran like a boy.

Allison had heard that great voice, and her heart leaped. Allison had had a bad time—such a very bad time that an account of it might make one sorry that Hugh Forbes had only suffered a small portion of what he deserved. She had been crying. She was crying now, but, game lass that she was, the tears were not altogether for herself. She had failed Hugh by foolishly losing herself, and her pride had reached a low ebb; she was imaginative, as red-haired women are, and she had been picturing poor lamed Hugh, tired of waiting, painfully crawling up that corrie and painfully hobbling down the valley. And now, here was Charles. Her own great Charles! The man for all emergencies—cool and experienced and so strong! Everything would come right now. Charles would take everything into his own strong hands, and she would yield her own intolerable burthen of anxiety. Her guards were down.

Charles came bounding round the flank of the knowe
—there was no mistaking that big figure hurtling through
the gloom—and she ran to meet him.

"Oh, Charles! Charles, dear," she cried through her
tears. "Hugh—poor Hugh! He is at Ben Bhreac corrie
with a sprained ankle." Bravo, Allison! remembering
your obligations first.

Before she was aware of it she was inside his great arms.
Leave them to it. Their explanations took some time.

IV

Hugh endeavoured to ignore Frances Mary, but he
reckoned without Frances Mary. His back was turned
to her, and he stood, as usual, on wide-planted feet,
hands deep in his pockets. He found himself inclined
to sway backwards on his heels, and hunched his head
and shoulders forward to keep himself from staggering.
If he took a stride he would probably fall before her feet,
and that would never do. He watched Tearlath till he
disappeared in the gloom between the knowes. "I would
never doubt you, Tearlath," he murmured. "A great
trouble I have been to you this night."

Frances Mary was now close behind his shoulder.
"And your Tearlath has been a great trouble to you too,
Hugh," she amplified with some sarcasm in her voice.

He turned his head a little. "Is that Frances Mary?"
he inquired mildly. "And what is Frances Mary doing
here?"

She was slow to reply. She knew that she had dis-
obeyed orders. She should not be here; and her being
with Charles must have spoiled whatever plan Hugh
had in his mind. Oh, but he was mad with her in that
unmistakable way of his. He gave her his hunched
shoulder to look at, and he was characteristically begin-

ning his suspiciously mild questioning before calling her some painful and opprobrious name. He could say the most outrageous thing like a caress and used commonplaces like a whiplash.

Hugh noted her hesitation, but he ascribed it to a different cause. She was probably too indignant to bandy words with him. Her blonde Bill Stark had probably arrived at Innismore before she left it, and—well, he might hide the black and blue of his ribs, but he could scarcely hide—what was it again? He could remember making long reaches for that high-bridged aristocratic nose, and he had a gash across a knuckle where a front tooth had cracked. Pity he had not stuck to body-lacing. Divil the doubt of it, but if Frances Mary once started she would have plenty to say. It was foolish of him to give her that opening, and he had better try again.

"Tell me, Frances Mary," he asked, "is this to-morrow night or is it the night after?"

Frances Mary understood. "Only to-night, Hugh. Charles knew exactly where to look for you. It is not midnight yet."

"Do you tell me that? But I might have known. When I was a boy I heard a Dominican Father preach a mission sermon. A good man it was that died and had only one hour to spend in purgatory, and after suffering the anguish of it for a year and ten years and a whole century of years he called God a liar, and an angel came and showed him that he had only been one minute in that place of dolour. A hell of a fine sermon that was, and kept me out of sin a whole week. I wouldn't as much as rob an orchard."

"Poor Hugh! But you did deserve your purgatory, didn't you?"

"I did," agreed Hugh firmly. Now she was going to

begin, and he might as well give her a hand and get it over. "I suppose big Bill was home before you left?"

"Vivian? No." Frances Mary was surprised at this oblique attack and played for time. "His gillie was, though, and with a good head—but not as fine a head as yours."

"Wasn't it, then?" The old quirk came at mouth corner and he shook his black head. If she only knew! If Bill Stark's head was worse than his own at this minute 'tis in bed he would be and the ceiling coming down on top of him. Bed was a good place to be in, and if Stark was there peace was ensured till morning. And many things might happen before morning. Meantime . . .

"I wonder how Frances Mary is out of bed herself at this hour," he mused aloud.

Suddenly Frances Mary got nettled. "Because you are what Charles said you were."

"A dam' fool! The meddling fool of the world surely, girl dear."

"So am I, Hugh," she cried, quickly relenting. "Please get it over and call me any name you like. Go on."

"Puddin' head! Will that do?"

"No. I got awfully rattled and spoiled everything. You see, when Wullie Mack arrived—and you and Allison should have been home before him—I did try to suggest you had lost the track. But mother was there, and—you know mother has second sight—she can feel things. Charles and I know that—we have seen it so often—during the War, heaps of times. 'No,' she said, 'Hugh is not lost, but Allison is.' The way she said it frightened Charles. 'What is it, mother?' he said. 'Allison is lost,' she told him, 'and Hugh can't find her.' I could see how stricken he was, and—he is my brother. And you know, for the first time in my life I did not believe my mother." Frances Mary smiled. "I knew you were on the track, and Charles was in such a way that I could not help telling him everything— everything I knew. And then we came looking for you. And now I wish you would hurry up and say what you have to say—but mother was right all the time."

"She was, girl, and you did the right thing. You couldn't do anything else. When Hugh Forbes sets himself up as a god he deserves to have the feet of clay kicked from under him. Only it was a great pity that the kicking did not stop at his feet—but, of course, his head is clay too. Ah! here they come, the two of them, and we'll have to make the best of it."

Frances Mary was ready to cry. Once more Hugh Forbes had surprised her. In the deep rumble of his voice was a tone so profound and so forlorn that she wanted to hide her head somewhere and weep. If only his shoulder was not so stubbornly turned from her his broad breast might be the haven; and he might soothe with his broad hand her flaxen head—and imagine it red. But she could do nothing against that hunched shoulder, nothing to help the hurt his voice showed, nothing to fill the emptiness of his heart. All she could do was to hold her own shoulders just as stiffly, hide her heart as patiently, nurse her secret till sometime it brought the solace of dreams.

Charles and Allison appeared out of the gloom, and Hugh looked at them intently and with some final shred of hope. Their coming told him nothing. Probably they were self-conscious and knew what was being looked for. And so they walked a whole foot apart, and their hands, that had an urge to cling, were held stiffly. Hugh made his own deductions. Tearlath would, of course, have held to his pig-headed obsession as to the fitness of things. Very likely he had no more than made light of the escapade and laughed at Allison for getting lost, and Allison, under the spur of that laughter, would have gathered up her shattered pride. He had failed, then, and Caroline Grant had leant on a broken reed. God! And he had to meet her yet. Broken and done-for and at the end of his resources—and nowhere to hide. And still he must maintain a still front and make no least sign. As the two came close he pulled himself to attention and saluted.

"Ye are welcome, the pair o' ye," he greeted, his brogue whimsical. "It has been a fine night, thank God, for a saunter, and a nice one we had, Allsoon. Let us be going home now."

He swung on his heel, steadied himself, swayed, and fell as a tree falls.

CHAPTER XIX

Slack goes the rein,
    The blood cools down;
Weary weary,
    Still must you clown;
Still your face and steel your eyes,
And say farewell to Paradise.

I

FRANCES MARY caught him as he fell, and his head struck her shoulder. She was as strong and as supple as a steel spring, but there were a compact one hundred and sixty pounds of Hugh Forbes, and it was lucky for her that the heather grew thick on the margin of Torran Moss. They went down together full length, and Frances Mary had her breath expelled with a sound very nearly approaching a grunt.

Oh, but strong and supple she was. Under the dead-weight of him she sat up like a spring, her arms round his shoulders and his face turned in against her breast. He was like a smallish boy getting a "sair hert" soothed, his knees drawn up, his hands limp in the heather, and his face hidden. Frances Mary looked up at her big brother.

"What is it, Charlie? Oh! what is it?" There was fear and something piteous in her voice.

"I—I'm not sure, Frances Mary." All that he was sure of was that Hugh was in the right place at this moment. Charles was not exactly surprised at the small man's keeling over, for he had seen him do it once before after—not during—a period of intense stress. He started to explain this to his sister. "He is very high-strung——"

Frances Mary snorted. "As if I didn't know," she said witheringly. And then she lost her temper with these two dumb people. Standing there like two sticks, and poor Hugh prostrate after failing to bring them together! "Oh you babies! You pair of big babies!" She squeezed and shook Hugh's shoulders in the force of her derision. "This is all your fault, and there you stand with your fingers in your mouths." This was untrue. "Oh, bah!"

"That's fine, Frances Mary. Give them hell." That was Hugh's voice. It was muffled, and Frances Mary felt its deep vibrations through her bosom. Her hands slipped off his shoulders, and, without help, he turned in the heather, got on his knees, pulled his crushed velour over one ear, and scrambled to his feet. She remained sitting, and looked up at him open-mouthed. How could a man come out of a dead faint to encourage her in contumely, and then get to his feet unaided? Had he fainted at all? But indeed he had. As with men of his kind, finely and intricately made, his sudden collapse was followed almost at once by as sudden a revival. And yet, no one could blame him for resting knowingly for a second (or ten) on Frances Mary's fragrant breast. It had been offered him as a final solace—perhaps as a final punishment, since the memory of it would be always too poignant.

The moment he was on his feet, and before he might even sway, the strong arm of Tearlath Grant was behind his shoulder and under an oxter. The small man let his weight lean against that firm crook and gave Charles a nudge with an elbow. "A pair of fools, you said, Tearlath. 'Tis so. But all the same you're the damnedest fool."

"You're a liar," said Tearlath firmly. "Ask Allison." Allison recognised the duty imposed on her, and did not hesitate. She came round Hugh's shoulder, laid her hand on his arm and lifted herself on tip-toe, so that her eyes, brought close to his, showed him the tender glow of friendliness, liking, gratitude. "Thank you, Hugh," she whispered.

"Allsoon, do I deserve thanks for what I did to you?"

"You do, dear. You had to do something to make this big baby talk."

"Was it all talking?" inquired the big baby boldly.

And then Allison's two fine small hands cupped Hugh's face, and she kissed him. "Now you know," she whispered.

"Well, now!" exclaimed Hugh inadequately.

Frances Mary was not in the least pleased with all this. She jumped to her feet and stamped a foot in the heather. "I hate Judas kissing," she cried unreasonably. "Let us go home."

Allison turned quickly, anger in the surge of her shoulders, opened her mouth to make warm protest, shut it again, and again opened it to laugh—a little wicked gurgle. "Poor Frances Mary!" she said, and there was more than pity in her voice.

"Bah——!"

"That will be all," commanded Tearlath. "You know the road, Frances Mary. Lead on with Allison."

Frances Mary knew that her brother must be obeyed when he used that tone.

II

Frances Mary and Allison did not say a word to each other. Frances Mary marched steadily, and frowned steadily straight before her into the gloom, and Allison, at her shoulder, smiled wisely and a trifle mockingly. Tearlath and Aodh, twenty yards behind, were not silent. The murmur of their voices reached Allison and made her curious, and tempted her to drop back and listen, and, if occasion offered, slip a small hand inside a big and welcoming one. But she dare not with Frances Mary forging so steadily a yard ahead, and so she kept her place and was not one bit sorry for the pain the tall girl was giving herself—so needlessly.

Charles's arm was still wrapped round Hugh, and the big man noticed, with some concern, that his friend bore down on that prop and that it often saved a stumble. He could understand the recent sudden collapse and quick recovery, but, knowing the indestructibility of the small man, he speculated uneasily on this persistent grogginess. There was his Allison moving lightly in front, and her ordeal had been no less. And yet! The night was not so dark as to hide from Tearlath's sharp eyes the marks on Hugh's brow and chin. A fall? But where? An awkward man might stumble on Ben Bhreac corrie, but not Hugh Forbes, and after the corrie was only heather and moss. Charles did not dream of asking the direct question, but he knew that enlightenment would come in its own way—or Hugh's way rather.

"Wait a minute," said Tearlath. "A drop of this won't hurt you." He took a wicker-clad flask from breast-pocket and unscrewed the nozzle with his teeth.

"I'm leg-weary," protested Hugh, "and whisky will make me worse. Wait till we get nearer home."

"Go on. Take a mouthful. Wullie Mack has two ponies within a mile, and we are just above Innismore. We'll be in by midnight."

"Midnight is a tarnation long time coming," said Hugh. His teeth clicked on the silver top of the flask. "Gosh! 'tis powerful stuff."

After that Tearlath had use for his strong arm

224

"You've run yourself ready for the gaff, small fellow," he said.

"I have. You'll not get me playing Jehovah again, my fine Adam."

"I have no kick coming," admitted Tearlath.

"Maybe not, but I forgot about the devil. There's always a devil—a big blonde devil."

Tearlath got that hint, and his arm tightened. "Viv Stark?"

"In that guise. Allsoon told you the trick I played on her? Yes? Well, she wasn't well over the corrie when Bill Stark turned up, taking the short cut. 'Halt, Lucifer!' says I. 'You're on the wrong road. Hell's round the corner.'"

"You were afraid he'd overtake Allison—and tried to delay him? Yes?"

"That's it. We were very polite, I'm telling you. 'Excuse me,' said he. 'Certainly,' said I. 'We have a saying in the Gaelic, 'tis a year and a day since my mother was drowned—if she went round by the road she'd be at home now. The glen road is the road for you, fine man.' 'Anything to please you,' he said—and off he went."

"Back the road he came?"

"As ever was."

"Just so, lad. And then by way of diversion—as you would say—you bumped your wooden head on a rock and gave yourself an uppercut in the angle of the jaw."

"Go to blazes!" Hugh told him, but without heat.

"Certainly." Tearlath's voice was a bark and a growl. "But first—this very night—I'll break Stark's neck."

"Why would you? Didn't he do what he was told?"

Tearlath began to see. "He didn't want to go round by the glen?"

"Until we reasoned it out."

"And then he went?"

"On his two feet."

"You Turk! You bare-faced Turk! Did you put it over thoroughly?"

"I disremember—but he went down the glen."

"Lord! I wish I'd been there," said Tearlath longingly, giving Hugh a hug. "How did you get inside his long reach?"

"I didn't—not for about a year, Lord help us. That's what delayed me and made me lose Allsoon."

"Of course. I was wondering. It must have been a whale of a scrap. Stark can box, you know."

"I know too dam' well. And there will be a bigger fight to-morrow—if I'm not careful."

"How?" Tearlath was interested.

"See that long-legs striding ahead. Think of the ramp she'll be in."

"Frances Mary?"

"Yes, Frances Mary," mimicked Hugh sourly. "How would Allison feel if you came down to breakfast, your nose looking round the corner at your ear, and you with no teeth to bite your toast?"

"You make me happy. As for Frances Mary, I'd spank her."

"You would so. Spank your red-head. I was beginning to like Frances Mary." His voice was ponderingly casual. "I was beginning to like that one, I say, and—and—well, I don't know what Providence was doing to let this happen."

Tearlath did not speak for some time. He was no longer in the dark, and he was puzzling his brain how to help. It would have to be done very carefully. "You are afraid of Frances Mary, I think?"

"I am so. I don't like facing her eye and a cold look in it—if it can be avoided."

226

"I wouldn't worry, if I were you."

"Mighty easy for you to take it calmly!" Hugh snorted.

Tearlath recognised that the time and occasion were not ripe, and that he would have to work out this problem carefully. "One good turn deserves another," was all he allowed himself to say.

Winding in and out along the edge of Torran Moss, they came on Wullie Mack and the ponies, and after that all was plain sailing.

III

Charles William Vivian Stark was in bed when the party reached Innismore. But Caroline Grant was not. She was waiting at the white pillared bridge, and in the half-dark she had no need for eyes. The soft white wrap round her shoulders stood out against the dark of the lawn behind, and Allison, riding on the first pony, saw her before reaching the bridge. The red-haired one immediately slipped to the ground close to Charles's side. She was nervous, and he felt her tremble. "You tell her, Charles," she whispered.

He placed his hand on her arm above the elbow and felt the cool firm flesh through the thin stuff of her sleeve. He pressed that arm to his side, and she came close with a little snuggling motion that invited the full clasp. Charles felt a thrill run through him. This was his own real Allison at last, not the strange flyting imp of the previous three weeks.

"It will be all right, small one," he whispered back into her red hair. "Mother will know."

Hugh, coming behind him, had slipped off his pony too, and Wullie Mack, with a murmured "*oidhche mhaith*" —to which Hugh replied "*beannacht leat*"—moved off down the river, with the little animals, to the lower bridge. The small man steadied himself on his feet, gave himself a dog-like shake, and drew in a full breath. That taste of whisky back there had helped him after all. The dizziness was gone, his head had settled down to a steady ache, and his ribs did not hurt him if he breathed with his stomach muscles. He saw Tearlath looking back at him over Allison's head and urged him forward with a throw of hand.

Frances Mary did not wait for anyone. She marched straight ahead without pause and without hurrying, and the floor boards of the bridge sounded sharply beneath her marching feet. She did not even pause when she came to the waiting figure, and though she brushed close by she did not reach out a hand to give that soft touch with which she was used to greet her mother. "All right, mother," she murmured. "They are all here, especially your private henchman. You'll be able to gloat with him." And she went on towards the house.

No doubt the mother caught the bitterness of her tone. Her face that had been intent in listening tremored into the faintest smile. There was sympathy in that smile, but not sadness. She said nothing.

Charles's firm feet thudded on the bridge and the sound of Allison's feet was lost. Anyhow, her feet barely touched the boards, for he drew her along like a quiet but strong wind. He halted before his mother and his arm brought Allison forward. "Here is another daughter for you, mother," he said.

"I know, Tearlath, son." Her arms found Allison and Allison, feeling the welcome in that embrace, forgot her embarrassment. "Mother, too," she whispered, and with a motion as entrancing as a child's, her soft cheek was pressed on the cool, softly flaccid cheek of the older woman.

His mother's hand touched Charles's sleeve. "Where is Hugh?"

Tearlath looked over his shoulder. "He is coming, mother."

Allison found herself moved into a waiting arm. "Go on to the house, you two—there's a hot meal waiting for you. Hugh will take me up."

Charles chuckled as his arm tightened. "I suppose you want to hear how the work was done, but don't keep him long—he needs a rest."

Caroline Grant knew that Hugh needed a rest. She knew exactly how much he needed and how much he deserved—and how much she was going to give him. She waited for him, her lovely blind eyes turned down the valley towards the pale north. How quietly the lad walked! Where Frances Mary's feet had clicked like castanets and Charles's boomed like a drum, Hugh's made only a soft pad. Like a wild animal he must move, with that lithe sway where one foot took the weight off the other as it touched the ground. Poor Hugh! Puir laddie! how solemn he was feeling after his long ordeal.

IV

Hugh came over the bridge without haste. Through the gloom he saw the white-shawled figure waiting for him. Old folks always waited for him. And why not? He was older than he thought, older than his years, and, for all the use he was, he might as well accept the inevitable and enlist himself in the wistful company of the old—but the not very wise. And a great pity he had not done so before—fool that he was, with his fancies and dreams and ideals inside an ugly black head. . . . He halted at Caroline Grant's side and faced down the valley with her. The north was lit with a glow that was wan and unfriendly, and above the glow was a cold ecstasy of green. The hills below that green were dark and strange, and the pine woods were blacker than black plumes. Hugh for very loneliness could have lifted up his head and howled like a wolf. Then he felt a quiet but firm hand inside his elbow, and he dragged his mind away from himself.

"I have been trying to imagine, Hugh," she said in her soft running voice, "the emphatic but reprehensible way you would sum up your experiences."

"Yes, ma'am! I had a hell of a time—and deserved it."

She chuckled. "You did," she agreed, "but I'll take share of the blame."

"'Tis your due, white lady. I was only your enlisted man—and I am now about to become a deserter."

"No, boy. I have enlisted you for life—but I suppose you would be thinking of deserting. You cannot do that, of course."

He expelled his breath quickly. "Can't I, Caroline Grant? If you tried me hard I'd break in your hands. Don't seek to hold me."

"Am I holding you? You have done your work."

"In a way. It was only luck after all. You know that, maybe."

"I know your stubbornness compelled luck. Pig-headed stubbornness, Hugh! Poor Vivian has gone to bed—not feeling very well in consequence."

"So you know that much, ma'am."

"I do." But she did not go on to tell him of the scene Vivian had made on his arrival. Vivian, alone with his aunt, had broken up strangely. His self-confidence had been shattered and his conceit snatched from him. And these gone, he was no more than a great immature boy who had been hurt grievously and wanted to unburthen

230

his hurt and his grievance and, especially, his sense of outrage. He wanted his aunt and High Heaven to explain why, when returning peaceably homewards, he had been set on by a murderous thug? What had he done? Nothing. What was the motive? Good God! There could be no motive any longer—except a brutal desire to hurt where there was hurt enough already. Coming home decently and unsuspectingly, and ordered to go another way! Kicked, too! Had not Forbes done enough already to be satisfied? Had not—? And so on—and so on, to the point of angry weeping. Poor Vivian was not really such a bad boy. Young and spoiled, certainly, and perhaps a little stupid; but in time he would develop into a decent, stodgy, useful member of society—like the men of his class who hid stodginess under the caste mask. Frances Mary, that wild bird of hers, would not be very happy as his wife once she discovered the commonplace below the strong front. Ah well! Frances Mary was no longer blind. . . . But Hugh was talking.

"I am glad he is in bed. I didn't want to meet Frances Mary and she knowing the things I had to do to him. Had to, ma'am. And how am I going to face Frances Mary? Can you tell me that, Caroline Grant?"

"I can, but I will not, Hugh."

"I believe you, seeing you are one of the few who, knowing a thing, are in no hurry to tell. Very well so. I was beginning to like that girl Frances Mary." He was again carefully casual. "I was beginning to like that girl, I say, and this day I have given her no cause to like me."

"Yes. Frances Mary doesn't like brawling, Hugh. I warn you now."

"Brawling! Wasn't I driven to it, woman?"

"I don't know whether you were or not——"

"The devil of it is, ma'am, I am not sure myself, either."

"Never mind now. You'll tell me about it again. And you know you have given Frances Mary plenty of reasons to like you. Come on, now, and have something to eat."

Side by side they went up the path by the lawn, and they leant on each other and were silent. Either Hugh's mood was due for a change or Caroline Grant infected him with her own quiet optimism, for suddenly he threw up his head and laughed, and there was neither bitterness nor regret in his laughter. The old resilient spirit was again supreme.

"For myself I was sorry," he satirised. "Dear, oh, dear! How sorrowful I was! Back there a piece I could cry for myself—for myself only. But sure what harm after all if I have given myself a prick that pierces like a wasp's sting. Between us, lady, we have done our work, and all hurts mend. Great people we are, the two of us."

"And worthy of our reward?"

"And not wanting any."

"I do, Hugh."

"I don't know what you may want, but the thing done with the hope of reward cries to heaven for vengeance. I want none. But sure, you have already rewarded me by your trust, and that I want to keep. You have no other reward you can give me."

"I suppose not, boy," she murmured quietly. "Your reward would come in spite of me."

"I don't know what you mean, ma'am."

"Not yet"; and then she put him a final query or, rather, asked him to make a final admission. "And wanting no reward, are you not sorry you came to Innismore?"

"Not ever, by God!" he said firmly.

232

CHAPTER XX

Oh, stark grey dawn!
The time is come,
When life ebbs low
And thoughts grow numb,
To bite grim-hard Will's iron bit
And do what is ordained by it.

I

HUGH FORBES, beyond all doubt, was a tough sprig of a tough stock. Aodh MacFirbis, Firbolg, Pict, Danaanite or maybe Gael—but not Nord—never Nordic. He waked sometime after dawn and had no more than a slight headache. Yesterday had been a hard day. He had brought down his stag, and whipped his man, and been lost and found, and now, after only five hours' sleep, he had no more than a slight headache. And perhaps that headache was not due so much to the jar of fist as to the kick of Glenmart whisky. "It feels like a morning-after head, anyway," he grumbled, sitting up in bed. He shut his eyes and shook his head slowly. 'Och and Ochone! 'tis morning, and vision is gone from me.''

Last night, before coming to bed, he had vision for half an hour or so. Tearlath and he had a talk and a drink—or maybe two drinks—after the others had gone to bed. He hadn't seen Frances Mary at all—she had gone straight to her own room. And then Caroline Grant, protesting that Hugh should be in bed and must stay there all next day, had taken her departure, leaving Allison only. Hugh had been about to rise and leave the sweethearts together, but Allison forestalled him and

233

went off herself, suddenly, with a side-glance at Tearlath. Old Tearlath had hesitated for a moment, self-consciousness in his eye, and then slipped out after her. In two minutes he was back, and there was still self-consciousness in the eye he turned on Hugh. But Hugh, stretched out in a low chair, kept his gaze fixed on his extended feet. "Ay! ay!" he murmured, and he gave full measure of satire to that Scots exclamation.

"Ay! ay! then!" Tearlath gave back. "Time you were to your bed, Aodh."

"Tearlath my son, let's have a dram."

"Right by dam'! We'll have two."

And they had two—at least two. Else how could he have this head? Glenmart is one of the very great whiskies; perhaps, next to certain four Irish ones, the greatest—of slow maturity, no more than reminiscent of heather and peat, holding the sun that sherry brings from Spain in its depths, hiding its kick under a mellowness that never descends to suavity, but with the very devil of a kick nevertheless: the right and proper drink for the northern Gael.

"Here's to the finest red-haired girl in the world." That was Hugh, lifting his glass.

"Leave red-haired out of that and the toast goes," said Tearlath. "Why qualify it?"

"Because I'm an honest man—in my drink."

"Just that," agreed Tearlath to the rim of his glass. "I'll drink it, then."

Both of them needed that first drink—and it could be that one drink is no good without a second, for, as Hugh said, no bird ever flew on one wing. They felt the effect of it almost immediately: that downy salubrity where the brain works with a faint buzz as of minute wheels, and life, though no longer precious, is no longer petty. The usual reticence of close friendship was no longer there.

"While I'm at it," said Hugh, "and while there's a mouthful left, here's to the luckiest girl in the world—and she's red-haired as well."

"It's what you believe, I know," said Tearlath, and added softly, "she could be luckier—I know that too," and laid his glass down convenient to the bottle.

"D'ye mind, Tearlath, that I said to-morrow would be a grand day?"

"Though it might snow and rain as well. Man, you had me guessing that time. I know what you meant now, Aodh—I know what you meant now, boy."

And that was how the talk started. Wise and witty they were and of extraordinary precision of speech, holding the scales of reason magnanimously even, finely convinced with their own conclusions; life—with a capital—Life opened its vistas to them and, for the time, their own private small urges and ideals were forgotten in a contemplation that was dangerously omniscient. And yet, not quite forgotten, perhaps, but driven deep down and, still as an undercurrent, affecting their flow of thought. For Hugh, in one of the many by-roads the discussion took, would develop a thesis that happiness was a static quality, measured out equally to the last minutest drop, not to be increased or depleted, equal and unchangeable in all lives—men or cabbages. He was even a bit sorry for old Tearlath. Tearlath was supping his happiness some quickly. Himself, now, was progressing more cannily, mixing mead with his metheglin, admiring the blown rose, avoiding a possibly pallid realisation, anticipating where he could, dreaming where he had lost. Lost! Wait now. Had he lost? And there, for a short while, he clearly realised that man was forever at war with Woman, and forever being defeated and forever accepting defeat as a victory. Here now was victory—real victory—in his grasp, and let him hold it.

By the Lord! he would hold it, keenly though it might sting. And, after all, since happiness was what it was, it could not be the aim of thinking men. What was the use of pursuing what was already dowered and sealed and given and had only to be spent? Look you, Tearlath, the thing to pursue is nearer pain than pleasure—pain, the agony of creation, the realisation of the inevitable, the clear-eyed sense of loss, the terrible ultimate of despair. Men had been too long worshipping a false god. . . . A whale of a great thing, whisky!

That was last night. And now it was morning, an hour after dawn, and the sun was yet below the eastern ramparts of the glen. Hugh sat on the side of the bed, ankles crossed, one hand gripping his thigh, the other smoothing the back of his head, and with that half-humorous, half-sardonic quirk at mouth corner. Alas! vision was gone from him—as it had often gone before—and he was not even sure that it had been true vision while it lasted. If it had been, then most of life was a stretch of arid dullness, and high thinking had to be paid for with a sore head. Well, there was no use in grumbling. It was the morning of another day. He turned his eyes to the open window and saw across the lawn the big beech, a dull copper in the toneless light; and the myriad leaves of it, stirred by the wind of dawn, trembled with some remote, secret, hopeless thought of their own. "It is late," he muttered deeply. "Six o'clock in the morning."

Late enough, perhaps, but surely an early rising hour for this small man, who was expected to stay abed most of the day. But though bed pulled him, he got out of it as of set purpose—as the toiler gets up of mornings—because he has to, poor devil. He was dizzy for just a moment, but that was all, and then he padded across to the door and slipped out into the big upper hall. H

lean strong feet made no sound on the parquetry floor
out there, where the only sound was the slow comfortable
tick-tock of a grandfather clock from away round the
corner of the curving stairway. The hall was wide and
high, and was lit from the ceiling by a big rose-window
of opaque, faintly-tinted glass. The morning light lost
its desolating wanness in here. The golden brown of the
parquetry and panelling warmed it and added to that
feeling of comfort, ease, quietude that is the atmosphere
of old and happy houses. Hugh could sense that quietude
now, but it was no longer any help to the dour will of
him. At the stair-head he leant over for a peep at the
clock. "Two minutes past six," he whispered. He never
carried a watch, but his time-sense was very nearly
perfect.

In the bathroom he took his cold bath with unusual
quietness this morning. Not that he had the reprehensible habit of singing or grampusing; but the first
sharp ecstasy of the plunge usually brought forth one
vibrant howl of a nature to bring down ceilings and
chimney-pots and summer rain. But now he did no
more than inhale and exhale gaspingly, and after that
lay still, his hands, only, making a screwing motion.
After a minute he let his head slip under for a second or
two, and came out to towel briskly. That brisk towelling
made him grimace. There were blue bruises on his left
arm below and above the elbow, a purplish patch
underneath the right nipple, a graze on his chin, a swelling above one eyebrow, and the towel hurt those places.
He said a small "hell" below his breath. That cold
bath did him a power of good and he felt the old vigour
flow back through him. He stood, feet together, lifted
his arms above his head and filled his lungs. Like all
good small men he buffed well. His strong neck sloped
into wide shoulders. The flat oval of his chest expanded

hugely at full intake of air, the long muscles of thighs and arms rolled smoothly under a skin more white and delicate than any woman's, and his lean calves looked hard as marble. He gave an impression of compact power carried on a hair trigger, and one might no longer wonder that Vivian Stark had found him indestructible.

Back in his room he donned his old suit of flannel and Donegal tweed, and repacked the rest of his luggage in his near-leather suit-case, which he pushed under the dressing-table. He took one final look round the room and left it—forever? He looked at a bedroom door across the hall, and made a gesture of farewell that had in it a fine dignity and a terrible finality.

His brown brogues made no noise down the carpeted centre of the stairs and only the smallest click-click on the polished wood of the big outer hall, where the morning light gleamed coldly on the polished stand of arms and glowed sullenly on the cairngorms decorating the plaid that a Grant had worn at the sack of Aberdeen that time Colkittoch showed Seumas Graham some of the arts of war. He smiled twistedly at his black velour hat that was now oldish and comfortably disreputable; and then, burberry over an arm and ash-plant under it, he tip-toed to the front door. He found it unlocked and not even shut-to. That gave him pause, and he turned a listening ear back into the house. But the only sound within the ancient walls was the slow tick-tock of the old clock, and that sound had now become obdurate and heart desolating—and was careless of his going. Probably old Tearlath was too lit-up last night to remember such trifles as locked doors; but it could be that this door was never locked. "Safe in and safe out" was the old Gaelic phrase before the urge of a false prosperity spoiled hospitality.

238

There was no one moving, at any rate, and he had better hurry.

He hurried, never looking back, down by the red-brick garden wall, and so round the corner to the white posts at the end of the foot-bridge. And there he stopped dead. Caroline Grant, in her white shawl, stood at the middle of the bridge, and her face was turned towards him.

Her dark wide-opened eyes seemed to be looking directly at him, but he knew that she did not see him. And he had come light-footed as a dog down the path, and she could not have heard him either. He held his breath. Wait now. Was this accident or design? Maybe Caroline Grant was an early riser—a priestess of the dawn drawing inspiration from its grey aloofness. Surely she could never have guessed or read what was in his mind. Ah! could she not? And what was he to do now? Slip down to the lower bridge and so away. He pivoted carefully on one foot, and Caroline lifted a hand in beckoning gesture. "Come, Hugh. I am waiting for you."

"Very well, ma'am," said Hugh Forbes resignedly, and he walked across to her side. "You white-haired old spider!" he said gloomily. "You ought to be tired of all the webs you spin."

She smiled to him sadly and laid her hand on his arm. In her other hand she held a neat brown paper package. "I am tired, Hugh, and you would break my last web. How quiet you were this morning?"

"And you quieter still, wise woman."

"And you thought to break my web?" she mocked him gently.

"No, lady. I am only going to my own place, and

239

you'll not be detaining me, if you please." There was firmness in his tone, but there was entreaty also.

Her head drooped in a small nod and stayed drooped. "I would never hold you against your will, but, I think, I hold you all the same."

"It is my body only that is going away."

"And that will come back too—later on, Hugh, later on. But we will not talk of that now. Listen, boy. I knew you were going, and I know you are going. You see I have been dealing with obstinate men all my life——"

Hugh Forbes was astounded. Changeable, wayward, inconsequent—however one might call it—that he was, he knew; but obstinate! "Devil the obstinate I ever was in my life," he interrupted her warmly.

She gave that pleasant ruminant gurgle that was the eternal youth in her. "But I know. The men of this house of Innismore are always that, and it is only the defect of their qualities. When they take the bit in their teeth they must be allowed to run for a little—not very far."

"Tearlath, you mean. That's him, sure enough."

"And now I am letting you run too—because I have to. Go, then—so far—and I do not even ask why you go."

"No, ma'am. There is no need between us to ask or tell."

She held up the brown paper packet. "See what I have for you. You came into the Glen with a famous parcel of biscuits and cheese, and you go out of it with the same, only this time I have added a bit butter for good hansel. It is the only hansel I will give you—this time."

"The kind heart of you! A bit butter is the finest hansel in the world. It is all I shall ask of you—ever."

"Foolish lad, who thinks his asking done!"

"Woman," he boomed, "what is the use of asking you for what is not mine—or yours either. Give me my hansel and let me go, who love you."

And being an exceptional woman she let him go with the last word.

III

When Hugh Forbes had gone, Caroline Grant leant on the wooden rail of the bridge and looked up the glen in the direction he had taken. Though she could not see him, she heard his softly swift feet crunch the granite gravel long after most ears would have failed to hear. And then he went round a curve of the glen, and there was only a thrush singing and a single rusty note from a gallant blackbird.

And still Caroline Grant leant on the rail and was not at all happy. She was only a foolish, groping, perplexed mother, she told herself, whom her children credited with knowledge—more than knowledge—an occult sense, wisdom, the power of accomplishing things. And against her will. All their lives they had looked to her to bring things about as a matter of course. Mother will see to this—Mother will do that—Oh! ask mother. And never for a moment did they guess how desperately, sometimes, she had to fumble in the dark to bring about what was demanded or—worse—often only hinted at carelessly. And it was her own fault, for, whether in vanity or from character, she hid under a calm front all doubts and fears. And in issues that touched them closely they gave her little help. There was her big Charles. For weeks she could feel his eyes dumbly beseeching her; could hear him, though obstinately silent, signal for help—a big baby wanting his mammy to reach him down the moon. And now he had got his moon, thanks to luck and that adequate small man re-

241

treating up the glen in good order. And her wild bird, Frances Mary, too! Lately, Frances Mary had been hanging on to her apron strings, saying nothing but meaning so much. Why could she not speak? How could a half-blind fumbler know what her wild bird wanted? And what could she know of a strange man coming from a restless island into their quiet Highland valley? Better know nothing. Why try and lose her wild bird? She had her now, more securely than ever with every mile that Hugh Forbes placed between himself and the house of Innismore. Be silent only, Caroline Grant, and you will not be heaping up loneliness for yourself. Moreover, after all the luck you have had in solving problems, the false solution is due, and the thing you contemplate now may be that. Do nothing, then. You have schemed long enough, and it is full time that you retired into inactive placidity. . . . But that might be the false move decreed by Fate, Caroline Grant. . . .

After many minutes she turned slowly and moved slowly towards the house. The morning wind had died and a plume of blue wood-smoke rose straight from one chimney. The old house was waking to its daily life. She entered by the side, went down a long passage, and pushed open a swinging green-baize door.

"Janet," she spoke gently to a maid at the big range, "I want you to make breakfast—for one. Tea, toast, eggs—in my work-room. Be quick, dear."

At the foot of the big stairway she halted, and an open palm rubbed over a small clenched fist. If her children could only see her now they would see perplexity and doubt and a good deal of chagrin. She was being driven, and she wanted to revolt. At last she went up the stairs and along the parqueted hall to a bedroom door, and there again she paused, her hands loose at her sides and her head downcast. Presently, by no volition that she **was** aware of, one hand lifted to the door-knob.

IV

"Hullo, mother!" greeted Frances Mary. "Hugh and you were up early this morning. What are ye planning this time?"

Caroline Grant smiled, and her mien was again one of quiet confidence. She went across the carpet and sat on the side of the bed, and at once her daughter's hand moved down over the coverlet and joined hers.

Frances Mary must have been awake for some time. There was no drowse of sleep in her wide-set grey eyes and nothing wan in the lovely cream of her face. Her flaxen hair was in waves about her ears, and her long neck gave a sense of soft delicacy, as if not meant to carry weight of brain. Both long fine arms were outside the coverlet, and her mother smoothed a caressing hand up the oval of a forearm to the cool flesh above the elbow.

"Hugh and I were up early? How did you know it was Hugh?" There was a quizzical note in the voice, and the mother noted the little electric twitch in the hand she held.

"I heard you, of course." As if she would not know when Hugh moved, quiet though he might be. "I had my fingers in my ears for his trumpet-blast, but it never came this morning. Where is he now?"

"Not very far away," replied Caroline Grant.

There was silence then while both were busy with their thoughts. A trace of faint but exquisite colour came into Frances Mary's cheeks, as if some wonderful contemplation coming from deep down had made her blood move faster. She knew that her mother had come to her bedside with some purpose in mind, and her own mind, set to speculation, turned to her dreams.

243

"You know what happened last night—on the moors?"

"Don't you, mother?"

"A good deal more than you know, girl."

"More? Did Hugh tell you?"

"Very little—but enough—and Charles and Allison told me a good deal—and Vivian too."

"Vivian! But he was not there? He was in bed."

"Before he went he had much to say—with a lisp too, as if a front tooth were missing."

"Oh, the little brute!" cried Frances Mary, at once jumping to conclusions. "Whatever happened?"

The cheerful chagrin in Frances Mary's voice was not lost on her mother. "Yes! a little brute," she said with irony. "It appears that he is deceitful too, for he pretended to sprain an ankle at the foot of Ben Bhreac corrie, and sent poor Allison the wrong road to get lost."

"Who set him his task, mother?" inquired Frances Mary quietly.

"Never mind. The complications began when Vivian, coming down from the loch, took the short-cut by Ben Bhreac."

"Oh!"

"It must have been immediately after Allison had gone, for your little brute tried to detain him."

Frances Mary stirred under the coverlet. "But he could not allow Vivian to spoil his scheme," she reasoned.

"He might have taken Vivian into his confidence, might he not?"

"I never thought of that. But no! Hugh would never do that—and he had to try and detain him."

"He did, too, and made him return by the long road. Your brother said it must have been a whale of a fine fight. Silly! Big boys—all of them! And it could have been avoided."

"But he had to detain him," said Frances Mary stubbornly.

The mother did not argue the point. "It apparently took him some time. That is how he lost Allison."

"I was wondering. Isn't he a terror?"

"And very much afraid of you this morning."

"And I shall talk to him too."

"You see, he takes things into his head—like you and Charles—and he knows—with such absolute certainty—that you care for Vivian."

"I know, mother," Frances Mary agreed, hopelessly calm. "I suppose he would."

"So he is trying to avoid you this morning; at least that is the reason he has given for avoiding you."

He had some other reason for avoiding her—a real reason? And her mother was here about it. She waited.

Her mother smiled sorrowfully. "Sometimes I am grieved that I have such stupid children," she protested. "And pig-headed too! You are quite certain, of course, that Hugh loves Allison?"

Frances Mary stirred. "Everything he said——"

"Well, he doesn't. He loves you."

"Mother!" Frances Mary said the word as a child might say it. She never thought of questioning. For a long moment her heart seemed to sink inside her bosom. No! not her bosom—into some profound emptiness unrelated to time or space. And then she felt a pulse beating in her neck.

"That is why he has run away."

Caroline Grant had broken her news cleverly and at the right moment. Shock counteracting shock! Frances Mary for yet a minute could not well realise anything but the one thing. Nothing else could matter very much. Her mother went on speaking quietly. "He hasn't put it in blunt words exactly—but there was no need. My

245

dear, you won him that very first night at Aunbeg bothy, and now you are twisted into every fibre of him. He has deeps for love, that boy. He simply could not stand it any longer, and has run away. He had to—and you caring for Vivian. He went away this morning."

"Back to Glounagrianaan?" Frances Mary put in quietly.

"Back to his Glounagrianaan. Up the glen, the road he came—with a fine packet of biscuits and cheese, and a bit butter for hansel."

"Mother, I am jealous of you," cried Frances Mary hotly. She sat up in bed.

She was jealous of her mother. Her mother knew too much. Ah! but her mother did not know everything, and she would not be told either.

"I think I'll get up, mother," she said casually.

Her mother's arm went round her shoulders, and the soft but faintly flaccid cheek was pressed to the firm cheek of youth.

"Oh, mother!" cried Frances Mary in a tone pitched queerly high. "Isn't he an awful obstinate little brute to cause us all this trouble?" And then the lump in her throat choked her.

CHAPTER XXI

Face you your grief
And do not cringe;
Know without fear
Thought's bitter twinge;
And having drunk your bitter lees,
God will yield your ecstasies.

I

IT was afternoon. High up in the south-west the sun
blazed through the hot thin haze of autumn; the great,
purple, curving slopes of heather slumbered in the heat;
the dust of the road was as fine as flour and nearly as
white—and Hugh Forbes leant on the parapet of the
high-cocked bridge over the Croghanmoyle and looked
down into the river, here feet deep in a still pool, and
showing every pebble on its green-grey bed. A ten-inch
trout seemed to soar, fin still, half-way down, but hardly
had the black head appeared against the sky than it
darted, too quick for eye, under the darkness of a ledge.

"God!" exclaimed Hugh. "Has anything at all happened?" How long had he been leaning over the bridge
and gazing into the limpid-green water of Croghanmoyle? Had time stood still, or, in moving, had it gone
full circle? Ah no! His face was turned the other way
now, but it would be better for him to have spent his
weeks looking into still water—for all the eddies he had
formed in his own life. Life! life! It could not flow
forever without an eddy. Perhaps the eddy was life.
Perhaps. . . . He found himself deep in the desolations of
abstraction, and presently some persistent thread of
association set his deep voice to an old tune:

> Sad I was and sore I was,
>   And lonely to the bone.
> Grey o' grass and green o' grass
>   And water over stone,
> Set a dream upon a dream
>   And washed away the lone.

And the great bass murmur of his singing seemed to vibrate in the grey stone of the bridge.

He straightened up then and shook his head slowly, and the sombreness of his face was not made any less sombre by the smile that twisted about his mouth. "The happy damn fool you were, Hughie, when you put words to that tune. 'Tis little you knew—little you knew. All the green slopes of Glounagrianaan, all the water shining down the wide aprons, what can ye do for me now—to-morrow—next year, and the year after? Ye'll be trying—ye'll be trying surely."

He stood lost in some strange dullness of thought for a full minute, and then went plodding down the road, and the white dust made a little mist round his brown shoon.

II

He came to a halt in front of the post-office at the corner of the village street, and looked through the open door into the low cool cavern of the shop. His lips formed the words "I may as well," and forthwith he went in under the low lintel. Inside, it was dusky and cool and had a pleasant fragrance of raisins, tobacco, nutmeg, bacon, leather, and toilet soap; and Hugh had again that small pang where a thing once pleasant is now touched with wistfulness.

The postmaster's black-fringed, bloodless face slanted by the side of the railing that guarded the sacred postal section near the door.

"*Dhia dhuit*, Highlandman," saluted Hugh. "Have you written that letter to the Postmaster-General?"

"Ah!" cried the postmaster. "Is it yourself, then? And have you been lost all this time on Cairn an Cludaigh Bhain?"

"Thanks to you I found that road, but—I lost myself too—and now I'm on top of my own road. Could you tell me was I in here about a month ago, and did I send a wire?"

The postmaster smiled and nodded. "I often feel that way too. Ay, were you."

"Wondering, I was. I am here again—now—for the second time—and I would be sending another wire."

"It can be done. To the same address?"

"The very same."

While the postmaster again fumbled for a telegraph form among his disarray of official papers Hugh wondered if disarray did not in the end become routine and normal—if, after all, disarray was not the ultimate normal.

As before, he ran his wire off without pause.

"*Safe over the hill Tearlath and making tracks for Glouna-grianaan—the fine time I had.*"

He paused, looking down at the words. Tearlath was wise and Tearlath would understand, as he had always understood when things went deep. No more need be said.

The old postmaster examined him curiously. Still the same safely-centred lad in the same careless dress, only, this time, that black hat was well worn and no longer incongruous. The mountain sun and wind had not added a line or a fleck of bronze to the fine sallowness of his face, and the character-lines of that face had, as ever, a gravely serene quality. A strong face guarding a reliant and understanding mind. A man you could be frank with. "You had a good holiday, I'm thinkin'?"

"I had so. And added to my experience many things I thought I knew already."

"Just that," agreed the postmaster; and added wisely, "A red-haired girl is hard to come by."

Hugh laughed. "Indeed, and that is true. And have you noticed how kind and friendly she can be, and how nicely she'll tell you to go to hell at the end of all?"

"I have noticed it. But maybe you are as well as you are."

"The thing to say. Could you tell me, now, if I can be getting a train down below?"

"At the Kirkton? You can. The up and down trains pass each other there, and you can about make it." He looked round the corner at his clock. "Yes! You'll make it."

"'Sort of plenty of time, but if you don't hurry up you'll be late,' as Wattletoes used to say. Then I'll be going."

"You'll be back this airt some time?"

Hugh was about to reply with an emphatic "No," but paused with his tongue pressed against his teeth and thought better of it. "One could never be saying. The glen I came out of is a hard glen to leave—but one never knows. An I come this road again, you and I will have a long talk."

"Ay will we! Haste ye back, then."

And with that Scots valediction in his ears Hugh went out the door. Before he turned the corner he gave a final glance over his shoulder. There, in front of the door, was where she had stood, a silken band round her flaxen hair and her brown shoes covered with dust. And he did not like her—and she had had her revenge. Good-bye, ghost!

And then he strode round the corner.

III

And that was the end of that—and that was the end of that—and that was the end of that. Life, real living—dammit, no! not all life. Let him be fair. All that he could say was that a new—and a greyer—aspect of life faced him once he had come round that corner, just as a few weeks ago a more intense appreciation had been given him on the other side of the same corner. Life would go on—for a woefully long time probably—and he would have to face it and do his work and make no sign. Let him, then, in the name of God, put the past behind him and start afresh. . . . And yet! Why should he put the past behind him?—even if he could. A man should be able to contemplate anything—by taking thought. The thing rigorously ignored became a fear that pounced. An appreciation of pain seasoned life. Overcoming cowardice was a man's duty, and had a finer aftertaste than a king's sherry. Ah! but had he not yielded to cowardice by running away? No, by the Lord! He had done what was demanded of him at Innismore—done his work and reaped his experience, and come away his quiet lone when every fibre of body and soul urged him to stay and hope dumbly for miracles. But, by the Lord again! he would never run away from his thoughts—and he would wear the sharp corners off them in time. Sharp corners! Sharp enough, but only because he was so darned sorry for himself. . . . And why not? He was just an ordinary sort of devil who fell for the usual lure, capable of great happiness—and of great sorrow in the losing of it. Let him be sorry for himself, then. There was nothing wonderful or noble in hiding feeling under a stoical front. The stoical front often hid rottenness and the glistening eye the brave heart. . . . He was heart-sorry for himself, that was all—with his back to Glen Dhu forever, and his face to Glounagrianaan. And if a tear fell on the toe-piece of his brogue, what harm? It was an infinitely quiet tear, welling up from deep down, a simple tribute to all the small urges, and corpuscles, and such, that had been deprived of what they clamoured for. It could not sway his resolution, and his eyes would be dry long enough—long enough. . . .

His chin was down on his breast between forward-hunched shoulders, and the road was blurred before his eyes. He blinked rapidly and shook his head. And then his breathing stopped in the middle of an intake and a thrill went over all his flesh. He had heard no sound. But someone walked at his right hand a little behind his shoulder. The thin evening breeze was making the birch trees whisper, and these feet must be lighter than the patter of leaves. He shut his eyes quickly and looked again, never lifting his head, his eyes looking downwards and a little back. Yes! He knew these brown shoes that made the white dust spurt as they touched ground lightly but firmly. They were grey at the points from swishing through heather. Poor shoon! ye have come far and foolishly. Fragments of surmise and thought fluttered in his mind. Was it pity? Was it good-bye—a friendly last act? Had Caroline Grant been foolish with her tongue? Easy now, Hughie. Keep your head. Keep pacing steadily down this Highland road and watch these feet for check and quiver.

"What are you doing so far from home, Frances Mary?" he asked, deep down in his chest.

The shoes never faltered, but she did not answer at once. He waited, one foot plodding over the other.

"Business of my own," she said at last quietly, but he sensed emotion behind her voice.

Business of her own! "Very foolish business, I think," he said sadly. "I expected you to have more sense, Frances Mary."

"I am afraid I was foolish . . . but . . . Oh! I am very tired."

The feet faltered then, and Hugh edged a little closer. "Steady, girl! We haven't far to go now. And could you tell me your business?"

Frances Mary replied after another pause. "You remember that first morning at Aunbeg—such a long time ago? You gave me a linen handkerchief as a diaper towel, and left it behind on a tussock. I always—well, I have it here for you."

"And is that all your business?" His voice was a little bleak.

"No, Hugh. You know I liked you—like you—and— there was no need to run away from Innismore."

"So you came to tell me that—and say good-bye."

"If I have to, Hugh."

He threw his head up then, but he did not turn his eyes to her, for his long lashes were still wet. "Oh, kind heart!" his great voice quivered. "You have come a long road to say good-bye to a churl. I like you too, Frances Mary." He paused and added, "That is why I am running from Innismore."

"Then there was no need to run away."

"But I was a coward. I was afraid I would get to like you too much."

"Only afraid?"

"If I grew to like you any better I'd—I'd burn up, Frances Mary."

He did not see the vigour come back to her feet. "And

still there was no need to run away." Finely serene was her voice at last.

"I suppose not," he agreed sombrely. Oh stubborn Irishman! anchored to your own pig-headed notions. Now she knew. And why should she not know? It was a good thing after all that there should be frankness between them before they said good-bye. "I was a coward indeed—and conceited too. It is only right that in these last few minutes I should hide nothing from you. But don't worry about me, girl dear. I'll have you in dreams always."

"And my hair will be red then?"

"Red as—no, by God! Your hair will be tow, and I wouldn't give one strand of it for all the red hair that ever flamed. My fine, kind-hearted brave one!—and whether you are or not, it does not matter. I'd still love you."

There was the final admission, and still Frances Mary said nothing.

"And now, Frances Mary, I can with peace of mind take the train towards Glounagrianaan and you the one for Innismore."

"I am not going back to Innismore without you," said Frances Mary with calmness.

Hugh was disappointed. "I am going back to Glounagrianaan," he said firmly, "and no one can stop me."

"Then I am coming with you."

He stopped dead, but did not turn round. Torn loose from its anchorage, his mind went, as it were, broadside for a moment. "Why—why—why?"

Frances Mary was still calm, because she knew. "You always said I had tell-tale eyes, Hugh."

He swung on her then. "God!" he whispered. His old burberry and ash-plant fell at his side. "Is it true, Frances Mary?"

"My dear!" said Frances Mary.

His hands went out. "Look, Frances Mary! Thinking had lost you, I was crying like hell."

The black velour hat fell with a soft whuff in the dust